THE ACTIVIST

THE ACTIVIST
Tanure Ojaide

AMV
Publishing

Published by:
AMV Publishing
P.O. Box 661
Princeton NJ 08542-0661
Tel(s): 6095770905 & 7326476721 Fax: 6097164770
africarus1@comcast.net & africarus@aol.com
http://home.comcast.net/~africarus1/site/?/home/

First published in Nigeria in 2006 by
Farafina, an imprint of Kachifo Limited

North American Edition Published on License from
Kachifo Limited,
25 Boyle Street,
Onikan, Lagos Island,
Lagos, Nigeria
Tel: (+234) 1 740 6741; 0807 736 4217
info@kachifo.com
www.kachifo.com

The Activist (North American Edition)
Copyright © 2010 Tanure Ojaide

Cover Photograph: George Osodi
Author's Photograph (Back Cover): Wade Bruton
Cover Design: Kunle Ajose

All rights reserved. No part of this publication may be reproduced, stored in a retrieval system, or transmitted in any form or by any means, electronic, mechanical, photocopying, recording or otherwise without the written permission of the Publisher.

This is a work of fiction and references to characters, groups, places, and incidents are purely of the author's imagination.

Library of Congress Control Number: 2010901098

ISBN: 0-9766941-4-X (10-Digit)
        978-0-9766941-4-4 (13-Digit)

In memory of Ken Saro-Wiwa

Acknowledgments:

Many thanks go to Charity Lami Adama, Joseph Ewubare, Theresa Jones, Anthonia Kalu, Joseph Obi, and Dike Okoro, who read the manuscript in its earlier stages and offered suggestions on its improvement.

ALSO BY TANURE OJAIDE

Fiction
Sovereign Body (a novel)
God's Medicine Men & Other Stories

Non-fiction
Great Boys: An African Childhood

Poetry
In the House of Words
I Want to Dance & Other Poems
In the Kingdom of Songs
Invoking the Warrior Spirit: New & Selected Poems
When It No Longer Matters Where You Live
Invoking the Warrior Spirit
Delta Blues & Home Songs
Daydream of Ants
The Blood of Peace
The Fate of Vultures
The Endless Song
The Eagle's Vision
Labyrinths of the Delta
Children of Iroko

Criticism
Poetry, Performance, and Art:
Udje Dance Songs of the Urhobo People Culture, Society,
and Politics in Modern African Literature (with Joseph Obi)
Poetic Imagination in Black Africa
The Poetry of Wole Soyinka

The bear went to the lambs. "Give me one of you and I will be content." The lambs answered and said to him, "Take whichever thou wilt of us. We are [thy] lambs."

-The Words of Ahiquar

PART ONE

THE RETURN

Life of Activism

The Activist slipped in one late Friday evening in mid-July. The KLM flight arrived on the precise time scheduled. There was nobody waiting to receive him at the Murtala Mohammed International Airport. His quiet arrival was most unusual, even unprecedented, for one who had been away for so long and then finally coming back. Almost all of his countrymen and women abroad had in Lagos friends or relatives, who waited for them when they visited or returned. In cases of a final return like his, relatives from distant towns abandoned their work and traveled for a day or two in order to come to Lagos for the sole purpose of welcoming home their illustrious son or daughter.

One became illustrious by travelling overseas and then coming back. Naturally, taking an airplane or travelling by ship to and from Europe or North America would distinguish one as belonging to the extended family's class of illustrious sons and daughters. Such a long journey needed a special welcome, which became a ritual for many who came to the airport with video cameras to film the memorable occasion. Others brought musicians to noisily sing the praises of the returnee, who danced with his or her people from the airport at the beginning of a month-long welcoming party.

But the Activist was a different type of person. He loved his people and their ways, but there were some of the ways he did not want to encourage. The ritual at the airport, when the returnee's community came to shout his praises, was one of these. He was not the sort of person who encouraged people to leave their tasks at home to come that tedious distance and wait for him. He did not consider himself important enough for that type of reception. It would be better if they remained at home than be on the dangerous roads and risk accidents that often bedeviled the country's travellers. If he could travel to various parts of the world without anybody waiting to pick him up at the airport, he would be able to find his way to anywhere in his own country. The deer will not be lost in the forest; it is its familiar haunt, he told himself.

He had visited home ten years earlier to bury his father and kept himself relatively current with the happenings in his country. He followed the political course of his homeland on a daily, if not weekly, basis in his immigrant home. There was much one could read about any oil-producing country in American papers and often news about Nigeria got into the papers and onto the screen, however small the space given.

Before he set out for home, the Activist knew very well that there were different types of taxis at the airport. He also knew that in Lagos there were many good hotels; some four- or five-star. He had slept in Concord Hotel at Ikeja when he last visited. That hotel was as comfortable and plush as any he had slept in elsewhere and, in fact, cheap compared to those of similar standards in foreign countries. He planned to still go there whenever he needed to sleep in Lagos.

The Activist chose to come in quietly because he did not want to add to the unprecedented crowds that made the Lagos airport one of the rowdiest in the whole world, according to a BBC correspondent. He was not sure of the accuracy of that observation, but he was one who would like to solve a problem rather than make it worse.

He had so prepared his mind for a long delay at the airport that he was pleasantly surprised that things went smoother and faster than he had expected. The luggage took some time to come out but that happened in many airports abroad also. He got his two luggage items fairly quickly. He did not believe in bringing from abroad what he could easily get at home. He did not even ship a car before he left despite repeated advice from his friends to take home one or two cars; one for his personal use and the other for sale. Instead, he sold his dark green Honda Accord and kept the money to buy another car when he got home. He shipped his books only a few days before he left and they would take several months to arrive because he mailed them bulk and surface, which cost much less than airmail but would take quite some time, according to the woman who had attended to him at the post office window.

And so at the customs checkpoint before exiting the restricted area of the airport building, the officer attending to those in his line asked:

"Where are you coming from, Mr. Man?"

He did not like being addressed as Mr. Man, a demeaning and rude appellation, but would not challenge the customs officer on this alone.

"The United States," he answered.

"America?"

"Yes," he replied.

"What do you have in your boxes?"

"Clothes and knickknacks," he explained.

The customs officer had not heard of the word "knickknacks," but he did not want to plead ignorance in his duty. He knew what information to extract from travellers with contraband that would make them helpless before him. He had been in the job for over a decade and cared less about the big words that some returnees to the country used to cut a grand impression.

"No banned textiles?"

"No," the Activist replied.

"No stereo equipment?"

"No," he again said.

"What did you bring to sell?"

"Nothing," he told him.

"Which kind man be this? Everything nothing! You no want make we chop?" the customs officer asked.

The Activist was confused. The officer realized he was dealing with one of those Nigerians who had stayed too long abroad and so did not understand the current language of survival he was speaking to him.

"You bring dollars?" he asked.

"No," he told him.

The Activist felt it was stupid for any customs officer to ask somebody returning from the United States whether or not he had dollars in his keep. There was no law banning him from bringing his hard-earned money into his own country. The days of currency declaration by Nigerians entering their own country had long passed.

"Make we search you and your luggage and if dollars dey we go seize am?" the officer asked in an intimidating manner.

"Mr. Man," the Activist said in a serious tone and paying back rudeness with rudeness, "will you please allow me to pass into my own country? What kind of shenanigan is this?"

Those questions made the male officer and his lady colleague to wave him off.

"Carry go, Doctor. You dey talk as if you no be our countryman," the lady officer said.

They had opened his passport and saw that he was addressed as a doctor. It did not matter whether he was a medical doctor or a Ph.D. holder because such people had friends in high places and should not be harassed in order to avoid unpleasant repercussions.

The Activist was relieved that he was free to leave. He could hear the two officers making catcalls and laughing as he rolled his cart that held his only two pieces of luggage. They must be thinking that only time would teach him that he should have brought back ten boxes rather than only two. How could he be returning finally from America, God's own country, without bringing in enough to last him his whole lifetime in Nigeria? What are clothes and knickknacks? He must be a fool to them. The Activist pitied them because they did not know that in God's own country, the Devil also reigned!

He had prepared himself for the big crowd outside made up of not only those who had come to receive friends and relatives, but also comprised of hustlers, thieves, conmen, and many others come there for their own reasons. He chose to take the expensive taxi, which you booked and paid for inside just before you got out of the airport building. It was expensive, but the company clerks made sure they took down your name, where you were going, and what you were carrying. They then assigned you a car and a driver to take you to wherever you wanted to go. This the Activist did. He paid three thousand naira for the fairly short ride to the hotel in the same area as the airport itself. He knew that outside he could get transportation to the hotel for only one thousand naira, but his personal safety would not be guaranteed, he believed.

He had heard stories of travellers who took unregistered and unidentified cabs and had been robbed of their money by their drivers. Some had been beaten unconscious and left on the side of the highway. And there were a few cases in which the returning travellers were killed and all their belongings stolen.

The Activist felt different the moment he stepped out of the airport building and breathed the outside air. His body tingled with excitement. There was something in this air that made him relaxed and comfortable. There was a fusion of familiar aromas, spices, and smells wafting in the dusk air. He felt a sense of exhilaration as he trod the hard soil of his motherland. "I have made it," he told himself. This was what he had always looked for - to return to his own country. He did not want to wait to come home to die or, worse, to die in America and be flown home for burial. While abroad, he always longed to return home and live among his own people. His dream during the flight across the Atlantic Ocean suddenly flashed again in his mind. He saw himself among a flock of migrating birds fleeing a cold climate and heading for a sunlit horizon.

The day the Activist returned to his home country was ordinary and unremarkable. It would not be in the history books, though he won a significant war that had raged in him for over a decade. He had overcome a fierce army of fear that had threatened to paralyze or kill him. He was a victor who relished his victory without being noisy about it. He did not need any victory drums, songs, and dance because he believed that in life one form or another of war was bound to challenge such a self-congratulatory celebration. As far as making his return home quiet and private, he was satisfied that things went perfectly well according to his plan.

The stars had gathered all over the sky for their nightly council and each shone with remarkable brilliance to impress anyone outdoors. There was a cheerful feeling in the air. It was one of those rain-free days preparatory to the August Break that really began in late July when there was a pause to the rainy season's heavy downpours.

As the driver passed the streets from the airport to the

hotel, the Activist saw makeshift outdoor restaurants crowded with people eating and laughing. The food was prepared outside, and he could see the blazing fire, big pots on tripods, and the smoke. He could smell some of the special dishes that made Lagos night life popular - pepper soup, isi ewu, jollof rice, akara, and moinmoin. "Blessed is the country with such a rich array of palatable dishes!" he chanted to himself.

Loud music was playing and some of the people were dancing and singing along. There was a combination of traditional and modern types of music assaulting the ears. He could pick up from the different types of music Fela's irrepressible voice in "Shakara Woman." He loved Fela's music, especially in its criticism of social and political ills of the country. Fela was the consummate artist, able to blend traditional and borrowed musical techniques to create a distinct Afro-beat voice of his own, he felt.

In the early night, people were moving up and down the streets like the columns of ants he used to see as a young man in his rural Niger Delta home. People were coming and going in a flux that made the night vibrant with so much life. This was a rare spectacle that soothed his heart.

The Activist planned to rest for two days in Lagos and then continue his return trip to the Niger Delta. He would stay in the hotel and spend his time sleeping to get over the jetlag, watching television, and reading newspapers to get acquainted with the developments in his country. He knew there would be a world of difference between hearing and reading about one's country from abroad and getting firsthand information at home. He had come to experience his country physically like a loved one.

The driver coughed. The Activist realized that the cough was meant to draw his attention.

"I hope you are fine?" he asked the driver.

"I fine? For Lagos nobody fine!"

"This is a beautiful and happy city," the returnee told the driver.

"E no be as you dey see am," the driver responded. "I come from Ibadan come drive taxi for here. But everywhere for country dry well well. E dry pass harmattan time self."

"Wetin happen make am so dry?" the Activist asked, switching to pidgin he had not spoken for a very long time.

"Business hard! Money no dey."

"Wetin happen why money no dey?"

"I no go lie for you. Na die we dey for here."

"E no suppose to be so with plenty money from oil," the Activist told him.

"Soja don steal all our money."

"That's sad," the Activist said.

"Water don pass garri for here."

"E go better," the Activist replied.

"We dey inside fire. If e no better, na die-o."

The driver paused for a moment to concentrate as a motorcyclist raced past, as if pursued by a dangerous animal. The motorcyclist meandered through the congested road as his engine rattled noisily and exhaled dark smoke and was soon out of sight.

"You no fit be somebody for dis our country now unless you steal. All the big men be thief!" the driver resumed.

"If you work hard, you go be rich too," the Activist advised.

"Not for here! If you work hard self and you no steal, na poor man you go die," the driver responded.

The Activist was thinking of what to say when he noticed that the driver had already entered the premises of Concord Hotel and was meandering his way through the brightly lit and flower-decked driveway towards the hotel's reception office that he seemed to be familiar with. He wished he had more time to dialogue with the driver and promote hard work over stealing, but the driver soon stopped and he had to come down.

"Thank you," the Activist told him, as he pressed a five-dollar note onto his chapped hands.

"God go bless you!" the driver prayed in appreciation.

"Continue to work hard. You go be rich."

"Oga self! You go see for yourself. Nobody go tell you say life hard for here. You no fit be big man if you no steal," the taxi driver reiterated before he drove off.

It seemed it was not a busy time for the reception desk because it was manned by a young man and a middle-aged woman who were chatting and laughing. Since there was no other guest around for them to attend to, things went fast for the Activist. After he filled the necessary forms and left a deposit of one hundred dollars, the young man stepped out to help him to the room; he rolled one of the two bags. The hotel worker led the way through a long corridor, at the left end of which he stopped. He opened the door to the room and placed the bags on a rack in a special corner of the room. The floor was comfortably rugged; the wall painted milk white, and the king-size bed was neatly made with flowery sheets.

"Enjoy your stay with us," the young man said, after showing the customer the luxuries in the room.

"Thanks," the Activist responded.

"We go see tomorrow. My shift don end," he told the Activist as he was about to step out of the room.

The Activist was happy to arrive safely at the hotel. As soon as he shut the door, he went to draw the two sides of the heavy curtain apart so that he could see the lit yard outside. He saw the different flowers at the back of his room. He also saw a tennis court and a swimming pool at opposite ends of the yard. He was pleased that the hotel management maintained the environment well. He looked forward to sitting outside the following day and reading newspapers.

He liked his room. It was big and had what he needed for the two nights he would be there - cable television, bathtub, and big bed. He drew the two halves of the curtain together and went in to bathe. He had a warm bath, which surprised him because he did not expect the taps to work; they not only worked but also had hot and cold water.

He was too exhausted to turn on the television. He fell asleep quickly in the big bed. He dreamt about police breaking up a protest he was participating in somewhere in the United States. The blaring loudspeaker cautioned everyone to step back but the crowd of protesters charged forward. The police unleashed water hoses at them but still appeared to be helpless before the zealous crowd. All of a sudden, they resorted to their last weapon of crowd control. They let loose their dogs on the crowd. There was a stampede as everybody tried to run away from the ferocious canines. It was at this point that a gentle knock on his door woke him.

"Who is that?" he asked.

"Office manager," the knocker introduced himself in a low tone.

The Activist could hear several other hushed voices beside the speaker's. He could tell that there were as many as three or four people at the door. He immediately suspected there must be something sinister going on. What was the office manager of the hotel doing coming to his room at two o'clock at night? He could see the time from the red light of the table clock beside the television.

"Wait a minute," the Activist said.

He did not open the door, but withdrew inside the room. He knew he had to act fast to avoid a robbery or some catastrophe. Fortunately, there was a phone in the room. He dialed zero, which he thought must be the number of either the operator or the reception desk. It rang four times before a sleepy-voiced man picked it up.

"Hello!"

"Yes; hello! Is the office manager around?" the Activist asked.

"No; wetin happen? You dey sick?" the coarse voice asked.

"No, there are three or four people at my door," he told the voice at the other end.

"He-e; they have come again-oo!" the man shouted into the phone.

"Where's the office manager?" the Activist asked.

He could only hear the hysterical cry of a loud-breathing man at the other end of the line. Meanwhile the knocking got a little louder. The Activist kept his cool. The people at the door seemed to be in a dilemma. They did not want to rouse the other people in their beds and yet they wanted to get in. They knocked harder but still not hard enough to awaken others from deep slumber at that time of the night. Once they heard he was on the phone, they gave a hard kick to the door which did not yield to their wish, and they hurriedly left.

Later that night, the desk manager told the Activist that he had seen the four men run out of the building into the yard and jump over the fence surrounding the hotel. Both the hotel manager and his guest were surprised at the fact that these intruders knew he was in that particular room. They must have tracked him from the airport in order to know where he was spending the night. He had taken precautions to avert this sort of happening, but evidently the taxi he had hired was not as safe as he thought. Could the driver who had brought him sold him to robbers? After all, he believed one could not make it without stealing. Or maybe the perpetrators had infiltrated a good company? The fact that the robbers came to his very door made him also to suspect that it could be somebody in the hotel that gave out the information about him. Could it be the reception desk's young man, who helped him to his room or his replacement whom he cried to on the phone for help that gave him out?

He felt lucky that the visitors were not hardened criminals who would have kicked down the door and tortured him to surrender his money. The story of his first night at home, if he had been murdered or seriously hurt and robbed, would have been circulated abroad to satisfy pessimistic émigrés who already felt he was crazy anyway and did not value his life for returning to his own country.

The following morning the Activist changed his mind. He quickly made arrangements for the hotel's minibus to take him to the Niger Delta Line station in Jibowu quarter. He was not spending a day longer in Lagos after the previous night's experience. Who knew what could happen the next night if he stayed? He did not want to imagine a worse scenario than had already happened to him. He used his one hundred dollar deposit as his payment for the night he had spent. He then changed two hundred dollars into naira in the hotel to take care of his taxi fare from Lagos to Warri.

The drive to the Niger Delta Line station was slow but smooth. Saturday morning did not carry as much traffic as any of the working days. At major intersections where traffic slowed down, hawkers of all types of items shoved their wares at the drivers and their passengers. These hawkers sold items ranging from toothbrushes, combs, mirrors, to canned drinks, snacks, artworks, calendars, and belts. The Activist shook his head in pity. Some hawkers carried items that, if all were sold, would not amount to one hundred naira. How did they come there? How did they eat from the pittance they made? he asked himself. Still the young boys and girls without any other means of livelihood carried smiles on their sweaty and anxious faces.

Fortunately a Peugeot station wagon was next to load for Warri. The Activist paid for the two back seats because the taxi driver told him that his two luggage pieces could not fit into the boot of the car; one was free and he had to pay for the other, considered as excess luggage. Within thirty minutes, the car was filled and the five-hour road journey to Warri began.

The Activist was one of those people described by American armchair psychologists as protest bugs that showed up wherever there was a big protest to attract media attention. He always tried to make time to join what he considered a necessary cause, and many causes were necessary in his view. He was on the mailing list of many organizations and more often than not responded to calls for major protests. To him, answering such calls was not a civic but a human duty. He had flown to Europe several times on chartered flights to carry placards against Bell Oil International and the Group of Seven over debt relief for Third World countries. He saw the World Bank and the International Monetary Fund as exploiters of developing countries. He liked ATTACK, the French activist group that believed in disrupting meetings of exploiters since the Shylocks refused to listen to anyone's plea for mercy. As he always put it, you don't debate with a madman! He loved the French organization's concerns for justice and fairness in economic and trade matters, especially in the developed world's attitude towards the underdeveloped countries. Its members were the true allies of Africa and the wretched of the earth, he told himself.

The Activist had also been airlifted in a Green Peace plane from Washington, DC, to Rio de Janeiro, Brazil. He identified with the concerns of Green Peace for the environment. Its objectives were in line with his for his Niger Delta birthplace. He had either paid to go to major protests within the United States or had been helped outright for international ones. He was not a rich man for that matter but he knew how to get to a place by Greyhound or Amtrak by negotiating a good bargain fare as early as possible; hence he participated in many big protests.

He believed that the FBI had files on him, but he was not afraid because he felt he was doing the right thing. The agents must have dismissed his type as idle people who sought the company of fellow idle ones in order to avoid boredom or depression. He had made many friends in the course of those types of protests, but many of such friendships, especially with the opposite sex, ended as impulsively as they had started.

He tried to forget his white girlfriend with whom he had broken up under disastrous circumstances. Amy wanted to be one thing depending upon her mood. She wanted to be a watermelon in the dog days of summer, a pumpkin during Thanksgiving, a comforter in winter, and a white lily in the spring. But that was not all about her. She tried every drug available in the street, drank, smoked, and suffered depression almost every season. She wanted him to make love with her as if he were a Kentucky Derby race horse, which he was not, and once when she sank so low threw a knife at him but he was fortunate to escape a direct hit; they struggled to possess the knife, which only grazed her right leg. The knife incident did not need going to the hospital for either of them.

Amy later told him that she was playing with him, an explanation he did not accept. In any case, one of them could have been badly hurt. One could not predict what a depressed person could do in a bad mood. If she had killed herself, he would certainly have answered many questions the police would pose. Ever since he broke up with Amy, he had not had a serious interest in another woman because he saw her in every potential girlfriend; he did not want to play with fire.

Photographs moved the Activist immensely. He had pasted to his bedroom wall photos of starving children and those of raped and battered women. He kept a file with newspaper cuttings of various forms of pollution clouds of smoke enveloping human beings in their homes; women fetching water from a greenish stream where the multinational oil companies worked in Africa and Latin America; and many more.

Whenever the Activist went to bed at night, he thought for a long time about the causes that he wished he had joined to change things for the better. There were many new causes that needed to be addressed to make the world a better and safer place to live in, he felt.

"Too many innocent people are convicted for crimes they do not commit," he told himself.

He dialogued with himself all the time about what needed to be done for a happy world.

"There are too many hungry people going to bed at night, even as too many rich throw away leftovers that would have fed the hungry. Look at hotels throwing away food, even as many people have nothing to eat!"

"There are too many homeless people sleeping under flyover bridges and in cardboard boxes in major cities around the world, even as rich and childless couples live in ten-room mansions."

"Too many women suffer battery at the hands of their men; too many helpless women are killed by psychotic men."

"There is too much oppression of the minority in the name of democracy in many countries."

"So many despots hold down large populations by rules of armed coercion."

He fell asleep carrying his thoughts into dreams in which laughter and tears metamorphosed into surreal landscapes.

The Activist thought about home a lot. "What am I doing here?" he started to ask himself after he returned from the trip home to bury his father. He used to be homesick but never as much as after that trip. The two weeks had opened his eyes to much he could not believe. Those people at home were more relaxed and happier than him that was supposed to be richer and in a developed society. The comparisons he started to make between his immigrant country and his native home also made him to reflect about his life. "What is a good life?" he asked himself. "Is a good life not a happy one?" he also asked.

He had lived in the United States for twenty-five years, but he did not consider it his home. Home for him was where his parents had given birth to him and handed to him tales also handed to them by their own parents. Home was his Niger Delta State in Nigeria.

He realized that he would make a greater impact in his own country than by following others to just swell up numbers of the crowds of people protesting in developed countries. He also realized that whether or not he joined protests in the United States, there were always enough concerned men and women there to fight a good cause. Most people were enlightened enough to know what was happening, unless they chose to be self-centered, as many were, and not care for others. The infrastructures were also there in the developed countries to assist in mobilizing opinion on the right track.

He saw the problems at home as a tug of war between the dictatorial military and the civilians, and the stronger side would triumph. He wanted to throw his small weight on the civilian side that wanted democracy in place of the tyranny of the gun.

Often the Activist did not want to revisit the circumstances that had brought him to the United States. It was always painful for him to do so. However, much as he wanted to avoid pain, he discovered he had to live with it. He had come as a refugee. Not a civil war refugee like many of his displaced countrymen and women who got compassionate consideration for American visas in the late 1960s, but because of the massacre of his people by soldiers and mobile police working at the behest of the military government and the major oil company. The two parties colluded to wipe out his village because his people had dared to bring in foreign journalists to document the degree of their exploitation and the pollution of their environment. With the publicized oil pollution in American coasts and the heavy compensations paid, it was so embarrassing that the oil company working in tandem with the military leadership decided to teach the people a lesson that would silence them.

Then a young man in secondary school and on vacation, the Activist narrowly escaped being killed. He survived with two bullets lodged in his right knee. It hurt but did not stop him from showing up when the American ambassador visited the site of the incident a few days later and saw for himself the degree of the atrocities. The ambassador randomly selected two young men to be sent to the United States to continue their education. That was the best the ambassador said he could do, since he had no control over Bell Oil Company or the military government.

Once in the United States, the bullets were removed from his knees, a medical feat for which he thanked God and his hosts. Nobody could now tell that he once walked with a limp from the pain of the bullets! He then went to complete his secondary school education. After that, he entered the university and in less than four years earned a bachelor's degree. He was not satisfied with the first degree and wanted to get as much education as possible. So he proceeded to graduate school for more degrees. Within another eighteen months he got a Master's degree. He performed so brilliantly that two and a half years later he successfully defended his Ph.D. dissertation.

But there he was a teacher in a black institution that was always threatened with bankruptcy, lack of accreditation, and closure. Barber College paid slave labor wages and did not tenure any teacher however long there, and the Activist was stuck with it. The college did not also enroll its teachers in a retirement program. There was also no health insurance program in the college. The Activist from the beginning knew the importance of good health and on his own enrolled in the state health insurance scheme.

Barber College was one of those liberal arts colleges that demanded so much teaching and personal attention to the students that you taught four or five courses a semester plus advising. Since the college did not emphasize publication, one soon learnt after being there for many years that one could not leave for another college with better pay. Other colleges or universities emphasized publication and one stood no chance against scholars from elsewhere that flaunted an endless list of publications.

The Activist drove from the city to the college twenty miles away in a small town. For a while he took to driving a cab at night in the city to make more money. With all the bills he had to pay and the money he had to send home occasionally, things were tight for him.

The Activist often reflected on the sorry plight of many immigrants. Was their coming abroad really worth it? For many, it was worth it, and for many others it was not. There was much ignorance of conditions at home abroad. This ignorance was very profound, especially in those who did not live well and so could not afford to visit home to see things firsthand. These people deluded themselves that at least they were better off economically than those they had left behind. They knew nothing about what really happened at home and believed wrongly that everybody in America was at least economically better than everybody in Nigeria. It did not bother them that they had to pick discarded mattresses, chairs, clothes, and utensils from garbage dumps to survive in America. Nor did it bother them that they had to shop at thrift shops and flea markets for what they needed. In those thrift shops and flea markets, they might be buying items of dead people, but that did not occur to their closed minds that were only concerned with cutting costs. The same could be said of those that drove round on Saturday mornings to yard sales for good bargains. Since some of them had also closed their minds to home, they could not imagine that some of the colleagues they had left at home had become bank managers, vice-chancellors of universities, state and federal ministers, and other high officials in government or business.

For the brave ones among them, they realized that they had made a mistake in leaving home; these ones cried in bed at night when nobody else saw them. There was the constant shame of imagining returning home without anything to show for the many years spent abroad; hence they continued hoping against hope for better days in America. They might go home but only after becoming rich in America! They realized the loss of respect and dignity in America they had to suffer bearing what they would not tolerate at home. Rednecks called them derogatory names. Other Americans made them to always feel that however long they lived there they remained strangers. They bore the taunts of the low and the high.

"If you so much love your home country, pack and go

home!"

"If you don't want to become American, go and be an African in Africa!"

"Better learn to speak American rather than that heavy accent!"

"You must be happy to be in America rather than in your tribal village!"

"Go and live on top of trees if you so much love your jungle country!"

"You must thank your God that you are enjoying peace in America rather than be maimed or killed by warring tribesmen!"

Those who claimed to be owners of the land talked at you and did not care whether you had something to tell them too. If you did not know it, they had to rub it on you that you were a second class person in their society.

But there were many other forms of self-inflicted humiliation that many African immigrants had to contend with. How would a Ph.D. holder in Africa drive a taxi at night? Such a person's relatives would believe that the person had been bewitched or had become crazy. There was no other explanation for sinking so low to make money when respectable or high-paying jobs were there for the asking. But there the Activist was, braving the night filled with violent crimes pursuing dollars to make both ends meet. There must be another way to live and he would try whatever way would be available in his home country, he assured himself.

A hunter goes out to hunt and returns home! It matters not whether he has shot any game; he always has to return home and not live in the wilds. A farmer leaves home for the farm and, at the end of the day, returns! It matters not whether he has completed the day's task or not because he has a home and so must not allow night to hold him hostage in the farm. One prays when about to travel to return safely. One goes to seek education, gets it, and returns, the Activist told himself.

One moody autumn morning, windy, cold, sunless, and with cascades of yellowish and brownish leaves falling, alone in his flat that had become used to his solitude, the Activist came to a decision. The decision to go home was a revelation that he had ignored for a long time. The vision of home beckoning on him to leave wherever he had taken refuge but was in fact a hell had always been there for him. If he lived any longer abroad, he would run the risk of becoming mad from the many conflicting thoughts crushing his mind. The long and acrimonious debate within him was over. He had won.

All of a sudden, he felt as one who had miraculously recovered from paralysis. He could feel a new surge of energy in his body. He wanted to exercise his free movement in a different atmosphere, which he knew would maintain his sanity and health. And the new state could only be exercised in his real home, thousands of miles away across the Atlantic Ocean.

For several years, his home state university had been contacting him to return and teach there. Just as the Federal Military Government drove professionals out of the country with its blatant human rights violation, so were state governments looking for ways to lure home their highly educated indigenes abroad. A reporter for Index on Censorship who wanted to remain anonymous because of possible harsh repercussions quoted the military leader as saying that anyone who wanted to leave his country was free to run away but that he would rule whatever number of people remained! That general was so power-possessed that he was capable of ruling a ghost nation, the Activist reflected.

The Niger Delta State University needed qualified indigenes of the state living abroad to return and to bring the institution up to a higher standard. A university always flourishes with knowledge from diverse sources, and the Activist's academic experience in the United States would be a great asset to the Niger Delta State University. He had even received a letter of appointment only months earlier and he was given six to twelve months to accept and report for work. Little had he known when he first threw the letter into a pile of papers on his table that he would one day look for it and take action on the offer of appointment!

That auspicious day he made several phone calls that brought him happiness because of his decision to return home.

By the end of that day, he had written to accept the teaching job in Nigeria and also had booked for his flight home. He was only obliged to give a month's notice at his place of work but he gave three months' notice of his intention to leave.

The alarm bells of his fellow Nigerian immigrants that he would leave behind continued to ring loud in his mind.

"Can you live in Nigeria again?" a fellow countryman asked.

"It's jungle life out there; can you cope?" another asked.

"Are you crazy; with all the armed robbers and those ruthless soldiers you still want to live there?"

"And the witchcraft stuff you hear about, how do you go into that voodoo land to live permanently?"

"You know what happens when one visits home, with all the relatives and friends bothering one to death with requests for money. How will you manage that situation?"

"With the rapacious women, can you find a partner there?"

"With HIV and AIDS spreading like a harmattan blaze, will you practice abstinence?"

"Without a single good hospital and the exodus of doctors, what will you do when you fall sick?"

"After being used to the Land of the Free, can you live in a militarized state?"

"How will you seek redress, if offended, in a land without law and order?"

The more questions they asked him, the more determined he became to return and take part in the tug-of-war. He did not consider himself a heavyweight but he would do his little best for the side he would throw his weight behind.

To him, all people could not be armed robbers; nor were they all conmen and women. Nigeria was not a nation of wizards and witches. Every woman in the country was not HIV positive or suffering from AIDS. Men, after all, also suffer from sexually transmitted diseases and he wondered why his dissuaders never thought about that fact. True, there were brutal and corrupt soldiers and policemen, but he did not count his life dearer than the lives of the one hundred and ten million people in the country. He was one of them and did not want to see himself as special. That mindset helped him to overcome the anxieties and fears pumped into his head by his émigré friends.

Each passing day, each passing week, as each passing month and each passing year would bring him more confidence despite inconveniences, which he had expected and so coped with. It was not malaria that he feared. He had bought a mosquito net, which he had fixed over his bed as soon as he got to his assigned accommodation. To avoid typhoid fever that was often mistaken for malaria, he washed his hands thoroughly before eating. He realized that the culture of handshaking helped spread the disease. He washed his fruits too before eating and avoided taking salad and ice block outside because these could easily be contaminated in the dusty environment. Cleanliness and properly cooking food would also prevent diarrhea.

The frequent blackouts did not scare him either. In fact, he had experienced them during snow and ice storms and hurricanes that brought down electric power lines in the heart of America too. There were hurricane lamps and rechargeable lights available and he had bought one of each to use in case of a blackout.

Two incidents rattled, or really shocked the Activist the first four weeks of his return. Within two weeks of his return, he attended a function outside the campus in Warri. There were many marriage and burial ceremonies and he wanted to gradually make new friends and to get to know people he could associate with. Fortunately, he had met a primary school classmate, Dr. Biribo Mukoro, from the history department. He jumped at his old classmate's invitation to attend the introduction of a young man to his future in-laws. It was one of the new developments since he left. There used to be a bride-price paying ceremony, but his people had continued to invent new ways of gathering to drink, eat, and dance, and the introduction ceremony was one of them.

Dr. Mukoro gave the Activist a ride in his meticulously maintained silver-colored Nissan car and steered the conversation towards how his former classmate could assist him to make contacts in America.

"Just connect me to one of your colleagues so that we can be exchanging letters," Dr. Mukoro told him.

"Is it a pen pal you want or what type of person?" the Activist asked.

"You know what I mean. Somebody in a university and in my field," he explained.

There was silence as the Activist thought of what to say next. He wiped sweat from his face. The air was rather hot as Dr. Mukoro had raised the windows up without turning on the air-conditioner.

"Can I lower the windows?" he asked.

"Don't worry, I'll turn on the air-con," Dr. Mukoro replied.

"Thanks," the Activist told him.

Like many others around, Dr. Mukoro believed that having a contact abroad increased one's chances of getting a visa; such a person could invite one or show one the way.

It sounded odd to the Activist that he had just come back to settle at home and yet his new colleagues wanted him to help send them out to where he had come from. He was certain they took him to be crazy or foolish but he was also sure they did not know what they were asking for. He pitied them in a similar way that they apparently pitied him for what they considered to be his meaningless decision to come back home.

In any case, the great embarrassment came when they arrived at the green-white canopied arena of the introduction ceremony. Dr. Mukoro introduced him as their American-educated associate professor who had just come to join them permanently at the Niger Delta State University. The group of men at the table, drinking an assortment of alcohol, stood up, moved in awe by where he had come from, and clapped for the Activist. They remained standing and stared at him as if he were an idol. It was extremely difficult to go to the United States, and therefore to see one of their sons back was reason enough for the dazing reverence. Dr. Mukoro gestured to them to sit down.

One of the men, a little more elderly than the rest, asked the Activist whether it was true that he left America where he was working to come and teach in Nigeria.

"Yes," he replied.

"Are you on a visit or come to stay with us permanently?" he further asked, as if he did not hear well Dr. Mukoro's introduction of the man he was asking the question.

"I am here permanently. I like it here," the Activist answered.

"Do you know what you are doing to yourself?"

"Of course, I took the decision to leave America and come home," the Activist answered.

"You took a decision to leave there for here?"

"Yes."

"I pity you," the man said.

"No, I like being here at home. No place is sweeter than home," the Activist explained.

"Do you like us as we are here?" the man further asked.

"Of course I do. You seem happy to me, and that is very important in life," replied the Activist.

"Black man happy in this black man's country," the man said in what was neither an exclamation nor a question.

The Activist did not know what to say or do next. The man stood up and, before the group, spat at the Activist, saying:

"You must be a fool!"

The saliva flew from the alcohol-smelling mouth, splashed on the chest of the Activist, and dribbled down lazily. It was thick and dark-colored; a mixture of Guinness Stout and Star Beer that the fellow had been gulping since he arrived at the ceremony. Again, the Activist did not know how to respond, but some of the men held back the half-dazed drunk and pulled him aside. Others instinctively took paper napkins from the table and wiped the saliva off the Activist's shirt. Three men led the fairly old man away to another section of the large gathering. The drunk was unapologetic and followed those dragging him away like a cow that had accepted its fate for slaughter but perhaps assured that he had publicly made his point.

Those that pulled away the drunk returned to tell the Activist that his assailant was a drunk, which he did not doubt but felt the man had gone too far in his drunkenness. He wondered how he would have reacted if this had happened to him in the United States. He would not have been as restrained as now but would have spat back or called the police. Here was he at home and powerless in reacting forcefully to such a terrible affront because he was not only newly come back but because it was done to him by a fellow Niger Delta person.

The group diminished by one sat silently. None was ready to begin a conversation. There were still many bottles of Guinness and Star Beer on the table, but none of them poured more drink into his glass. A fly buzzed past the beer smell without attempting to land on the table or any of the foaming glasses. Soon the silence became rather disquieting and within a short time the others gradually melted from the table, each with his bottle and glass. Only the Activist and his lecturer friend who had brought him remained there.

The Activist, who had not taken anything before the assault, drank bottled water at the ceremony and did not eat the fried chicken and rice that were served. The ill-mannered drunk had destroyed his appetite for the food. He did not dance either. Okpa and his group were playing "Catch your Gulder," a piece that brought almost everybody out to dance. Men and women danced seductively; the women baited their male partners with their backsides.

"This is our traditional disco," Dr. Mukoro explained to him, as he went for a female partner to dance with.

This type of music was new; a fusion of dance club music and traditional music. The Activist was moved by the percussion rhythms but he held himself down.

"Enjoy yourself. I'll look after our table," he told Dr. Mukoro.

The Activist watched the dance outside. Most of the dancers appeared to be in a trance as they danced for over a half hour non-stop to Okpa's latest piece. As those outside were transported by music into frenzied dancing, a group indoors went through the new tradition of introducing the soon-to-be bridegroom to the future bride's people. As would be expected, there was abundance of kola nuts, bottles of gin, and fried meat for them to consume in the process of the introduction. To the Activist, this was the longest and most entertaining introduction he had ever seen.

The Activist and his friend remained at the ceremony till its close late in the evening. It intrigued the Activist that he did not see the bride-to-be. Nor did Dr. Mukoro introduce him to the groom-to-be that they had come to support. It appeared as if they came to just enjoy themselves. People mingled and talked but there was no formal procedure for those outside who occupied themselves with drinking, dancing, and eating.

The trip back to the campus was somber. The two men were rather taciturn, because the Activist did not want to respond to his old classmate's request for a connection with some of his former teaching colleagues in America. He did not want anyone to remind him of Barber College. He would not help anybody to get a ticket to hell. That was what Dr. Mukoro was asking for without knowing.

The Niger Delta State Line taxi that brought the Activist from Lagos took him straight to the university campus to drop him at his residence. The Registrar had already informed him of his temporary residence, which had been prepared for his arrival. Neither the driver nor the Activist knew the campus well and once inside asked the first person they saw coming towards them for direction and that person happened to be Ebi. She was walking towards the main gate to take a taxi or bus to town.

"Just continue until you come to the set of flats painted brown. Those are the transit quarters," she explained, as she pointed at the three rows of buildings that they could see from where they were.

"Thanks," the Activist told her.

Two days later they met and recognized each other.

"Were you not the one who showed us the way two days ago?" the Activist asked.

"It looks like yesterday. Yes. You were the one in the taxi. You are new, it seems. How are you adjusting?"

"Still finding my bearing but should be okay soon," he replied.

The second time they had exchanged greetings along the corridor of the big building, he had ventured to introduce himself. Of course Ebi also had to introduce herself. She appeared very mature; she carried herself with a certain dignity. He did not see any ring on her hand and guessed she was not married. He had observed within the few days he had been at the university that while the married men did not wear any rings, the married women brandished their gold rings as a status symbol.

Ebi soon found herself in the midst of those second-guessing about the Activist's reasons for coming home. In a country where so many people wanted to get a visa to leave for North America or Europe, everyone said it was insane for somebody who was not kicked out of America to leave that God's own country. People were stealing, prostituting, killing, and committing other heinous crimes to make money to look for devious ways to go abroad. And here was somebody already there and working coming back!

"To do what?" they asked.

"If he wants to help Nigeria, he is of better use outside than inside," one lecturer told another.

"He should help to take his relatives and friends away from this damned country, rather than come back," another said. "He has made plenty of money there and now wants to compete with us for the pittance we are earning here," a senior lecturer said.

"Let him live in our hell and see whether he can survive."

"Don't say you heard it from me. I understand he was selling drugs and he came back to escape an arrest warrant," one said.

In the last several years, many Nigerians had been deported from Europe and North America for drug-trafficking. Many had also been repatriated for unknown offenses, though many of such were prostitutes in Italy and The Netherlands and also illegal aliens in America in states without more spaces in their crammed prisons.

"They said he jumped bail after being convicted for tax fraud," another said.

This lecturer had heard about tax fraud as an offense in America but did not quite understand what it meant in a country in which only government employees paid taxes but often underpaid after bribing tax office workers.

"I also heard he impregnated two white women who knew each other at the same time and they threatened to kill him," said some other lecturer.

"I believe something serious that really threatened his life made him leave. I learnt one of the white women fired a gun over his head and said if she saw him again he would be dead," a professor said.

"And, of course, don't forget the witchcraft of his people here. He might no longer have a father or a mother alive, but that does not protect him. His relatives certainly have the ability to call him home; he must have heeded a powerful call, a diabolic one for that matter," another explained. Ebi felt it was wrong for them to speculate wildly as to why he came back from America.

"Is it now a sin to be back in your own country?" she asked.

"Why are you defending somebody you don't even know?" one of her colleagues asked.

"He's not a criminal; he might have been homesick and he chose to come home," Ebi told the group.

"How do you know? How can you tell that somebody is not a criminal?"

Ebi saw herself pushed to the position of defending somebody she had greeted several times on the corridor but did not know well. Why should they not give him the chance to show the type of person he is? she asked herself.

The Activist's relatives had at first wanted to invite him home, but on second thought decided to accord him the courtesy of going to him instead. After all, they had not gone to Lagos to wait for him. He had not told them that he was coming back home, but they would make up for that lost chance of singing his praises from the airport to their home. They also wanted other lecturers and the entire Niger Delta State University community to know that their son had proud relatives. In a university with a multiethnic population, they wanted it known that they had an American-trained lecturer among them. They hoped that, after this trip, many gates on campus and the entire state would open to them if they mentioned their son's name. They did not want to spring a surprise upon him as they did among themselves and so sent word to him about their proposed visit. They expected him to prepare to receive them and he did so as best as he could.

When the Activist received the notice from his relatives that they were coming to visit him, he wondered what he would do to entertain them. When visitors give you notice, they expect much from you. He wanted to give them a pleasant surprise, if he could arrange it.

His options were limited. He knew only one woman around and that was Ebi Emasheyi, the art lecturer, whom he had met several times. He decided to ask her to help him out in the quandary of preparing traditional food to surprise his visitors. He had doubts as to how she might respond, but he was not the sort of person who failed to try things for fear of failure. He would speak to her when next they met at the corridor of the huge hall.

"Do you have a minute?" he asked her.

"Yes," Ebi answered with some anxiety.

In her mind, she wondered what this stranger wanted to discuss with her. She had learnt to always listen rather than refuse to do so. They stepped to the side of the corridor.

"I need your help," the Activist told her.

"What type of help is that?" she asked.

"My relatives are coming to visit me and I want to receive them well. That reception will not be complete without their eating," he told her.

"So what do you want me to do for you?"

"If you could help me to prepare the best traditional food possible for them, I will forever be grateful."

She was very surprised at the request to cook a special traditional dish. Why would someone want to treat his visitors with what he could not prepare himself? she asked herself. He must be helpless to ask somebody he had not known well for this task, she felt.

"When are they visiting?" she asked.

"Next Saturday."

"Let's buy what you need by Thursday," she told him.

"I can't thank you enough, Ebi," he told her.

"Let me think about what I will prepare. By tomorrow, I'll give you a list of the things we need for the soup."

"Thanks a million," he told her.

Ebi knew that her presence would mean more than cooking

for the visitors. She had to prepare him to follow the customs of welcoming his visiting elders.

The fourth week of the Activist's return, the delegation from his village came to visit him. It was made up of five men. The Activist was disappointed that none of their wives, sisters, or aunts was in the delegation. Poko, as his name suggested, was plump like a pig. Despite his huge size, he looked very agile. If he did not introduce himself as the oldest of the five, the Activist would not have known.

Poko introduced Dafe, the cloth merchant, who was prosperous by village standards. Tebu was the fisherman, who knew the creeks and rivers as one knew one's own backyard. He was rather gaunt in appearance and looked older than Poko even though he was really much younger. Dafe and Tebu were uncles to the Activist, who had met them ten years ago when he returned home to bury his father. A few times he had sent money to them for their personal upkeep or for their children's school fees. Macaulay was the hunter and was famous for not missing his target. He had, despite his marriage of six years, not fathered a child and some of his relatives had advised him to stop hunting in order to assuage the spirits of the animals he had killed so that he could bring forth life. The youngest among them was Sodje, a farmer of yams. He was spare in shape and hardened physically.

Ebi had coached the Activist on how to receive his relatives. Once they were seated, she placed a plate on the small table in front of Poko, the eldest and leader of the delegation.

"I am happy that you have come to see me," the Activist began. "Here are three kola nuts, a bottle of Schnapps, beer, soft drinks, and five thousand naira as token of my appreciation of your visit."

Poko felt overwhelmed with what the Activist offered them and started a flurry of praises.

"Doctor of knowledge, you know everything in the white man's books!"

His fellow visitors would not be left out of the praise-chanting.

"You who have achieved so much that you lack nothing!"

"Son of Isaba, Ubi, Aje, you know honour and embrace it."

"You are the back of the cat. It doesn't touch the soil."

"You are the great hunter. You know where to shoot the elephant once and it falls."

The Activist was overwhelmed by the praises. "Thank you very much," he told his relatives.

"Let me not leave him to walk this path alone; he needs company," Ebi told the delegation, as she added three hundred naira.

"Thank you.

You are the moon in the night. No stars will outshine you," Poko told her.

Dafe accepted the kola nuts, drinks, and money on behalf of the delegation.

"We did not come here expecting you to overwhelm us with hospitality. At the same time, you will not be our true son if you did not know what to do to make your relatives very happy and proud of you. We are very satisfied with your reception and we will relate your kindness to our people at home. We can only pray that God will bless you a hundredfold and replenish the purse you took this from. We also thank our daughter."

"Bring the plate," Poko said, beckoning to Ebi.

She carried the plate to the eldest man, who prayed over the kola nuts and drinks.

"God will bless the kola nuts and drinks for us. Let Him give us peace, prosperity, and long life. We want educated children that will carry our names to the farthest parts of the world," he intoned.

Poko split the kola nuts and handed to each according to the person's age. Of course he gave Ebi last.

"May the kola nut and drink bless your womb so that you can give us plenty of children," he prayed as he handed her a piece of the kola nut.

"Amen," she replied politely.

Once they were settled and had unwound with shots of Schnapps and chewing kola nuts, members of the delegation looked at each other to signal that it was time for them to start business. They had come to visit the Activist with a message. Speaking for them, Dafe said they wanted to give him a welcome party in their village.

"But I have been back a month now," he told them. The Activist knew from their custom that whatever they spent on a welcoming party, he would have to pay for at a later date because the reception would carry an obligation he had to fulfill.

"Yes, but that is a short time. Do you know where you have gone to and returned from?" they asked him.

It was a distance they could not measure in their language. To them, America was farther than the spirit world. They mingled with spirits in their folktales, and some claimed to have gone and returned from the land of the spirits. None of them in the village before the Activist had gone to and returned from America. It was a place one could not walk to. Nor was it a place one could ride a bicycle or take a bus to. You could only take a ship for weeks or fly for days. No witch or wizard among them had ever confessed to successfully flying to and returning from America. The Atlantic Ocean was an impossible barrier that mocked their invisible craft. Without having been there, they could still imagine the great distance.

The Activist knew that his relatives did not expect him to answer the question. Saying he travelled to America and then came back was too banal under the circumstances.

"Do you realize how long you lived in America?" they further asked.

Their question reminded him of the long time he had spent outside. Twenty-five years was a very long time. His mother had died within two years of his leaving for America, and his father had also departed to join her in the other world ten years ago. There were young ones, boys and girls, he had not met and all grown enough to marry and have children. He had cousins, nephews and nieces, who had written him and he had sent them money to help them to buy books as they requested. He had not seen any of them since he returned. In the twenty-five years he had gone away a patient cook would have boiled a stone to become soft, in the parlance of the old.

"We want to give you a welcome party, but we also want to advise you. We want to acquaint you with our latest songs and dance steps, since you might only remember outdated ones. Since you left, goru dance had come and gone; so had kparikebe music. Ikpeba is on the decline, but tuetue has stuck with us. But we also want you to go back to America. We are proud of you over there more so than your being here," the spokesman said.

"Is that all?" the shocked Activist asked.

"That is not all, but that is our advice," Dafe told him.

The Activist thought that they had come to rejoice with him for returning home and he was ready to encourage them to send their children to the university where he now taught, but apparently that was not important to them. They preferred more to boast about his being overseas than to see him living close to them and helping to train their children.

After they had chatted for long, the Activist signalled Ebi to bring them food. Entertainment of visitors from a long distance is not complete without food. Drinks and kola nuts do not fill the place of food in the stomach. The aroma of the food could not be contained in the kitchen; it filled the air. Poko sniffed the aroma noisily and others salivated in anticipation. Ebi placed the food on the table and also set smaller plates there for each person to take his portion.

"Food on the table is like a woman who has removed her clothes; you don't have to look her in the eye for too long again before going into action," Poko told his men. As the oldest of the visitors, he had to give permission for them to start eating and after his metaphoric foray he expected them to plunge into the food spread on the table.

"There's water in the bowls to wash your hands," Ebi told them.

The members of the delegation enjoyed the palm oil soup with starch and yam. Ebi had used smoked mudfish, tilapia, crayfish, and special spices. The soup was thick and perfectly done, and so delicious. The starch was prepared with a little palm oil and was soft and ideal to cut with fingers. As the visitors ate, they kept quiet; they licked their fingers and were very impressed.

"How did you know our desire?" the spokesman asked the Activist.

"I am one of you and I know what we enjoy," he told them.

"You are our true son," Tebu said.

"But it is my colleague, Ebi, who helped me. All the praises should go to her," the Activist explained.

"Is she the keeper of your keys?" Poko asked.

The Activist was confused. He did not understand the question and so did not know what to say. Poko realized the Activist was too young when he left them to understand this deep expression.

"Is she your wife?" he asked.

"No, not so soon; she is a colleague and she has been kind enough to help a stranger to take care of his people he left many years ago who have come to visit him," he further explained.

They looked at Ebi, surveyed her from head to toe and nodded approval of her stature. She possessed the qualities they admired in women. She was neither thin nor fat but on the slender side and had a height that suited her size. Ebi wore a three-piece traditional dress that fitted her very well. She carried a dignified mien that added to her physical charm. The Activist was embarrassed, but there was nothing he could do about his people's mannerisms.

"The Great Maker has been kind to her," Dafe told the Activist.

"She's Mami Wata," Poko declared.

"What does that mean?" the Activist asked.

"If she loves you, you will be blessed," Poko explained.

They all laughed. The Activist liked the comparison of a wife to the keeper of one's keys. He knew that a man loved by his woman must consider himself blessed.

"Where is she from?" Poko again asked.

"I think she is from here," the Activist answered.

"Do you know that your father once spent many years with his senior sister married to an Izon man?" Poko asked.

Poko then spoke Izon to Ebi and she spoke back the language. Then she spoke fluent Urhobo to say that she was from Okwagbe, which made them believe she was Urhobo. She did not want to explain her complicated background to strangers.

Before they left, Dafe, as spokesman, again raised the issue that the Activist should return to America, where he could be taking their children one by one to work there.

"If you don't want to earn dollars, go back and send us dollars every month. We are roasting from hardship here. You have just come and may not yet feel the heat tormenting us," Poko told him.

"But things are going to get better," the Activist told them.

"This is a bottomless hole and nobody can fill it up. Go back and help us from there," Dafe pronounced in a pleading tone.

"You can take our daughter along with you there," Tebu said, referring to Ebi.

The Activist reminded his visitors that he wanted no welcome-back party, an idea that lost steam once the members of the delegation knew he was steadfast in his decision to stay in Nigeria rather than return to the United States. Members of the delegation rose to leave, scratching their heads in disappointment at their illustrious son's stubborn resolve to stay permanently among them. To Poko, the Activist had inherited this dogged determination from his late father, who could not be moved to change his position once he had arrived at a decision.

When the Activist wrote to a friend of his in the United States about what was happening, the reply was expected: "That is Nigeria for you!" Still he had no regrets for coming home. He was heartened that someone had helped him beyond expectation.

The Genealogy of Area Boys

The Niger Delta that the Activist returned to had changed so much from what it used to be, even as it remained the same landmass. It had been seriously scarred by Bell Oil Company whose emblem of a red-rimmed shell of yellow flames was seen all over the area. In the company's inordinate hunger for more barrels of oil to ship out to increase yearly record profits, the landscape was gradually turning into a wasteland. Residents of the oil-producing area had become helpless before the monstrous power of their overlords, the oil company and the military government. But there were many other changes too.

The boma boys of the Activist's childhood days were gone; in their place were area boys now assuming the roles the boma boys used to play. Many rural people still produced palm oil that once made the area to be called the Oil Protectorate but they could barely meet local demands. The new oil, petroleum, had drastically diminished the economic importance of the once invaluable palm tree that the Action Group Party had chosen, and not the cocoa plant closer to the party's core area, as its symbol.

Since the Activist left, Nigeria's oil production had risen from about four hundred thousand to more than two million barrels a day, and the country had joined the Organization of Oil-Producing and Exporting Countries and had remained ranked sixth among them. Bell Oil and the other oil companies had been given a free hand by the military rulers to do all it took to continue increasing production. While that meant more money in the government's coffers to sustain the dictatorship, it also meant total disregard of the Niger Delta people and their environment.

The Activist would discover that his Niger Delta had a new face, an ugly or rather sick face that was different from the pristine one he used to know. The signs were already there before he left, but the disfiguration then was child's play compared to now. He returned to witness the wake of a destructive hurricane as far as the environment was concerned. He would also meet and make friends with people that he had least expected would be his partners in the tug-of-war that was taking place.

Soon after his return the Activist started to hear about the area boys. He had not read about them in Nigerian papers that got into American libraries or posted on the Internet. Why did the journalists not report on them? From the way the community was divided in praising or cursing the area boys, it was a crime of omission that the journalists did not write about them. But the longer he stayed in his homeland, the more he would learn about the journalists and so would understand their omission of the area boys from their reporting and write-ups.

The law enforcement agency saw the area boys as a menace to society. From the police profile, until you met or saw them, you would think they were ogres out there savagely attacking people for no reason other than for personal gratification from doing evil or mischief. The police could not be trusted for anything; this included the way they described their so-called suspects. The police had arrested some area boys for petty stealing and misdemeanors and tortured them into admitting to other heinous crimes they had not committed but to help them claim success in their steadfast war against crime.

The area boys had their own story to tell, and, from their perspective, they were fighters attempting not only to reclaim what had been robbed from them but also holding firmly to what was theirs that others were attempting to snatch away. They were dedicated to Egba, the god of war that helped his devotees to take back what had been forcibly taken from them. Egba was also the god of revenge and restitution. The area boys were also called Egba Boys, a name that evoked mass hysteria because of the god's fearful nature. They treated those who agreed with their robbers the same way they treated the robbers themselves. They saw no contradiction in robbing those who had robbed them.

By the end of the civil war in 1970 the boma boys, members of local gangs, would not only lose their glamorous status but also their clout in society. For decades before the civil war, the port cities of the Niger Delta, especially Sapele and Warri, were hotbeds of the glamourised group whose members were collectively called boma boys. They built their identity on two foreign traditions: cowboys and sailors.

Boma boys wore Texas cowboy paraphernalia: high boots, tight blue or black jeans, large belts, flannel or denim shirts, and big hats. This dress code they had apparently copied from old American western movies. Sapele, Warri, and Port Harcourt had many cinema houses then. Delta, Odion, Rex, and later Olympia cinema houses, operated by Lebanese and Syrian entrepreneurs, were in most towns.

John Wayne was the major idol. The worshippers of the swashbuckler John Wayne became boma boys, toughened inner city boys whose daredevil behaviour and actions soon became their trademark. They loved the shootings and killings of the so-called Red Indians. The boma boys lacked the critical acumen to interpret artistic works, and so they took the side of the white adventurer who did not care about other people's lives against the victimized Native Americans, who were slaughtered in a very nonchalant manner, just like the buffalo that roamed their grassy plains. The history of the strong and armed taking over the resources of the weak started very long ago. Inhabitants of the Niger Delta would have their turn also of being robbed of their resources decades later. Colonization was the first stage, but the oil exploration would be the crowning glory of the modern swashbuckler no longer an individual John Wayne but multinational corporations known as major employers and manipulators of local and national governments.

The boma boys walked with the swagger of sailors, who came to town to seek women in clubs. The long absence of sailors from land had starved them sexually and they came onshore to fulfill their libidinous cravings. They spent whatever it took to take to bed the club ladies that dressed fancifully. The oversexed sailors sometimes went to Okoye Street and sought outright prostitutes, who became their girlfriends until they went back to the sea.

The young men flaunted their fancy clothing as a wand to overcome difficulties. They loved riding motorcycles and performed different stunts to impress girls. They liked girls in a romantic sense, and so impressed them with their manners rather than raping them as the police maligned them of doing.

The boma boys assumed the responsibility of policing their neighbourhoods and their tough mistreatment of suspected thieves earned them the status of heroes. The very old of Uguanja quarter in Sapele looked back with nostalgia to the days of the boma boys.

When the Biafran forces entered the Midwest Region in 1967, the Nigerian Army posted to defend the State's borders melted away and the invading forces that called themselves liberators took over the entire state. It was only in Sapele, the headquarters of boma boys, that there was robust resistance against the humiliation. The boma boys organized themselves into a kind of guerrilla force and took on the rebel army that invaded their town. They not only killed many of the rebel soldiers, their rising sun uniforms still trophies among the old, but also succeeded in driving them out of the town. Sapele was the only town in the entire Midwest Region that was not occupied by the rebel soldiers.

In the wake of the successful defense of Sapele, almost every boma boy escaped through the Ethiope River and adjoining creeks to Lagos, where they joined the Federal Army that would later liberate the captive state. By the time the secessionist rebellion collapsed, there were no boma boys left - they had all virtually become veterans of the civil war, husbands of war-ravaged girls, and parents in a new society.

But the vacuum created by the absence of boma boys immediately following the civil war's end would be filled after the oil boom turned into doom for the Niger Delta people. The proceeds from the oil went to Lagos to build a festival town for the black peoples of the world to celebrate their culture and arts and also to construct unending bridges to connect water-separated parts of the teeming city. Other oil gains also went to build an entire new capital on rocks in the windy and dusty savannah.

The oil-producing coastal people were left in the lurch. Children of boma boys dropped out of school and those that graduated from secondary schools had no jobs. Areas in which boma boys had lived lacked social amenities and the government failed to address the problems. The Federal Military Government operated a quota system that favored inland states that inflated their population by counting their cows, dogs, and goats as humans. That was what they believed a national census to be all about. Since they had population advantage, the people of those states enjoyed the oil prosperity at the expense of the hard-toiling farmers and fishermen and women whose lands, waters and air were polluted by oil slicks, blowouts, and permanent flares that made hell a daily experience of the Niger Delta people.

So the boma boys resurrected with a new name - area boys. The cinema houses had all closed because of austere economic measures that had killed all forms of entertainment. New churches, businesses, took over the old cinema houses. But that's another matter.

The government and the oil corporations brought in people from other states to fill the jobs in the industry that was destroying not only their environment but also their sources of livelihood. The area boys saw themselves as a reject caste thrown out of their paradise that had become a haven for others. They were a bitter group and they would die to wrest a few naira from the outsiders.

The poor economic situation promoted armed robbery. The area boys were not mindless robbers but hardened locals who felt they had to share in whatever they could from the economic life of their communities. They were jobless urchins, capable of robbing, killing, and doing any type of dastardly act for pay to survive the hard times. Their morality and ethics were convoluted by the socio-economic dictates of the time, but they knew very well the experience of survival. Call it hustling, harassment, blackmail, or extortion, they were ready to take on the outsider to eke out a living.

These area boys were worshipers of Egba, the god of war, revenge, and restitution. Each member of the area boys' group was initiated into the association at Egba's shrine by a huge and ageless iroko tree.

"I accept Egba as my protector," the initiate said after the ritual chief. "From now on, I will give all I have, including my blood and sweat, to obey the commands of Egba, who knows my needs. May Egba make me realize my rightful destiny!" he repeated.

"Egba, burn your enemies!" the gathering chanted.

"Egba, give your enemies no comfort," they also shouted.

It was an infectious atmosphere and the newly initiated area boys, after drinking local gin mixed with some other potions, danced deliriously proclaiming Egba as the helper of orphans and the victimized. Then they swore to avenge or take back whatever had been robbed from them. The kidnapping of expatriates working in the oil companies was a major preoccupation of the area boys. They built up personal wealth from the proceeds of ransoms, which the companies paid secretly even though they publicly denied dealing with armed gangs and terrorists.

Ebi's Past

Ebi Emasheyi was thirty-seven years old when the forty-year-old Activist returned finally from the United States. She was blessed with a youthful physique and good looks and so could easily be taken for a twenty-eight-year-old lady. Everything about her belied her true age. She walked in a zestful manner that displayed her athletic agility. She took good care of herself by eating right and regularly. She would often walk rather than accept a ride to be physically fit. She had been an athlete in secondary school and did very well in both the 200-yard and 400-yard races. Her main exercise now was keeping busy at home and walking whenever possible.

   Ebi already had a Master's degree in art education and had been teaching at the Niger Delta State University for four years. She wanted to have the highest degree possible in her field and had registered in a doctoral program in art. She was doing it part-time as she taught at the university. She knew it would take some time but she could not afford to do the program faster and fulltime without her employer's assistance. She regretted that the university had stopped paying its teachers to pursue their doctoral programs fulltime. It was an arrangement that could have been very convenient for her. However, she could understand the university's decision, since many beneficiaries of the special scholarship abused the kind gesture by deliberately prolonging their studies to have free pay and no teaching. A few sent abroad even refused to return home to serve the time required after their studies in the staff development agreement.

   Ebi always wanted to be able to take care of her needs - she had nobody else to do that for her. Many men had begun to consider her over-ripe, but she was not bothered. She dismissed the societal norms concerning marriage as a patriarchal effort to continue to place women in a subordinate position. She loved the path of education that she had chosen and knew she was better off educated than marrying more than ten years ago without education. Many men would like such uneducated women to be their wives, but she wanted to be equal with or close to her future husband's status.

She saw many young women leaving school to marry and wondered whether they thought clearly about their future. Her own mother often taunted her.

"When are you going to bring home a man to introduce as your prospective husband?" she would ask her daughter.

"Am I to go out into the street and kidnap a man just to bring him to you as my husband?" Ebi would ask back.

"A woman's prime runs out fast and you should bring somebody soon," the mother would counsel.

"When the right man comes my way, you'll know," she would tell her mother.

Her mother often gave a sigh of exasperation whenever she talked about waiting until the right man came her way.

"Are you waiting for the President? Men are men."

"Marry that stark illiterate? And a soldier for that matter! He's not my type! All men are not men as all women are not women," Ebi would challenge her mother.

"What do you need a man for than to have children?"

"I need a man for more than children."

"You modern women don't understand. We married young and had our children early and fast."

"I want my husband, if he comes, to be my friend and companion at the same time."

"A man will prefer another man for friendship to his wife."

"Don't you think that a man can say the same thing of a woman that a woman will prefer another woman to her husband for friendship?"

"Men's friendships are stronger than women's."

"I think it depends on individuals," Ebi said.

"You will learn with time that men are men," the cynical mother told her.

"I believe some men are different as some women are also

different. A man will only appeal to me if he is really different in a very positive way," she said.

"The sun is already gone far."

"It's still morning despite the sun," Ebi countered.

To Ebi, her mother did not just get what it meant to marry. But that did not bother her at all. She would not succumb to this type of intimidation, however persistent the harassment from her mother or relatives.

Ebi wanted a man whom she would love and who also would love her, a companion for life. So, despite the taunts from her mother, which would have driven a weak-hearted and desperate lady to marry the first man that approached her for marriage, she did not want to marry for the sake of keeping up appearances as a married woman. Instead she did what surprised her suitor many years ago.

Udoma had married Jessica for seven years and they were still without a child. He appeared to have lost hope of their ever having a child together after so many fruitless years. He began to listen to some friends and relatives, who asked him to "try another leg," by which they meant that he should take another woman since his current wife had failed in her reproductive role. Not too long after, Udoma was won over by the argument of having another woman to prove his virility and fertility.

Udoma thought of the marriageable women in the community. They were not many because the young women were betrothed almost as soon as they were seventeen to eighteen. He was not that young and so needed a woman that was also not too young. In his search, his gaze fell on one unmarried lady who could fulfill his desire for a child. Ebi was there for him, he believed, and so he came to her to make a blunt proposal.

He had known Ebi from a distance for many years. On her side, Ebi also knew him as one of her townsmen. When she was in a grammar school and on vacation, she had attended some dance parties that Udoma had also attended. At the time, he liked her but could not bring himself to talk to her. He graduated from the university as Ebi was entering. So, he knew Ebi but not much.

Neither before this time had attempted to bridge the gap

between them. Udoma had, among his fellow men, talked about Ebi several times as a beautiful woman without a husband. To them, she was too selective to settle on one man for a husband and that might have caused her not to be yet married. "Is she waiting for a complete gentleman?" they asked. Sooner or later, she would have to make do with one of the men around, the gossiping men believed. To Udoma, that later time had come.

Udoma did not attempt to introduce the matter subtly or gradually. He did not want to waste time in courtship. He felt he knew what he wanted and no subtleties were needed.

"I am interested in marrying you," he told Ebi.

"What of your present wife?" she asked.

"I want to be frank with you, Ebi."

"Yes, tell me what's on your mind."

"I have been married for seven years and I am still without a child. I want to marry you," he told her.

"Do you simply want me to bear you a child? What type of proposal is this?"

"I want you to be the mother of my child or children," he retorted.

"But is that enough reason for us to marry?"

"It's more than that. I really like and love you; hence I want you to be my wife. I have known you for many years and really like your manners. You are also very beautiful. It's only the woman that a man loves that he will want to be the mother of his children."

"But what if I do not have a child for you in time too, what will you do?" she asked him.

"You will certainly give me a child. Your family's women are always fertile. I know the fact that I already have a wife must bother you, but I'll take care of that problem, if a problem is what it looks to you. After I have married you and you have given me a child, I'll gradually let Jessica go. Everybody will understand."

"Are you planning to have me as your second wife? Count me out," she told him, as she joined her right thumb and the middle finger to circle her head and snapped the fingers in the air. It was a signal of her complete and forceful rejection of his explanation of what he intended to do with her and Jessica.

"Not quite that."

"You will wait for me to conceive before letting Jessica go to where?"

Udoma was quiet, perhaps thinking of what next to say. He did not expect to be asked so many questions by a woman he thought would jump at his proposal. But Ebi knew the type of man she wanted. She would not give him the chance to impose his will on her. She believed in asserting herself in matters of this nature in which someone would want to take advantage of her.

"How will everybody understand? What of her? How do you know the source of the problem is from her and not you?"

"It can't be me!" he said with an authoritative air.

"There's no way of knowing short of a medical examination," she told him.

"Let's talk about first things first. I am interested in marrying you."

"I don't know you well enough. Also I won't marry an already married man. I hope this is clear enough."

"Think more about it," Udoma persisted.

"I don't need to think more about it. I won't marry you."

The bantering went on, and neither changed the other's feelings or views. But, as in such things, Ebi knew that Udoma would bring up the matter again soon. His type of men did not take no for an answer, as if the woman must accept whatever proposal was brought to her. She was not the type that could be taken for granted.

When Ebi jokingly told her mother about the proposal, she responded that it was her life and therefore she should know what to do, but not to forget that she was getting to be an old maid. The mother, of course from a different generation, was not bothered that Udoma was already married. She had been socialized to believe that women compete for a man's affection. If she had a problem at all, it was something else and she told her daughter what it was.

"No woman wants to put her head into wherever that woman's family member has married. I know them. It will be like thrusting your hand into a viper's nest. Their women are so jealous that they are capable of hurting the other woman in their lives."

"I don't need to hear that because I am not interested," Ebi told her mother.

"I have to let you know this. As long as she is from the Egube family, that Udoma's wife will use any means necessary to hold onto her man and not allow another woman to share him with her. Their means are often diabolical," she explained.

Still, Udoma's proposal to her was an offer that she should use her discretion to accept or reject.

"You are not growing younger. You are educated enough to know what is right for you," the mother again counselled.

"I certainly know what's good for me and that's why you should leave me alone in this matter," Ebi told her mother.

"You told me about his proposal and it's not such a bad thing, but I'll leave you to decide for yourself," she replied.

Unknown to Ebi, her mother, gladdened that her daughter had got a suitor however unimpressive, took the proposal more seriously. She desperately wanted her daughter to be married. She was tired of seeing her single; a spinster. How many more years before her reproductive life would be over? Would she not be happy to be Mrs. Somebody? Had she herself not been attending the marriage ceremonies of her friends' daughters? Was it not her turn to invite others to her daughter's wedding? Though she did not marry in the church, she would like her daughter to be dressed in a flowing white gown and wearing white gloves and exchanging rings and vows with her husband in the church. Then it would be her turn to brag as the bride's mother at the reception after the church service.

Ebi's mother told her brother about the proposal. Pesu, Ebi's uncle, made inquiries about Udoma's birthplace and his parents. He went to secretly investigate the Udoma family and came back with a negative report. Udoma's was not a family to marry into no matter how much one wanted to have a son-in-law. They had frequent divorces. The men beat their wives and did not live long. They seemed to be jinxed with bad luck; hence they were dwindling and were not prosperous. Udoma was an exception in some ways, but he was still relatively young and his family genes might still manifest in some unpleasant ways in his life. After all, he was already being plagued since his wife of so many years could not conceive in a society where seventeen-year-olds conceived from their first sexual encounters.

"I don't support your marrying him. He does not come to you out of love," Uncle Pesu told Ebi with finality.

Ebi was surprised that his uncle knew about this at all. She told him that she did not want the man at all because he was already married and she would not share her husband with another woman.

Ebi also jokingly told some of her friends, who advised her to accept first and think about it later. She objected to playing with such a serious matter and said she had to think first before acting. She knew what she wanted. She wanted to marry when the right opportunity came, but this was not a good opportunity. She could not imagine herself being a second wife.

When Udoma came back to Ebi, she had made up her mind to be very blunt in rejecting him and still helping him in any way she could. It was not that deciding her response was difficult. She also thought of what she could do following her decision.

"I will help you to be a happy father," she told him.

"Thank you. I can't be grateful enough. I trusted that you would agree to marry me," he told her.

He felt he had won over a new bride fairly easily and it remained for the details of the marriage to be worked out. He had enough money to take care of the customary requirements. He had kept his bank savings a secret from his wife and occasionally complained of being broke to give the impression that he had no money. He was a cunning man and had a fairly good sum in his bank account.

"I am saying that I will help you to achieve your desire for children or your wife's conception, your reason for trying to marry me," she told him.

Udoma was confused. Was this woman shy and trying to make things difficult? Or what did she mean? Was she not mature enough to be direct on issues of marriage and sex? Or she just wanted to be his girlfriend and not be his wife? He wondered in his mind. He had no other way of interpreting

Ebi's readiness to assist him in getting a baby without marrying him.

"I will take you to somebody who will help your wife to conceive. He has a very good reputation in such things," she told him.

Ebi had told Clara, her girlfriend, about this weird proposal and, inthe course of their conversation, learnt of a medicine man that helped couples with difficulty in having children. Ebi relayed this to Udoma who had been jubilant a short while ago that he had got a new bride. He was interested in Ebi's suggestion to see the medicine man, and they arranged for a day to go and see him.

Accompanied by Clara, her friend, Ebi set out with Udoma to consult the healer. The famous man lived in a hole; his house was tucked inside the bush. Udoma's Peugeot 504 car could not go through the dirt path and so he parked the car in a small village on the way. The three walked a mile to the healer's house. It was during the rainy season and the soil was soaked with water. They had to walk through mud to get there and they were happy that the healer was at home.

After Udoma explained his problem, Ezeani promised to do his best. He said that his best efforts had always worked for his many patients. He charged him a ram and fifty thousand naira.

"I will prepare a mixture for you and your wife. Taken by both of you every other day from the seventh day after your wife's menstruation about an hour before you go to bed, your problem should eventually be solved," Ezeani, in a self-assured manner, told Udoma.

"Amen!" the happy Udoma intoned.

Udoma was happy that the humiliation of his inability to impregnate his wife would soon end. Then, he could beat his chest among men who were strong enough to impregnate their wives. He often felt that some relatives and friends doubted his virility. Some might even be speculating that he was impotent and just using his wife as a cover. Others might be suspecting he had "kerosene" sperm which was not thick enough to make a woman conceive. It would be no small relief to impregnate his wife and later have a baby. Once he had his child, he would be free of invisible jeers and taunts.

But Udoma soon thought about the charge for the medicine. He was a rather tight-fisted man who grudgingly released money for anything no matter how important to him. He complained that the fee charged him was too much and asked to pay only twenty thousand naira. Ezeani told him that he was not used to bargaining about the amount he charged and that the task was worth the money. The healer explained that he was not asking him to pay the whole amount at that time. He would only pay in full after his wife conceived. Still Udoma was not satisfied. At a point when Udoma still wanted to negotiate the charged fee, Ezeani asked him to go away and think about his offer and let him know if he still wanted the treatment. Surprisingly, Udoma became angry, got up and started to head back to his car. Of course Ebi and Clara followed him out.

Ebi had to plead with him along the footpath to seize the opportunity and try the man's treatment.

"The money is not too much, if you get what you want! Are you telling me that Ezeani's fee is more important to you than having a baby?" Ebi asked him.

"It's a lot for what you are not sure of. You know these medicine men like to impress but one cannot be sure of the result of their work," he said.

"Ezeani is an experienced healer and you must trust him to get the desired results," Clara told Udoma.

After all, she was the one who told Ebi about the medicine man. Ebi had asked her to accompany her and Udoma to show them the way. She did not want to travel with Udoma alone too. More so, to a medicine man's place!

"But he told you to pay only after the medicine had worked. What can be a better assurance for your money than that?" Ebi asked.

Ebi reflected about this man who, if she agreed to marry him, would spend ten times the amount Ezeani had charged him for the marriage ceremony so that people could drink, eat, and dance. Was this man serious at all? she asked herself.

They came back to the car, got in and were about to drive back, when reason suddenly came into Udoma's head and he heeded Ebi's counsel. They trudged back the muddy path to the herbalist, who though amazed by Udoma's action, still agreed to help him overcome his doubts. He prepared a curative from herbs, which he asked Udoma and his wife to drink only on days they made love, but must be seven days after her menstruation.

"You can give me whatever pleases you for now. However, after you have taken the medicine and after your wife delivers, bring me a ram and fifty thousand naira; that's the total cost," he told Udoma, re-stating the agreement.

"There will be no problem. You'll get more than one ram plus the money if you can help me have a child."

"You should be calm. Don't be anxious and use the medicine as I have directed," the medicine man explained to Udoma.

For about a year after they returned from Ezeani's, Ebi did not see Udoma. She guessed he must be busy. Everybody was trying to make a living by doing extra jobs, if available, in the hard times and he must be struggling to make his family comfortable. She did not go to ask about him for fear he would misread her intention. Any man he asked about Udoma would inevitably pass the word to him. He might feel that she had reconsidered her rejection of his proposal and changed her mind to marry him. She also did not want him to be emotionally distracted from his wife. All these concerns and the need for her to maintain her dignity restrained her from asking about him.

Weeks passed. Then months passed. A year had almost passed. Then one early morning Udoma arrived in his newly re-sprayed milk-white car. The sun was up that early and he was in a very cheerful mood. He wore a suit, which was a rarity for him. There must be something in the air, Ebi guessed. He did not even greet Ebi before going straight to announce the good news.

"Jessica delivered a baby boy three days ago. Both the mother and the baby are doing very fine and are back home."

"We thank God for his wonderful mercies!" Ebi chanted.

"It's a miracle," he said.

"I am very happy for you and your wife."

"Thank you."

"Why didn't you tell me that Jessica had conceived?" she asked.

"My pastor ordered me not to tell anybody," he told her.

Ebi wondered whether Udoma told the pastor about meeting a traditional healer to help him have a child. She was sure he didn't.

"You have to take the ram and fifty thousand naira to Ezeani, as promised," she reminded him.

"We are born again in the blood of Christ. We are now members of the Redeemed Church of Christ and the pastor, who is a prayer warrior, prays for us," he told her.

"Did you take the medicine that Ezeani prepared for you and your wife?"

"Yes, I did, but it was God's power and not the medicine that helped us."

"I don't doubt God's power, but as long as you took the medicine you have to pay for it."

"We are paying God with our monthly tithes."

"That's not enough."

"What do you mean by not enough? The Bible stipulates that."

"You better take the ram and money to Ezeani as promised, if you don't want to lose your child," Ebi warned.

"With the blood of Jesus, we will overcome all fears and superstitions," he replied.

Ebi felt happy for him that the medicine prepared for him had the desired effect. Ezeani had really proved to be a knowledgeable and experienced healer, as Clara had told her. His kind should be very few these days when many healers announced their trades with signboards and advertisements in newspapers in order to make money. Such medicine men ran a litany of ailments they could treat. She was happy that both Udoma and his wife, Jessica, were now parents and should be content with their marriage.

Ebi was ready to live a single woman all her life, if a suitable partner did not come her way. She would not be one of those women on campus flaunting their Mrs. before their names at every opportunity; they were always very keen to impress unmarried women rather than the male population that took them for granted and trampled on them. She was surprised at the women with Ph.D. degrees calling and signing their names as Dr. (Mrs.), while the men were just Dr. and not Dr. (Mr.). She pitied those women. Women could often be their own worst enemies, she reflected.

Ebi worked hard on her doctoral program while she taught full-load and performed other departmental duties assigned to her. She wanted to pursue a career at the university so as to be well established to take care of herself and assist her immediate family. She realized that without the doctorate degree, one's prospects in the university were very limited. She wanted to rise to the highest possible position and be able to stand on her own with pride. It is when women are unable to take care of their needs, she realized, that they go to men they do not even like or marry whatever man they do not love, but believe can provide materially for them. Such women soon discover that material comfort alone cannot make up for lack of love. She thus set herself on the path of self-reliance. If a partner came to supplement her income, fine. If nobody came to her, she was prepared to live independently.

For several years, Ebi knew that her mother's health was failing. Her regular visit to Warri Central Hospital had not helped much because the doctors were unable to point out what was really wrong with her. She did tests whose results pointed to no ailment known by the doctors. Old age must have exacerbated whatever unknown illness she suffered from. Ebi took some days off her work to be with her at the Central Hospital when the sickness became critical.

When her mother died, Ebi felt relieved from being taunted about marriage by one who was supposed to show her love unconditionally. She believed her mother would have loved her more as a married woman than the single woman she was. Why should her mother not be proud of her education; more so because she was one of the few women teaching in the university? She grieved for her and wished she had married before her death, even if only to fulfill her mother's dream of having a son-in-law. Because she had no husband when her mother died, there was no son-in-law to bring a dance troupe to perform at the burial ceremony. But she felt that did not matter; she could not help what was beyond her control. With her father long dead and the mother now gone, she became more determined to take her academic career even more seriously.

Suspicions

Someone from the United States of America would be the last person to be welcomed warmly by the area boys. Their respective interests, one would expect, should be far apart. America presented a dilemma to the area boys. On the one hand, they admired America and many of their idols were American. They loved American stars ranging from Michael Jackson, Eddie Murphy, Michael Jordan, to Bill Cosby and Janet Jackson. Many of them wore baseball caps turned the other way around to show what they described as "guyish," a mark of sophistication. They also wore blue jeans, which they saw as American. Some area boys carried boom boxes; they played and danced to the music of many African-American artists. Many even spoke with a ghetto accent, which they mistook for sophisticated American English. Some also had posters of thin white American blondes and superstars on their walls. So, many of the area boys loved American products and lifestyles.

But, on the other hand, they knew that America owned O&G Company and worked hand in hand with Britain, Holland, and Bell Oil Company. The oil companies, to them, were brothers; they were all owned by white people. It did not matter whether it was O&G or Bell Oil; they were all oil companies, even though they bore the most grudge against Bell Oil. That multinational oil company brandishing its yellow flame logo covered the entire Niger Delta area in its operations and was blamed for the oil spillage, blowouts, and gas flares. To the area boys, Bell Oil Company stole their wealth to develop its owners' countries overseas and left them impoverished. They had heard the news reports that foreign retired marines were training the national army to protect the oil installations; a sugar-coated way of asking the mercenaries and the national army's brutal soldiers to kill any protesters against Bell Oil Company under the guise of securing oil wells. They realized that somehow America had joined hands with their local enemies, the oil companies and the military government, whose activities destroyed the people and their environment by spreading fire all over the oil-producing region.

In recent years, Bell Oil Company and O&G Company had each begun employing a senior academic of the area as a community development officer. The holder of this office was expected to liaise between the oil company and the local community and suggest and implement ways of "developing" the area. Those who benefitted from the practice praised it as a concession to the Niger Delta people. Usually the oil companies gave the academic an astounding salary; over five times what he received in the university, while on sabbatical leave. No strategy could be more effective at winning over the top academic class of the community to the side of the oil companies. With this type of salary offered to the academic that he could only have dreamt of, he simply became the company's sidekick, assuming the role of Member in early colonial times. Member often collected taxes and helped to chase his own industrious but impoverished people into the bush for not paying the British-imposed taxes. The people loathed him like a vulture for the traitor they saw him to be, but he enjoyed the trust of his white boss, whom he obeyed like a dog its owner.

The metamorphosed Member with an academic qualification wrote the situation report about whatever the chiefs were up to, what the area boys were contemplating, the direction the academic staff were taking, and so forth. He gathered information about his people and passed it to his new employers to earn his huge pay.

Oftentimes the petroleum industry would build a block of buildings for the local primary or secondary schools, which they opened with fanfare. The oil companies made sure that their public relations officers cultivated a warm relationship with the press and that meant that their charitable activities were trumpeted in the media for as many people as possible to hear about. They promoted the image of a development company rather than the exploiting one that the local people saw them to be. The local pressmen and women, who did not understand the home cultures of the oil companies, knew nothing about packaging, which made lies and dirt to look attractive. The companies' image-makers worked very hard to control their public perception with flattering write-ups.

These public relations officers stuffed large padded brown envelopes with money, which they gave to the newspapermen and women to buy them over to their side. They even went as far as writing for the press what they wanted reported - what in Europe and North America would be called infomercial, which the companies would have paid heavily for to be published or broadcast. From what the press wrote about the oil companies, one would think they were charitable organizations like Oxfam and Caritas among a displaced people. Also, if the claims of the oil companies were true about their development projects, the Niger Delta would have, over the decades of oil exploration, transformed into a European province or an American state in Africa. The companies thought that the people were stupid and loved money so much that they had no sense to realize that they were being robbed. But the area boys were wiser than the foreigners thought.

The area boys knew that charity in the form of tidbits thrown about to a desperate crowd should not take the place of justice and fairness. They also knew that those among them that should fight for them, such as the academics and chiefs, were interested in lining their individual pockets. They wanted a formal share to develop their area and compensate the people for their occupations destroyed by the oil-prospecting activities. They also wanted the oil companies to return a fraction of their profit to restore the environment that had been devastated by various forms of pollution. In their minds, that was not too much to ask for.

So, to the area boys, half-educated as some pompous academics might dismiss them, America was beautiful and ugly. America was a friend and a foe at the same time. It was with this ambivalence that they viewed the Activist, the

Johnny that had just come to town. To them, returning from America made him an American. After all, he had been there for twenty-five years; many of them were not even as old as that.

The area boys were therefore wary of the Activist. They saw one more educated man from the area that could be on the pay roll of the oil companies. They believed it was a matter of time before the oil explorers recruited him as a community development officer to sell his people for pay. After all, what was a community development officer other than an overseer for the white man in a global age, used by the outsiders to stop his own people from demanding justice and fair compensation?

Various area boys heard about the Activist. They listened to him at the barber's shop as he railed against the powerful countries that were stifling small ones to maintain their high standard of living. They heard him talk about their Niger Delta people being cheated of their inheritance by the multinational corporations. They liked what they had heard so far. But he remained a stranger to them, an inscrutable man who had left America to come and suffer with them in the Niger Delta. He was not only from America, but he was an academic; two points that counted against him as someone that they should trust. In their struggle against multinational companies and the Federal Military Government for "sovereignty" over their natural resources, the area boys did not trust every homeboy. People had to prove themselves, and they watched every step the Activist took, as they thought he also watched them.

Pere's Trials

Pere fought his way to the headship of his area boys' group. This was done beyond the pale of public eyes. Since the inner core of the area boys' association operated like a secret society, only very few would know Pere closely; he might be doing some job in the day but that was often a cover for his real important position among the area boys. Neighbours and relatives would not know his real identity; he would remain just a neighbour or a relative.

Pere escaped many assassination attempts to reach the top post of the association; survivors led by intimidation. Where the area boys got guns from and kept them the public did not know but they had more sophisticated weapons than the police and soldiers did. They possessed AK 47s, magnums, .50 caliber rifles, and all sorts of powerful guns. The many factions fought against each other fierce battles that brought the civil war battles of Abagana and Ehor to mind. Once they engaged themselves in combat, civilians in long trails left town in a manner also reminiscent of civil war days.

Pere was an impressive young man in his early thirties; he commanded much respect. To come to his position, he had kidnapped five white expatriates, and the heavy ransom gained through secret negotiations had enriched him and his group. He did not kill because, according to him, he wanted to live and so allowed others to also live. The struggle, to him, was to be allowed to live. Outsiders were not allowing him and his people to live and so he would make life hard for them in their paradise, his hell. He would force them to concede that he and his people had a right to live on their God-given resources. He was a true Egba Boy. So, the threats of executing kidnapped expatriates were negotiation strategies to wrest as much money as possible from the oil company's hands.

"If we cannot live on our water, land, and air, then we are finished," he reasoned.

"Those who take away our wealth must pay dearly for it," he often told his fellow area boys.

"We obey the dictates of Egba!" they would chorus.

His people needed the fish that had sustained them from the beginning of time. So also did they need the farmlands to cultivate cassava, yams, and other subsistent crops to live on! They also had to grow much needed vegetables. And, of course, they had to live a healthy life. The air used to be cool because of constant rain and the luxuriant forest, but oil slicks, blowouts, and gas flares had destroyed that life. Even the rain that fell was so soot-black that no more did anybody drink rainwater, which, of all waters, used to be described as God-given water. The people had lost their green refuge as well. Their forests used to have deep green and lush foliage, the pride of the tropics, but that had changed, since fires often followed oil and gas accidents.

Pere's mother was once married to an ex-soldier, the term used after the civil war to describe someone fending for himself after being discharged from the Nigerian Army and abandoned by the government. She often left and returned to the man, who eventually became insane. The ex-soldier had been a boma boy of the olden days and one of the unsung heroes of the Niger Delta's liberation. He recovered his dishevelled boma boy's attire, which he alternated with the uniform of the army he had been discharged from. The dresses were too tight but he wore them anyway to either do a military drill or do a sailor's walk. Children followed him and enjoyed the spectacle of his free performance.

"To Keep Nigeria One!" they often called him.

"Is a task that must be done!" he would respond to complete the wartime slogan, on his happy days.

"Attention!" they shouted at him, and he would stop abruptly and stand to attention to salute a phantom officer.

"March!" the children ordered, and he would start marching.

"Shoot!" they again ordered him.

In a flash he would take an offensive position and aim his imaginary gun at the ghost of one of his civil war victims. He would jump up in jubilation, shouting "Hurrah!" But all of a sudden his mood would change; he would turn menacingly serious and run clumsily after the children who soon broke up and disappeared into their familiar streets.

The elders shook their heads at his terrible sight. To Keep Nigeria One continued his performance till the uniform got torn and then he disappeared from the streets and was presumed dead. With seemingly healthy and sane people disappearing from the streets now and then, his relatives did not waste time looking for him. Where would they begin or end their search? His beautiful wife left their home, a one-room hovel, after he disappeared and was rather generous with her attractive body until she died with the secret of her only conception that brought forth Pere.

As Pere grew into boyhood, he became very impatient and irascible. While in elementary school, without provocation he would beat his classmates and insult his teachers. He was inattentive and unruly. The teachers would report to his mother and father who would scold him, but that did not change him. His father barely came to the mother's house and the boy did not go to his father's house often. He had no space in his father's compound.

Nobody was surprised when he was expelled from school. In his second year in the grammar school he fought his classmate so fiercely that he broke his teeth. The boy was in hospital for three days. The headmaster, Mr. Joshua Temile, had to call his mother and father to relay to them the expulsion decision.

Only his mother showed up.

"We have decided to expel your son from our school before he commits murder here," Mr. Temile told her.

Titi only burst out in tears in response. She took hold of Pere and led him out of the headmaster's office and they went home. On the way home, neither mother nor son spoke to each other. They would forever remain silent over the expulsion order.

There was no attempt to beg the school authorities to

rescind the draconian decision or reduce it to a suspension. Neither was he placed in another secondary school to see whether he would change his bad behavior or not. He had nobody with a stubborn resolve standing forcefully for him to continue with education. Not long after, his mother died from snakebite while weeding her cassava farm. From then on, Pere knew he had to survive as a motherless child in a very hostile and unkind world.

What happened not long after his mother's death rather than break him, in fact, strengthened him. His father, Omishola, shocked him with his actions. Rather than bring him to his house, he left him to cater for himself in his dead mother's room in another street. As if that was not enough, he called him to deliver him a bombshell.

"I called you to tell you what I have always wanted to tell you. I have to tell you this, however bitter you may feel about it. You are not my son," the person he had assumed to be his father told him.

Pere stood silent. What reply should he make to one denying him paternity? What knowledge of his own birth did he have to tell him that he was wrong? He waited for more revelations, but his stepfather, if he was not his biological father, did not say more immediately about him or his own relationship with the mother. The man paused for a long time; he then closed his eyes, as if exploring a landscape within, before continuing his revelation.

Pere was never close to the man that his mother told him was his father. He lived with his mother but not in Omishola's compound; they lived in a different street far away. Pere always wondered why his mother often admonished him not to bother his father. The man helped him and his mother but not wholeheartedly as a man taking care of his wife and son would normally do. His mother did not say anything else, and since they did not live together, there was always some distance between him and his father.

"Papa, are you telling me that you are not my father?" he asked.

"Yes, you are not my son," Omishola restated.

"I am not surprised," Pere told him.

"I am sorry about what this disclosure will cause you, but I have to tell you the truth," Omishola said, as if telling the truth would assuage the psychological wound he had already inflicted on Pere.

The elders, who took such matters seriously, heard about it but did not meet on Pere's behalf. Since he bore no physical or moral resemblance to the man who disowned him, the elders did not want to humiliate him further with a meeting that would not help matters. Nor did they want to publicly air their suspicions that his mother might have slept with her ex-soldier husband even when he was already out of his mind. The old folk kept quiet about such things.

What was hard on Pere was that the man he thought was his father waited for his mother to die before calling him and telling him that he, Pere, was not his son, that his mother had told a lie to cover the true circumstances of his birth, and that he rejected paternity of him. He did not explain to the young man that his mother was known to be generous with her body for some time and that she was pregnant before they met. It would have certainly raised many eyebrows if people had known that he was sleeping with a woman who had already conceived for another man. While they never talked about it, Pere's mother knew that her lover knew that her pregnancy was from another man. But so strong was their attraction to each other at the beginning of the relationship that they were ready to break taboos in the name of love. Both lived with the secret.

If he did not know who his father was, Pere decided not to continue living a lie, as his mother had made him to do till her death. He gave up the Omishola name he had used at school and took his mother's father's name, Ighogboja. He did it not only to spite the father he thought he had but also to have a sense of where he truly belonged. A child belongs to its mother, who carries it during pregnancy and then delivers it. His mother did not reject him, whatever reason she might have had to place his parenthood on the undeserving man. A mother does not reject what comes from her womb as not hers. Never! Pere reflected.

Pere found his way in a hard manner into adulthood. He had

to work himself out to earn a living. He started as a Pools agent and assisted Yeri Daibo, who had a big gambling business. He was poorly paid, because his boss complained of paying out too much to his winning customers and having too little money left to maintain the office and pay the workers. Pere knew that his boss also betted but could not tell whether he used his personal money or part of the business's money. He could not challenge his boss or ask for higher pay with the constant complaints of being in the red and so, after two years of working there, he quit for what he envisaged would be a more paying job.

Such jobs were not many, and in fact he found none. He soon discovered how hard the job situation was. At a time he regretted losing his job however small the pay. But he put that behind. He sat at home and with an empty and groaning stomach thought deeply of where he could do anything to survive. If he did not find some other way to make a living, he might be forced to beg. But who would give him, a healthy-looking young man, money? Two weeks without a job, his situation became desperate. At night in his wooden bed, he thought of something he had not realized he could do. He was ready to do any job that would bring him money to sustain himself.

The following morning he went to the motor park to assist drivers in attracting passengers to their cars or buses and also helping to load them. He took the work seriously because that was the only means of sustaining himself. He knew the job of an agbero needed a tough-minded and physically strong person. In a few weeks, he developed these skills in his determination to survive.

He stood at the motor park's entrance, dressed in his worn-out Bata shoes, secondhand trousers, and frayed flying short-sleeve shirt long bought at McIver Market. He observed keenly and greeted those coming into the motor park that he suspected to be travelling. After he asked and was told by the travellers where they were going, he would take their bags and lead them to the car or bus setting out for that place. He knew how to stuff the boot of a car or bus with the luggage items of travellers. He even marvelled at how he was able to arrange passengers' bags and other items into whatever space was available in the vehicle. Many drivers called him to assist them in arranging their loads. What Pere Ighogboja could not do in the task of arranging loads in the car or bus, no other agbero in the motor park could. On many occasions, passengers travelling with heavy loads gave him a tip to avoid paying for double seats. He so impressed other good-natured passengers with his dedication to his work that they also gave him tips. And these were in addition to what the drivers gave to him - the little commission he gained from assisting them.

Pere joined the association of road transport workers and paid his dues regularly. He made friends with many fellow agberos and they were like a family ready to help each other if the need arose. He soon found out that on a good day he could make more than a hundred naira. He lived a frugal life and took home his money, abstaining from drinking and smoking, a lifestyle that helped him to save much of his earnings. He prepared his meals and ate at home and did not join the others when they went to the food sheds around, where one was bound to spend much to impress fellow workers. He saved and got married. He wanted, with time, to set up a provision store for his wife, Tosan. He hoped things would continue to improve. His first child was a son.

Nobody at the motor park knew he was also an area boy. He had started to build a career in the association which a friend of his took him to.

He was climbing without being noticed. He was living a normal life at the motor park and at home. He spent his off-duty time with his fellow area boys. Tosan trusted him and did not care where he went after work. His not drinking and smoking made him to be trusted as a simple man. But he was complex. The police that dealt with area boys and thieves knew him but did not know his status in the area boys' association.

Pere so adored his child that he would do anything to make life comfortable for his son as well as for his wife and himself. The boy was like an egg that he handled with so much care and he also wanted other people to handle him in the same manner. The elders who noticed this did not mince words and told him that he was too young to pamper his child. Only those who had children late in life or who had thought they were incapable of having a child but got one miraculously, did what he did. He did not beat his child even when he did wrong such as disobeying him but only talked to him and without raising his voice. He reprimanded his wife for the few times that she spanked the boy. He was proud of his son and wanted to give him what he had received from no father.

As his economic condition improved, he continued to be thrifty and saved much of his earnings from the double sources. He was a caring husband and a loving father. One day he came back from work early and saw his child lying by the fireside and covered with clothes. His wife was reluctant to tell him what had really happened because she knew how attached he was to their son. She feared his response because he would take personally whatever was done to the child.

"Tosan, what's wrong with Tonye?"

"He developed a fever all of a sudden," she explained.

Pere felt the boy's forehead, then his stomach and legs. He shook his head to indicate that he knew that something else was wrong with the child.

"Does fever not go with heat? His body is not hot."

"I don't know what's wrong with him then. He just fell sick."

"How long will you keep me from knowing the truth about my son?"

From the way he stared at her, Tosan was scared and told him what had really happened.

"Pabor's son beat him when they were playing," she at last revealed.

"What really happened?" he asked.

"Their play turned into a fight."

Once Pere learnt that another child had beaten his son that day, he went into a rage.

"Why did you allow Efe to beat him?" he asked.

"I was not there. He was already howling before I knew what was happening outside."

"Why did you not look after him outside?"

"I was cooking."

"Is food more important than Tonye?"

"It's not so. Nothing can be more important than our son."

Pere went straight to Pabor's compound nearby. Did this fat and older boy want to kill his child or what was he up to beating him?

Efe was at home alone; the parents had gone out since morning.

Pere first held the frightened boy.

"Where is your father?"

"He has gone out."

"What of your mother?"

"I don't know where they have gone to."

That the boy's parents were not in did not stop Pere from taking any immediate action against him. Pere was expected by the communal rules of living to report to the offending boy's parents first and wait for their action. If Pabor and the boy's mother failed to discipline their son and apologize, it would be after then that Pere could take his own action against Efe, small as he was. But, to Pere, nobody should hurt his son. He went ahead and beat Efe mercilessly. The small boy cried from the pain of the beating till his parents came home. As Pabor asked him what happened, Efe had a seizure and collapsed; he was taken to hospital where he died the following day.

Neither the child's parents nor anybody else believed that he died from convulsion. A child outgrows convulsion, the saying goes, and Efe was almost getting past the age of convulsion episodes that had plagued him since infancy. Even the doctor who confirmed that he died of a seizure said the thrashing he received triggered the attack.

The deceased boy's father used his connections to bring soldiers to beat Pere before handing him over to the police. The police saw an opportunity to get rid of a hoodlum, as they saw him. They threw him into jail, where they expected him to rot or be condemned for murder and hanged. They wanted him to learn a lesson from the mosquitoes that would feed on him daily, especially at night. Bedbugs too would find a good source of their daily nutritional requirement in him. The poor prison food would certainly take a heavy toll on him, the police and Pabor believed. In fact, very few people survived their prison terms or long detentions in the nation's prisons because of their extremely unsanitary conditions.

Pere was one of the few detainees that graduated from Okere High College, as the maximum security prison on Okere Road was called. He used to cut grass and sing the common song:

I never chop since morning
I dey Okere High College

Man dey suffer o
I dey Okere High College

Okere High College!
Okere High College!

The rhythm of the song made the prison inmates to forget the hard labour. Sweat covered their bodies in the blazing sun. They certainly preferred the period outside while working to when inside the prison cell or yard. They even developed a sense of camaraderie among themselves; it looked as if they enjoyed their time there.

"Wetin man go do?" they often asked themselves.

To break the boredom of prison life and to exercise, they had mock military marches. Right, left, right left, they marched. They did frog jump, pushup, and other exercises. Some of them had been in the Army and were group leaders in these exercises that the warders overlooked. They often mimicked the prison warders in their authoritative demeanor shouting out orders.

Pere was never accused of the crime for which he was thrown into jail and was never tried and found innocent or guilty. He remained in prison until a district judge, in his clemency inspection before Christmas, freed him after seven years. He considered himself lucky to be released without further trial.

In the prison he had plenty of time for reflection and he did an abundance of it. He realized that he ought to have reported to the parents of the dead child, but felt that his plea for forgiveness afterwards should have been heeded. He had sent several relatives to the boy's father to apologize, but they were not given any audience. He knew he was too hasty in beating his son's attacker but what happened was an accident - he did not set out to kill the child but just wanted to teach him a lesson. Besides, the convulsion episode developed long after the beating. In any case, the hot temper that had plagued him from childhood, he now realized, had caused him education and a jail term. He promised himself that he would be a different man.

Boating Downstream

What began as playful talk between the Activist and Ebi on the corridor of their office building was about to take them into deep waters. After she had assisted him in entertaining his visitors, the Activist was profuse in his gratitude to her. With her assistance, he gained pride among his relatives. With her first-class cooking, she made him a cultured man among his people. With her support, he was not a lone man. She was the angel sent to save him from disgrace. She was his expert guide through the labyrinths of traditional customs that he had nearly forgotten. She was his saviour goddess.

Ebi was overwhelmed by the compliments. How many men around praised women for whatever task or achievement? She had felt that one who had come home after a long stay abroad should be helped to get his bearing before being left alone. The Activist might consider himself to be a homeboy, she felt, but he was at that time a stranger at home. "Be kind to strangers," she had heard the elders say. She was doing nothing extraordinary in preparing food for the Activist's guests, her own way of being kind to this stranger of a homeboy.

Ebi and the Activist greeted each other whenever they happened to run into each other. With a little more familiarity between them, they just waved at each other and sought the opportunity to do so. At other times they greeted and looked at each other and smiled without starting a conversation.

One Friday afternoon they met after their separate classes. The Activist felt like engaging her in a conversation.

"Any plans for the weekend?" he asked her, after they greeted.

"Like what?" she asked back, not wanting to say something stupid.

"Are you free this coming weekend?" he asked back in explanation.

"No, not free!" she told him.

"Really?" he asked.

"Yes, I already promised to visit a friend in Warri on Saturday and I will spend the whole day there, and Sunday should also be busy," she explained.

He was quiet. He did not even know why he wanted to know whether or not she would be free the following weekend. They stared at one another, each expecting the other to say something.

"But the next one I should be free," Ebi said.

"Let's do something then," he told her.

"Like what?"

"Something silly; something like we used to do when we were boys and girls," he suggested.

"Are we no more boys and girls, eating rice and beans?" she asked, referring cleverly to the jovial slang in secondary school of calling rice and beans "boys and girls."

"Not that kind of boys and girls," he told her.

"Tell me which one!"

Suddenly an idea flashed in the Activist's mind. He would like to go downstream towards the ocean, but he was not sure what her response would be to such a daring proposition. His fear of her response did not stop him from asking her.

"Why can't we have a picnic somewhere on the Great River by the ocean if you won't mind taking a boat with me?"

"Let me think about it. I'll let you know my answer in a short while."

Ebi really had nothing for the following weekend but wanted to control her own space and time. She felt she did not have to jump at any invitation to do something, as if her time was always free. Besides, she had learnt over the years to cover her excitement with caution.

She soon realized she had not indulged herself in that type of fun for a very long time. How many times since leaving secondary school had she gone down the creeks? In fact, she had not got the opportunity to fish since then. The Activist's invitation had woken in her the yearning to do the things she used to do as a young girl until education stopped her from doing them. She could no longer swim in the river, where all young girls used to strip and have fun in the water.

By the time they met four days later, Ebi had subdued her excitement and was calm.

"I thought about the picnic. It will be fine with me next Saturday," she told him.

"Thanks, Ebi."

"It will be a pleasure going down the Great River with you," she said.

"We'll go as far as possible."

"That's no problem with me."

"I can't wait for the weekend to come," the Activist said.

"Me too," Ebi told him.

Ebi had the experience of not just rowing a boat well but also of fishing almost into the ocean. On many occasions, she was the leader of the fishing girls. She had known how to swim at the age of two. Her mother told her that she had thrown her into the water, where she struggled to keep afloat. She gulped drafts of water and often came close to suffocating and drowning before her watchful mother rescued her. That was how she learnt to swim from a very young age. She could swim underwater for several minutes and would resurface a good distance away from where she had dived in.

She and her fellow female fishers started fishing from the smaller creeks that flowed into bigger creeks that soon turned into streams. The different streams, like fingers of a hand, raced into the big river that widened as it poured into the ocean. The easy part was going downstream. Coming upstream could be dangerous because it involved going against the strong currents. But Ebi and her female age-mates had learnt from their elders how to cope with strong tides and currents in their way.

On his part, the Activist was tormented by a passion for water that he could not fulfill while abroad in crowded beaches. As a small boy, he used to take a big uhovwe plank to a flowing creek and steer it to the small river that raced to merge with the big river. He knew the different types of wood that would float or sink. He bathed in the water; he fished both day and night in the creeks and streams. He could recollect while in elementary school going in a group of three to a river to fish - itwas a common practice for a child not to go alone to the river; there must be company. As they fished, a thunderstorm crashed on them. The water rose to overflow the banks. They were all confused, but fortunately they managed to find their way through the entire area that had become a water scape. As he grew bigger and a few children were lost in the water, his parents forbade him from going to the rivers. He went behind their backs to satisfy his avid passion for water. The creeks, streams, and rivers were enchantresses that he, like other boys of his age, could not resist. Now he looked forward with longing to the appointed day.

The early January day was bright but cool. There had been showers the previous day, which at that time of the dry season meant they had a pleasant day ahead.

Ebi knew that gossip was a major preoccupation on campus. She could imagine the questions some people would ask about this journey should they see them together or hear about it. She did not care; more so since the Activist was not married, even though his age-mates on campus had already fathered many children.

She wanted to have some fun, and having it in the company of somebody new but fairly familiar would be thrilling to her. How many single men around ever thought of rowing a boat from the creeks to the ocean? she asked herself. They were not interested in that sort of excitement. The only kind of fun that they wanted was drugging you with beer and then making love. They could not imagine more exciting ways of enjoyment or pleasing a woman, she thought.

Ebi recollected how as a young girl she and her mates used to row far to the mouth of the ocean and go to a small island where they secured their boats, took off their clothes, and swam in the salt water. The ocean water and breeze were very soothing to the body. The air, as one came closer to the ocean, was cool and salty. It had a special recuperative and enlivening effect on them. If on this trip they got to the island by the ocean, would she, as she did as a girl, take off her clothes and bathe naked in the sun? She was not yet sure of what she would do, if they got there. For now she just wanted to row downstream and experience that exhilaration of girlhood days again.

In his khaki trousers and T-shirt, the Activist went to meet Ebi at their arranged meeting point. They had hired a strong canoe that would comfortably accommodate the two of them and what they would take along for the journey.

Ebi was in control. Her memory of the waters was sharp.

"Look at me," Ebi told her companion, as she rowed the boat. "If you handle the paddle this way, sway it in a semi-circle from the front to the back of the boat with minimum effort, the boat just moves fast and glides on the water effortlessly," she explained.

"Can I try it?" the Activist asked.

"Not yet. See this too. There's a way of going against the current, tide, or waves and also a way of slowing down when following them and just getting carried along," she said.

"It's your turn now" she added.

As they entered deeper and wider waters, Ebi behaved like a guide explaining the history and geography of the waters. She was as excited as the Activist in the widening and deepening waters. Ebi reminded the Activist of the rule of boating that she knew and practised when young - when one person was captain, the other assisted. When she relaxed into conversation, she signalled to the Activist to be in command. They had to be alert at all times to avoid an accident.

The magnitude of the desolation of the water shocked them. Where were the flying fish that used to shoot out of the water into the air and then somersault back into water? That spectacle was now confined to memory. The water was no longer the herb-dark draught that she liked to dip her hands into and wash her face with. It was light green, greasy, and smelly. The large fish population had either been decimated by chemicals from oil industries or migrated downstream into the ocean. Where were the flocks of storks, kingfishers, and many exotic types of birds that filled the airspace as one approached the ocean?

Ebi and the Activist passed the riverine small town of

Enekerogha that used to be famous for fishing. Markets inland used to sell fish brought from Enekerogha, whose residents were known as catchers of big fish with the special nets they prepared themselves. Now at the river port of the fishing village, Ebi and the Activist saw big boats, powered by Yamaha engines, bringing imported frozen fish from Warri to the most interior villages by the water. After offloading the many cartons there, smaller boats fanned into the delta to sell the "ice fish," now the main source of protein for these riverine people who used to take their fresh catches to Warri and Port Harcourt for sale.

The two continued their journey and entered ever-widening waters. The transition from fresh to brackish water was revealing. The thick rain forest flaunted gloomy-faced aburas, black and white afaras, irokos, and mahoganies. The beginning of the brackish water coincided with the omnipresence of mangrove trees. The river cut through the mangrove forest. As the sun shone, the shadow of the trees danced on the racing current.

It was a great spectacle looking at the ocean from a distance. Ebi steered the boat by the side of the wide river close to shrubs. That way the current did not affect the boat much. They eventually arrived at the small island that Ebi had visited several times in the company of her friends. Beyond there was too dangerous to attempt crossing. The waves clashed thunderously ahead of them and left a white cloud of foam.

They went ashore, pulling the boat onto the beach sand. Shells of different types and sizes littered the sand. The picnickers picked some big shells, which they would take home as mementos of this day. They spread a mat on a sandy expanse and beside it they placed the bags they brought. Each walked to a different spot, and for more than ten minutes they both silently just stared at the ocean in front of them to marvel at the grandeur of nature. The salt-scented breeze was strong and they enjoyed its soothing touch.

The sun was shining with far more zest than when they took off from home. The waves clashed and splashed in the sun. A rainbow appeared suspended in the air and disappeared once the risen waves fell. After a few minutes, Ebi and the

Activist moved back towards each other.

"We made it!" the Activist exclaimed.

"It's a long way here. I wish this moment could last forever," Ebi said.

"This is certainly grand and so fulfilling," he said, as if talking to himself.

They looked seaward at the sun. They were just two puny human beings in front of this grand expanse. The excitement of the journey and the arrival had made them lose track of time.

"I hope you have not forgotten that we brought food?" Ebi asked.

"Of course not, but we eat all the time. We don't have this experience all the time," he answered.

"I just want to remind you that we brought food."

"In this beautiful landscape, food is not a priority for me," the Activist told her.

"Things have changed so drastically that we might lose everything we knew from our youth in just a few years to come," she said, as one who knew the area very well.

"The oil companies are discovering more oil onshore and offshore. We are in for disaster, if nothing is done to save our waters, land, and air," the Activist said.

"It's something we have to pray for," Ebi said.

"This will take more than prayers to resolve. We, the owners of the place, have to force the oil companies and the Federal Military Government to start doing something about it before it is too late."

"Our people watch their waters turn to poison, their land become crust from blowouts and the air become hot from poisonous gas. They do nothing to stop the hands that want to strangle them," she lamented.

"We have to do something, and we can," the Activist said, as one trying to win support for a cause he wanted to fight.

The Niger Delta was part of its people and just as the land, air, and rivers were being poisoned so were the residents themselves, the Activist believed. He had observed in the short time since he had returned the epidemics of dysentery and worm diseases that afflicted the people. The paradise of the olden days was degenerating fast into a kind of hell. The water that used to be an elixir had become a poisonous brew. Something had to be done to detoxify the water so that fish could once more feel safe to breed there.

The Activist remembered when he was young.

"Whenever my mother wanted to prepare a meal with crayfish, she literally put a pot of water on the fire and took her scooping net and went to the nearby lake to catch fish. She returned within a half-hour with just enough fish to prepare a delicious palm oil soup. Those lakes and wetlands have been filled, first with rubber trees, then new roads and developments that left the people hungry, diseased, malnourished, and alienated from their roots. Now the oil companies are pouring poisons into them, giving these natural sustainers of the people a final deathblow."

Ebi recalled a list of luxuries of the past.

"What happened to our oil-beans, breadfruit, mushroom, urhurhu grapes, owe apple, and otie cherry fruit? Either gone or barely available! Where are the water-leaf, greens, water yam, ikpaho groundnuts, lemon leaves, plantation peas, okpeyin yam, taro roots, and sweet cassava that were such a pleasure to eat? Now there is an increase in the number of stomachs that need food and yet the supply is diminishing at an alarming rate."

"There was no famine in the years of my childhood," the Activist said, "people were robust and healthy. One did not need to buy so many good things; they were either readily available from the soil and waters or bartered for from someone else," he recalled.

They ate their corned beef sandwich and drank from both the water and the Coke bottles they brought. It was sunny and windy, and they enjoyed sitting on the mat in the sun. Their bodies came close without touching and they looked at each other as they conversed.

"I want to return to my childhood," Ebi suddenly told the Activist.

"How?" he asked.

"I came to this spot many times in the past, and I always swam in the cove there," she said, as she pointed to a spot west of where they sat.

"If you won't mind my swimming too," he responded.

"If you trust your swimming, you can follow. But it is not swimming really. I just want to splash myself with water. The water is still good here, and who knows when I will come here again? I may as well take a dip in it before the pollution covers everything, including the adjoining ocean water," she said.

"The ocean supertankers taking the oil away discharge much sluice in the water too and the ocean shores will not be free of pollution either in a short while," the Activist added.

"Let's seize this chance and enjoy it," Ebi said.

Ebi led the short walk to the cove. The water narrowed and then enlarged into almost a full circle. By the time the waves reached the cove, they had lost their clashing power. The water was relatively placid. The two entered the water, which was warmer than the water around. Ebi told the Activist that it was a secret among the girls to come here and bathe in order to become full women later in life. Many of them started menstruating after their first dip into the cove's warm waters. Before many married, they came there too to dip into the water of the cove, which was supposed to enhance good health and fertility.

Ebi remained standing, pulled off her scarf and blouse and then threw them onto the land. The Activist for the first time saw how smooth and glowing her skin was, but he did not rivet his gaze on her. Ebi then waded into the water; she splashed herself with the salt water. The Activist pulled off his T-shirt and threw it onto the sand. His chest was covered with hair and his arms were muscular. He also splashed himself with water. A little to the side was a log that looked like it had been brought and placed there for rest. They sat on the water-washed log and dangled their legs in the water.

"I have to do the right thing," Ebi suddenly said.

"Do it," the Activist implored, without knowing exactly what she wanted to do right.

She pulled off her skirt, folded it, and threw it towards the land. It fell just at the water's edge but on land. Bare-bodied except for her white bra and underwear, Ebi dived into the water and swam underwater for some distance and emerged, shaking water off her hair. She clasped her hands over her breasts as if out of coyness but soon dropped them and waded back smiling to the Activist. She was such a shapely figure. Her stomach was taut and flat. Her black long hair spread in the air, her figure transformed into a calm female deity. She wore red tiny waist beads that defined her contours seductively. She also wore the same type of beads around her ankles. She sat on the log again, dazed as if possessed by the water, staring ahead at the ocean whose breadth and depth filled her with wonder.

All of a sudden the Activist could inhale her body odor, the fragrance of an un-named flower nursed into full bloom by an experienced gardener. Something passed from her to him that filled him with a pleasant fever. His body quivered in her presence. Here was Mami Wata before him; here the Great Maker's masterpiece! Ebi had assumed a physical form that he had never been as close to. She was more than a mind with whom he discussed or conversed at the corridor of their office building. She was both body and soul in her divine body.

"I didn't know I asked Mami Wata to accompany me here," the Activist told her.

Ebi raised her forefinger over her mouth to shut up the Activist. She wanted to watch the ocean ahead of her in silence. The Activist understood her unspoken message and kept quiet. He gazed at the transformed woman who appeared to be transported into another realm that she did not want to be brought down from. After about a quarter of an hour, she broke the silence.

"Forgive me for asking you to be quiet. I did not mean to be rude. I heard you when you said that I was Mami Wata. In fact, at that time I was listening to the quiet voice of Mami Wata."

"Did you hear her?"

"Yes. She was not talking but singing in the clashing waves and muttering wind."

"You must have a sharp ear."

"We all have sharp ears and can hear the voice of silence."

"I wish mine are as keen as yours," he told her.

"They must be, if you want to listen," she replied.

"The air is so refreshing," the Activist added.

"By the way, I am no Mami Wata. If I were, I would be

wearing a python on my neck as a pendant."

"You are beautiful!"

"Thanks," Ebi responded with a coy smile.

They waded back to the mat on the sand. With the sun and salt wind, their wet clothes that clung to them from the cove soon got dried. Ebi put on her cotton skirt.

They told water adventure stories about their childhood and really warmed up to each other. Ebi was happy that she made it to the cove. The Activist was happy he was born again, as he put it. He was most pleased that Ebi had brought him to the oceanfront.

They rowed back with a little more difficulty than when they had come, because the currents and waves were stronger and against them. But Ebi was experienced and used all the skills she had acquired from her seashore people's life over the years. As they rowed homeward, they talked about the villages they passed. They deliberately slowed down since they knew it was a moonlit evening and they wanted to enjoy to the utmost this rare adventure. They could hear travelers in boats singing, sometimes in Izon and at other times in Itsekiri or Urhobo.

By the time they entered one of the fingers of the Great River, there was relative calm. The chorus of some insects, birds, and animals entertained them. They heard the woodpecker still working on its parents' coffins so late that day; it had had a boil, according to the myth, when its mother and father died. It had to work overtime to get two coffins made before long to give them a befitting burial! The hyrax and bush dog were barking in the distant dark. Ebi and the Activist heard squirrels and other animal voices they could not identify.

The sky was star-studded and beautiful. Ebi showed the Activist the "blacksmith" star in the sky. That star was always shining very bright because of the bellows it was blowing, according to the elders. But the closer they drew nearer home, the less animated the environment became.

Enclaves of oil companies were floodlit and dazzled from a distance. Outside those secluded zones, the indigenous people continued to live under primitive conditions. The Activist thought of what Green Peace described as the law of mutual preservation: one should not harm nature if one does not want nature to strike back. Outsiders were callously destroying the environment, but nature might not be able to discriminate and retaliate against only those doing the damage.

It was an outing that both the Activist and Ebi would not forget.

"Thanks for this great favour," the Activist told Ebi.

"Thanks also for the invitation," she replied.

"You don't know what you have brought to my life. I am happy that I came back to the Niger Delta. Thank you. I just can't thank you enough for the joy that I feel."

"I have done nothing special for you. I enjoyed the outing and feel honoured that you invited me. You could have called on somebody else, but you asked me to go with you. I appreciate that."

"You are a wonderful lady."

"And you are a thoughtful man."

They looked at each other with a new fondness. The Activist stretched out his hand and Ebi did the same and they shook hands. They could feel each other's warmth. They held each other's hand clasped for a moment.

That night in bed the Activist was restless and thought of looking for Ebi the following day to tell her "I love you." She was surely divine. He fell asleep gazing at her figure, the waist and ankle beads shining like stars.

Ethnic Fusion and Fission

The following day the Activist did not find Ebi to tell her that he loved her.

But they soon started seeing each other regularly at home. It began casually when the Activist saw Ebi by her flat. It was a chance happening. She was returning from town where she had gone to buy provisions and the Activist was going out. There was some distance between the transit flats where the Activist lived and Ebi's junior staff complex. The university operated a hierarchical society in which professors were at the top of the social pyramid, followed by associate professors and senior lecturers. Lecturers I down were junior and treated accordingly when it came to dispensing university privileges.

"I didn't know you live here," he said.

"Here's where I hide," she said jovially.

"At least you have a permanent place to hide. I can be driven from my temporary home anytime."

"Unless there is a big house ready for you," she said.

"But that may take another two, three, or more years."

"You'll at least leave for a big mansion, however long it takes."

"Thanks for being optimistic. And you are bound to leave here too to a bigger house. The opportunity is there for everybody."

"It's going to be a long ladder for me to climb to get to your height."

"You'll make it."

"Amen," she replied.

They talked for some time outside. Ebi only pointed at her flat but did not invite him inside. She knew how nosey her neighbours were and did not want them to jump to conclusions about their having a relationship even before it started.

But week after week in the corridor of their office building they greeted and got more familiar with each other.

"Can I visit you one of these days?" the Activist asked.

"Nothing will bite you in my flat. You will be welcome," she said.

"Expect me this Friday evening."

That evening the Activist went to see her. Her two-bedroom flat was neatly arranged. The sitting room was rugged brown, the same color as the curtains. Huge earthen pots of different styles sat at corners of the room. Two of the big shells she collected during their picnic adorned a side table.

"You have a beautiful flat. I like these pots."

"I made them."

"You made these pots?" the Activist asked, quite surprised.

"When I have the time, I make earthen pots and plates."

"You are a great artist. I didn't know you make pots. I only thought you just taught about pots."

"That's how life is. Until you get close to people, you never know what they are capable of doing," she replied.

"It is a privilege to know you," the Activist complimented.

Ebi smiled at him in response to the compliment. He moved to one corner of the sitting room to touch and feel one of the pots.

"Sorry, I ought to have asked for your permission before touching your work. Can I lift this pot?"

"As long as you do so with care, there's no problem."

"Surely, I will be careful."

"As long as you are careful, do what you like with it."

"A pot is like a woman."

"That's a good metaphor," she said.

"Yes, one handles with care what one loves and cares for."

"I am happy you know that. I don't know whether the same can be said of most men around," Ebi said.

The Activist lifted the big pot with his two palms held together. He raised it up as if delivering it to some deity.

"The pot is life," he declared.

"We all carry pots without knowing," Ebi said.

"Pots full of what we desire."

"Also pots of sacrifice," Ebi added.

He put the pot down and sat on a chair. Ebi brought him a cold Coke to drink. They chatted about the university and the campus community in general. Before he left, the Activist told Ebi to feel free to visit him.

After she made up her mind to visit the Activist, Ebi waited for dusk or twilight to go to the Activist's flat. She did not want peering eyes to catch her entering the Activist's flat. She knew that on campus many people watched what men the single ladies visited. Rumour and gossip soon flew around from such observations that were often embellished. She did not want to be seen and scandalized.

By her third visit, Ebi bought groundnuts and corn and took them to share with him. It was the season of fresh corn and groundnuts. The girl who roasted and sold them sat under a big almond tree from morning until late evening. Ebi knew the Activist who so cherished homegrown foods would like fresh groundnuts and corn. She opened the wrapped groundnuts and corn on a side table.

"What have you brought?"

"Roasted fresh corn and groundnuts," she replied.

"That's kind and thoughtful of you."

"I like them and thought you too might like them."

"I don't just like them; I enjoy them," the Activist said.

"I enjoy them too."

"But don't stir the hornets' nest!"

"How?" she asked.

"Better be careful," the Activist said, making a knowing face and smiling sensually.

"You self!" she exclaimed.

"Dis no be guguru and groundnuts?"

"Na im."

"I better warn you make you no say I no warn you-o. Abi you no know?"

The Activist spoke pidgin rarely but he appeared so relaxed and warmed up that he spoke familiarly.

"What is he up to today?" Ebi asked in her mind.

She liked the Activist's conviviality. He could be very jovial and witty. He behaved as if he had not lived in America for so many years. He talked as if he had always been around in the Niger Delta.

The Activist drew closer to Ebi where they sat. Their bodies touched and they could feel each other's warmth. The Activist held her hand. He drew her to himself and looked at her eyes, as if to seek permission to go further. Their hearts pounded heavily and they breathed fast. The Activist stretched out his tongue and Ebi reciprocated; they kissed.

They began to rub each other excitedly. They had been transported into a passionate planet in which they appeared to have surrendered their bodies to each other. After a while, Ebi pulled away.

"Enough!" she said feebly.

"Sure?" the Activist asked.

"Not yet."

She could not bring herself to make love with the Activist yet. Her love for him had grown gradually, but she still wanted to hold on for some time. Where this would lead them to, she was not sure but she knew that something was pulling them together.

"Maybe next time," she told herself.

She was not denying him the pleasure of her body, but they needed to know each other more, she felt.

The Activist and Pere Meet

The Activist initiated the first meeting between him and Pere. Both men had been suspicious of each other.

Pere asked himself many questions. Was this American returnee genuine or playing on his people's intelligence? Was he not, as gossip had it, thrown out of the United States for some unknown reason? How could he have left the United States willingly to come to this warfront of a place? Pere felt if the Activist consciously chose to return in order to face poverty and the stress of underdevelopment, then he deserved to be not only listened to but also applauded. Time would tell what type of person he was. His actions and behaviour would also tell whether he was for the people, as he claimed, or for the outsiders, who were capable of recruiting insiders as agents to infiltrate them.

Pere and the Activist first met at the barbershop and they talked as they waited for their turns. Pere noticed the Activist's interest when the talk shifted to Bell Oil Company.

"Bell Oil na imself e dey look after, not to us!"

"We never reach dem place but we know say e better pass here," Pere responded.

"Na dream world dem dey live for their place; we dey the hell they create for black man," the Activist had also said.

The Activist talked as one who really knew something about the exploitative nature of Bell Oil Company. Pere felt there was so much he could learn from the Activist.

When they met at the barbershop a second time, they talked more familiarly. The Activist did not speak the bombastic language of the academics. Nor did he speak American slang that many who had not even stepped into America spoke among them. Rather, he spoke simple, lucid language and interjected pidgin at times. Pere could forgive him for not speaking pidgin well because the language evolved every year with new terms being absorbed into it, and the Activist had been away for too long and therefore knew only how to speak the older version. He started to look forward to talking with the Activist, whom he was learning some deep things from. He would observe him, talk with him, and watch how he carried himself.

The Activist wanted to know Pere too. His several visits to the barbershop always gave him more information about local celebrities. He had asked his barber, a young man in his mid-twenties, about Pere when his name first came up in their conversation. He was curious to know this leader of the area boys. Pere had come out of the shadows and was now known and respected. There was a certain mystique about Pere that he wanted to unravel, if possible. Then he met him at the barbershop. He carried himself with a certain pride based on having gone through suffering and absorbed everything with dignity. Sorrow or suffering had not crushed him. In fact, suffering and pain had strengthened him into a veteran fighter. He was the champion of the local cause of holding Bell Oil Company and the Federal Military Government accountable for what he saw as going wrong in the Niger Delta.

The Activist had heard the story at the barbershop of Pere's seven-year detention and his coming out stronger and more than ever determined to succeed. It was such people that he wanted as friends and allies.

Raining that late afternoon, the Activist defied the inclement weather to call on Pere. They had jokingly invited each other to the other's home and both had agreed to take up the invitation. The Activist was not one of those people who blamed others for not fulfilling what was a joint responsibility. He would take the first step and see what followed.

"You come visit me?" Pere asked in surprise.

"I say I must see you today," the Activist replied.

Pere shook his visitor's hands with vigor to express his delight. In his mind, he asked how many academics called on common people. He knew they visited one another and did not make friends outside their university group. You found them occasionally at their relatives' places in town, but they were in a different class from the people outside the campus fence. They were often full of airs about their positions, members of the Senate and Council and other such committees. Pere was very pleased. The Activist had freed him from going to the university campus to ask for him. That trip would have been intimidating to him, but no longer so when he would pay a return visit to the Activist sometime.

Pere treated his guest to a traditional welcome. He presented the Activist two big kola nuts, a bottle of Gordon Gin, and several bottles of soft drinks. He also added a one hundred naira note to complete the custom. Tosan supported her husband with fifty naira to welcome their guest. The Activist was delighted by the warm reception. This was one of the many strong features of his native culture that he admired. Visiting somebody without an appointment and yet the host would treat you as if he had been expecting you and so prepared for the visit. It was spontaneous and natural.

"You shouldn't have taken this trouble. After all, I didn't even inform you that I would come to see you this afternoon," he told his host.

"It's no trouble. It's a pleasure. And you don't need to inform me to call on me. We are brothers. You are always welcome," Pere told his guest.

"Na because of dis money people dey travel go abroad. Good that I come back. I go dey visit friends like you when I get broke," the Activist said in his mangled pidgin.

"We dey wait for you. But we go come storm your place too and you go release all the dollars which you pack from America."

"Any day feel free to come," the Activist replied.

The Activist on his part was a good guest. The host and his guest started with social pleasantries and laughed over a few things. Pere thanked him for making the great sacrifice to return from America to teach in their university and help uplift the standard of education in the state. To this the Activist replied that it was the responsibility of every individual to give back to the society that had nourished him, and he was doing his little best in paying back. Even though he got his many degrees from outside, it was the Niger Delta that made him what he was, he explained.

Gradually they began to talk local and national politics.

"Why you no join dem for government?" Pere teased the Activist.

"Me, they go fire me the first day I join dem; they go say I be rebel."

They laughed.

"I be rebel too-o," Pere told him.

"If you no dey with dem, you be rebel. No mind dem."

Tosan seeing the men engrossed in their conversation felt left out and so went inside.

"Why you no join Army self? You for don become military governor!" the Activist asked Pere.

"For where? Who dash monkey banana?"

"Every time they promise election, they go postpone am. Why?"

"Go ask God because nobody with sense know wetin the military dey do," Pere replied.

"Na our oil dey make dem no want commot for power."

"And the oil still dey boku."

Pere and the Activist soon found out that they had common goals, which they had discovered but not told the other - either to push out the outsiders or be accepted and treated respectfully by them as the owners of the resources that were being carted away. They also wished they could isolate and diminish the ranks of the treacherous insiders, who colluded with the outsiders. The outsiders would always find it difficult to succeed without the support of some insiders.

Pere told the Activist about Chief Ishaka. This chief was different from the other chiefs around. From his views and actions, he was on their side and they wished more of the chiefs would think of their people's interests and not of their own pockets.

"What a change it would be, if many lecturers were like him," Pere told himself after the Activist left.

The Activist Moves in with Ebi

Ebi and the Activist first saw each other's nakedness in Ebi's flat. The Activist was surprised at Ebi's chastity.
"How were you able to hold on for so long?" he asked her, after they got out of bed.
"There's a time for everything," she told him, smiling.
"You are a jewel. Thanks for keeping this for me."
"Thank you too for being patient."
"It's a pleasure. I will always cherish this privilege," he told her.
"I will also cherish it all my life. It is one of those things that a woman doesn't forget."
"You are a strong woman," he complimented her.
"I'd better be strong to survive," she said, as she took off the blood-stained bed-sheet to soak in a bucket of water in preparation for washing.
"You are a miracle to me," the Activist further told her.
"I think you are the greater miracle," she responded.
"Thanks for the compliment that I do not deserve."
The aftertaste of the sexual experience made them to cling more to each other. They stayed longer in each other's place when they visited. It was a matter of time for them to take far-reaching decisions about their relationship.
Three weeks later.
"I have been meaning to tell you something," the Activist told Ebi.
"Please tell me," Ebi responded in her characteristic manner.
"Why can't you move over?" the Activist asked.
He had approached her and held her right hand, a more frequent happening now than before. They used to avoid

physical contact and the Activist treated her as a sovereign body and Ebi treated him the same way. It would be through mutual agreement that the two bodies would surrender their sovereignty and be involved with each other.

"Move over to where?" Ebi asked back, as if she did not understand the full implication of the invitation.

To underscore this, she moved to his side of the table. The Activist smiled to show that she had missed the point.

"Instead of this coming to-and-fro, don't you think we may as well live together, if you don't mind?" he asked.

"See me see trouble-o!" she shouted.

"I beg your pardon," the Activist said.

"You say if I don't mind what? Are you crazy?" she shouted at him.

She wanted to hear how he would receive her response to his invitation. He had invited her several times to his flat for an evening of conversation and food together. In more recent visits to his, she ended up preparing traditional dishes that he relished. She came in when he was about to cook, the foodstuffs ready. After one or two visits, he would get everything ready and waited for her arrival, if he wanted a traditional food, be it Itsekiri, Izon, or Urhobo. She was a first-class cook of all dishes of the three groups.

Their main foods were prepared with fish and taken with yam, starch, or garri. Ebi's pepper soup was one of a kind; a symmetry of the talents of all three groups. So were her banga and palm oil soups. Blessed be that mother who imbibed her daughter with this great cooking talent, the Activist often said in her praise. Blessed is she who cooks what the gods would scramble to taste, he also said. He always ate voraciously what she prepared for him.

The Activist was at peace with himself the way he had never been before all his life. He felt relaxed and happy. He laughed a lot while with Ebi who enjoyed his jokes that had become more imaginative. Even if he lived in America for fifty years, he would not have come close to this fulfilling experience that Ebi gave him. He did not want to think of his girlfriends in America who always resorted to ordering pizza or Kentucky fried chicken whenever he was visiting them.

Home is really great, he thought. Who knew that home was a paradise? If many of his countrymen suffering abroad knew this, they would seize the next available flight and return. Let those who were speaking ill of Nigerian women abroad come home and see an unsurpassable lady in Ebi!

Ebi also ate what he prepared and was impressed by his culinary skills in the curry stew and fried rice he prepared that they ate together. The Activist prepared chicken kebab, which they took with jollof rice. Few men could impress women with their food as the Activist did; more so as men in the area were not trained to cook. Here was a son of the soil who not only knew how to cook but really cooked very well. She thought his American experience and many years of living alone must have made him acquire this rare skill. She knew such men would not be many to come by in the entire Niger Delta.

For the generality of men, their sick wives still had to cook before they ate at all. Many did not enter the kitchen, not to talk of cooking to eat even when starving.

"Sleep over it," he told her of his suggestion that both of them should start to live together.

"It's something I really have to sleep over," she responded.

"We have to do something about our relationship," the Activist told her.

Ebi did not stay till late at his, nor did he too stay late at hers. They did not want to give the campus community more to gossip about. University teachers gossiped so much to occupy their spare time. If it was not about promotions and appointments, it was about something else. Academics and administration workers second-guessed what the Vice-Chancellor and the Registrar did. The University Club was the gossip and rumour mill. There the sex lives of the community were exposed, analyzed, and debated. Alcohol often fuelled those in the club to imagine what they had not heard and to expose what they ought to keep mum about. They laughed hilariously as they talked about others or teased one another about their sexual escapades. Ebi and the Activist did not go to the club.

When they met again at Ebi's three days later, they

embraced and held to each other for several minutes without talking. They listened to their hearts beat for the other. They broke the embrace to look at each other's eyes satiated with desire for the other.

"Okay," Ebi simply told him.

"Thanks a million," he responded.

Implementing the decision to live together would be more difficult than agreeing to do so. Were they going to marry? Each did not yet know what was on the other's mind on this. As for the Activist, he worried whether Ebi would like to live with him without going to church, court, or doing a traditional marriage. In any of those ceremonies, if she were the conventional woman, she would invite her friends and the public to watch her take a man; and that would make her proud. Would she not ask for a ring? But the little time he had known her, she was far from the ordinary woman. Ebi was an exceptional woman, and she would not like such superficial trappings in order to impress anybody.

As for Ebi, she did not know what this living together would turn out to be. Wouldn't he ask for a church wedding in which she would wear a white gown and gloves and he a blue or dark suit? That would be a masquerade spectacle that she would prefer to forego, she told herself. She wanted a stable relationship, married or just living together, but would this man be the right man for her? After waiting all this long to take a man seriously, would this be the God-given man? She knew there were some things you did and did not care about their consequences, and this was one of such for her. She loved this man and wanted him and would live with him no matter the consequences.

"You have to move over here," Ebi told him rather casually.

She expected an argument. Or would he just resist for a while and then give in? Would he persuade her to move to his flat? She also expected a lecture about the culture and what obtained in a man-woman relationship. The Activist did not contradict her.

"No problem," he replied.

Ebi was surprised but pleased. She could not explain to herself why she wanted him to move to hers rather than her to move to his, but something deep inside her had made her want it so. There was no argument and this made her feel that the man was really serious with her.

"Thanks," she said.

"I should thank you for this. You have brought happiness to me."

"You have brought me the same."

"You have made my return home the best decision I have ever made."

"You have brought me a new life."

They held each other's hands again, came together in a passionate embrace, and kissed. They could feel each other's heart beating a happy drum. They were relieved of the anguish they had carried in their hearts for months.

The next weekend, the Activist moved into Ebi's flat, which was small in the sense of having only two bedrooms but was still larger than his one-bedroom transit quarter. He had been expected to stay in the transit room for as many years as it would take for a permanent accommodation to be available in a period when the military government was not interested in funding higher education.

It had never happened in the area that a man abandoned his flat or home however small or unimpressive and moved into a woman's home.

"Is that what happens abroad?" one lecturer asked his colleagues.

"That happens only with useless and uneducated black men who do not take jobs but live on women. When one woman kicks them out, they look for another woman to move to and it is so easy to live that way with so many women and so few men around," a lecturer who had studied at Wisconsin in the 1970s proffered.

"No wonder he came back! He had no other woman to move to when thrown out. I can now understand his madness."

"He must have taken after the worst of his black brothers abroad!" the Wisconsin alumnus again said.

"Is he a serial lover or what do you call that type of man?"

"Who knows whether there is a term for this unusual

practice?"

"The world is large and strange things happen far from one's place."

"He shouldn't do that here!"

"But what can we do? This is a university and he has the freedom to attach himself to a spinster lecturer."

"It's the woman I blame. Has she no shame?"

"That will be Ebi's problem when the serial lover leaves her to move to another woman's flat," one of them said.

"Why blame the woman? What of the stupid man, the woman-wrapper?"

No man around would like to be called a "woman's wrapper," one manipulated by a woman to please her fancy. The man was the head of the family and the woman went to him rather than the other way around.

The community wondered what would be next in the Activist's cache of surprises to unsettle not only the campus but also the society beyond in the name of returning from America. They braced themselves for strange lifestyles that the Activist would propagate among them.

"Very soon he will be going to the market to buy foodstuffs for his wife in the name of love or civilization," the gossip went.

"That's not a bad thing," one of the lecturers challenged. "Helping our wives when necessary is different from their marrying you rather than you marrying them," he explained.

"Don't be surprised if he blended pepper, tomatoes, onions and other ingredients and cooked while his wife sat crossing her legs and watching television or video films. He would place the food on the table for both of them to eat and wash the dishes afterwards."

"He will soon ask a man to be escorted to the woman's place rather than the other way around, as has always happened in the land. After all, he has given himself to the old maid. She should ask her people to pay bride price to his family."

There was grumbling here and there, not because Ebi and the Activist broke any law or hurt others by their action but because of jealousy for their bold action of doing what they desired. Those who grumbled did not do so in the presence of both or either of them.

The Activist and Ebi were under attack from many quarters. The female students saw their spinster lecturer as a robber. In their opinion, she took over a man that should be their prize. They believed that one of the female students ought to claim the hand of the American-trained lecturer as either a boyfriend or a husband.

To the female lecturers, Ebi had grabbed to herself the man that they all should have openly competed for. It was customary for women to compete for the love of a man and a bachelor for that matter. The ways women competed to win a man's heart continued to change, but it was a tradition that came from their mothers to them and they wanted it to continue. Whether through good cooking, good manners, chatting, or the ultimate one in bed, it had to be competition. But from the beginning, according to them, Ebi schemed to have the Activist to herself alone. She broke the law of competing on a level field, they gossiped. Her "open-eye" desperation to have a man was unprecedented. How would a woman invite a man to her flat, as Ebi often did? They heard that, before he moved in to live with her, she had invited him many times to hers and prepared delicious fresh fish dishes for him. She spent so much money to cook to impress the Activist. Once he had eaten her food, the gossip went, the Activist no longer responded to greetings from other single women on campus. What a charmer Ebi was! How were they sure that she did not add something else to the fish in the food she prepared specially for him? Even when he was not passing the night at hers, as far as they could tell from their jealous observations, who knew what they did even in daylight in her flat? Some gossips had reported that whenever the Activist visited Ebi, one type of music always played until he left. Was that not a ploy to cover their love moans? the jealous ones asked.

Before the Activist moved to hers, Ebi had also been dressing so elegantly in recent times, the embittered women said among themselves, for the sole purpose of attracting the man. She must be spending more than half her salary on buying fine clothes to please the Activist, they believed. She came to class in a new dress almost all the time. She alternated between traditional and Western dresses and whatever she wore fitted her elegantly. The gossiping women said her braids were now much longer, thinner, and more sophisticated than they used to be. Though Ebi had always used simple makeup, it was now that the women started to notice her mascara, pencilled long eyelashes, and others. What couldn't that woman do to get a husband? they asked. She must be so desperate, even those older than her believed.

A casualty of the friendship between Ebi and the Activist was a female prayer group. Many of the unmarried mature ladies had increasingly become very religious and prayed for everything they wanted and dreamt of. Most of them said that they were betrothed to Jesus. Eunice proclaimed she would not sleep with a man again until she got married, even though she got a baby before passing out of secondary school. Grace daydreamed about marrying a man that she would sing Christian hymns with before and after going to bed. Maria talked little but was known to be friendly with a Catholic priest; nobody really knew the nature of their intriguing relationship; a love affair or something else.

After Kevwe left for Holland to practice what rumour said was sex entertainment, the "sisters" began to suspect each other. Ebi's fall was the latest in the backsliding of a once cohesive group.

The most fanatical among the single ladies expressed open displeasure at Ebi's relationship with the Activist by making snide gestures and comments.

"She was just pretending; she was never born again."

"She always prayed loudly with us but still went out to do something against God."

"I never trusted her from the beginning."

"When she appears before God, let her not lie to the Almighty."

"Why did she not have the patience to study the man for a year or more?"

"I can't believe that Ebi has chosen the Devil after God has been protecting her!"

"I am sure both of them will burn in hell after Judgment Day."

Ebi's former colleagues saw her as a fallen angel that was

damned and condemned eternally to hellfire. How could she forsake Jesus for the man with a mental problem from America? How would she leave the pure relationship with God for a carnal one with an infidel? After all, they knew the Activist did not go to church on Sundays.

The Activist's male colleagues were furiously jealous too. Many had tried so many times to date Ebi and failed. How could this woman that was not moveable like the Rock of Gibraltar change so suddenly to be like a butterfly seeking to be everywhere the Activist found himself. Was it his American perfume, aura, or what? He wore a French perfume whose origin they could not identify but felt must be American. Or was Ebi after his money? Whoever came from America must be rich, they believed.

The two companions had soon introduced a new angle to their friendship. The Activist invited Ebi to visit and talk to his class, and he also visited and talked to her class. The students enjoyed these classes in which they collaborated. A few times they disagreed on issues and held their grounds. The students had keenly watched the mini academic debates, as each attempted to explain a point of view. But their co-teaching, though refreshing to the students, stirred jealousy and envy among their male and female colleagues. What were these two trying to show or prove to students? they asked.

As Ebi and the Activist bonded more and more, they left the outsiders in no doubt that they were in love with each other. Love, after all, is a magnificent fragrance that cannot be hidden - you scent it in whoever it touches!

"Sorry, love," Ebi told him in a rather public place when she stepped on his shoes.

"No problem, sweet one," was the response.

Ebi and the Activist became "darling" and "honey" to each other and the women who wanted to experience this type of romantic relationship gossiped the most about them.

"Dis na love in Tokyo or abi wetin?" one asked.

"Na wa for dem o-o," said another.

"Na love in New York, this one be-o," one explained.

"No, na love in Hollywood," another said.

"Na wa-oo! We never see this kind love before," somebody

else said.

"This one pass Romeo and Juliet-o; e pass Anthony and Cleopatra-o," one with knowledge of Shakespeare said.

"How did she learn these manners?"

"I am sure she has been very secretive with men. She must be one of these Don't-let-my-mother-know girls."

That the Activist and Ebi did not mind and behaved so naturally fuelled the gossip for several months, until the campus community grew familiar with their love expressions and gestures.

Soon the women workers and female students demanded of their men to treat them as in New York or Hollywood, by which they meant more romantically as the Activist treated Ebi. The Activist rubbed Ebi's shoulder and back in a very gentlemanly way. He gave her a seat when she came in and there was no other vacant seat. A little chivalry here and there, the others noticed. And, of course, Ebi's "Thanks!" mattered to the men also; they saw and heard how a woman responded to a man's graciousness. Their reciprocal relationship was not lost on anybody and became the talk of the campus. It was no longer frivolous talk, but individual yearning for good manners from the opposite sex.

Ebi and the Activist hungered for any opportunity to be together. Whenever she knew he would be at an event, she abandoned whatever tasks at hand to be there with him. For his sake she kept her schedule as flexible as possible. Similarly, whenever he knew that Ebi would show up somewhere, he put aside any other thing and went there. Some spirit they could not resist pulled them together. They gestured to each other from a distance. They were gradually developing a code language with which they could communicate without being heard by others. They spoke with their eyes and each gaze spoke a thousand words in their secret love language. As the relationship grew stronger, they became much happier and more cheerful than before.

Their separate neighbours were stunned into silence after weeks of wild gossip. They had not believed that this would be possible, but it happened. Ebi and the Activist did not need their approval to live the way they wanted, they soon realized.

The Activist informed the university in writing of his quitting the transit quarter, which could now be re-allocated to somebody else who needed it; he would accept a permanent house when available. The American and the old maid, as many in the university community disparagingly called the two companions they found difficult to describe and understand, were living together. There was nothing they could do to separate them.

Chief Tobi Ishaka

Not all the local chiefs were captives of corruption. Nor were they all partners and friends of Bell Oil and O&G. The oil companies, to silence the local population from demanding compensations for their despoiled environment, built palaces for local monarchs. They not only paid the monarchs and chiefs monthly stipends but also catered for their luxuries that included big cars and jeeps. The multinational oil company directors expected the elderly chiefs to keep a strong hold on their people because the well-fed dogs would not bite the hands that fed them. But some dogs refused to be distracted and fiercely kept their sentinel duty.

Tobi Ishaka was an exceptional chief. He might be strange in some ways, as anyone familiar with him would observe, but he was not tainted by oil and blood money. He refused to share in the big payoff envelopes that the oil companies frequently sent to the monarch and his chiefs. The tall chief, often compared to the slim onoge palm tree, railed at his fellow chiefs who saw truth and deliberately bypassed it to embrace lies.

At the last council of chiefs' meeting, he was almost isolated by his fellow chiefs.

"When have elders become afraid of telling the truth?" he asked.

There was no response to his question.

"The white robe of chieftaincy and the coral beads we wear set us apart. But we seem not to know our responsibilities. We are supposed to be the clean ones, but I am afraid we even stink. We secretly eat forbidden foods and wipe our mouths; we cannot deceive our ancestors and they will surely not forgive us," he declared.

"Can you just speak for only yourself and not for all of us?"

Chief Dogho countered.

"Money does not smell. If you are comfortable enough to reject a gift, that's your loss. When I am offered a gift, I take it. You know that it is not customary to reject a gift," Chief Tebele said.

"Not from your robbers or enemies," Chief Ishaka responded.

"Who offers you a gift cannot but be your friend," Chief Tebele again defended.

"There you go wrong. Who gives you some types of gifts can be taking more from you than he is giving you," Chief Ishaka told him.

"We have no robbers or enemies here," the monarch intervened. "Bell Oil is our friend and partner in progress,"

"Your Royal Highness," Chief Ishaka replied, "I will like them to be friends and partners, but they are not now. Unless we are unequal partners that they take away our wealth and leave us tidbits to quarrel over as we are doing now!"

You could count on Chief Ishaka to tell the truth and for knowing that the people were being shortchanged in the oil wealth. He was the only one in the council of chiefs that saw the change in their environment as negative rather than positive.

"Oil brought wealth, but how are we better off without farming, fishing, and hunting that are no longer viable?" Chief Ishaka asked.

He noticed that all of a sudden his people had become recipients of charities from their own children in the cities because there was no way of generating enough money to live on in their rural homes. And the worst part of it all, they could no longer produce food to feed their families. They travelled outside to buy what they used to produce plantains, yams, beans, and cassava. They used to give yams, plantains, palm oil, and garri to their sons and daughters visiting from the city. But now they depended on money sent to them by their sons, daughters, and other relatives working in the city to survive. "How can reducing a once self-reliant people to a dependent population be a sign of development?" he asked himself. To him, it was only the outsiders that gained from the oil exploration in the land.

How things have changed! The current state of things was an omen of worse things to come. This was what Ishaka told the monarch and his fellow chiefs, who saw the money from oil as superseding these negative phenomena. He saw development in a different light from them. To him, development meant using modern tools to farm and fish more efficiently for a good harvest and catch respectively. Development meant modern ways of storing and preserving excess yams and fish for a season of need.

"How can we be developed with complaining stomachs?" he asked.

"Are you telling me that people are not hungry in Europe before they eat?" Chief Fatakpa asked.

"People overseas surely will be hungry before they eat but there's abundance of food available to be eaten. When we are hungry, where's the food?" he asked back.

"There's always food in the market," Chief Fatakpa answered.

"The food in the market is not yours and so you cannot take it away without paying for it. Why will you go to buy something that you can produce?" he asked out of exasperation.

"If you don't have enough money to buy food, why can't you take your brown envelope? Why should a needy man be so fastidious about receiving assistance from whatever source is there for him?" Chief Okiti asked.

"I do not need plenty of money. I am fine with what I have and do not need to accept money from those robbing us," Chief Ishaka told the chief.

Chief Tobi Ishaka wanted the local roads tarred, drainage done in the towns so that whenever there was a heavy downpour, as often happened, they would not be flooded. These fresh ideas fell on the deaf ears of those who always smiled broadly whenever they saw the money bags from the oil companies.

The other chiefs dismissed his concerns about development and always had a ready answer to counter his complaints.

"Are there no floods in America or Europe?"

"Does it rain as much there as it does here?"

"You will soon tell us that white people in developed countries don't urinate or shit."

"Does the shit of those people not smell?"

Ishaka knew that his fellow chiefs missed the point with their frivolous comments and questions; their hunger for money that the oil companies satisfied made them not to be reasonable.

"I have not travelled to Dubai or Saudi Arabia, but others with oil look far nicer than we do. We even lived better in days before this abundance of oil," he told his fellow chiefs.

"Don't you see those skyscrapers, the headquarters of Bell Oil and O&G? Are they not the houses of gods in our folktales?" Chief Fatakpa asked.

"Do we live in those houses?" Ishaka asked back.

"So you want to live in a house of glass?" Chief Fatakpa again asked, making jest of him.

"What else other than the tall buildings housing the oil companies can we boast of?" Chief Ishaka asked back.

"Are the oil companies your own? When you have a business, do you share the profits as these companies are doing?" Chief Tebele asked.

Arguing with his colleagues did not bridge the gap of understanding between them; they were too far apart in their respective attitudes towards the oil companies. Let them continue to accept payoffs from the companies until some day when they would be asked to disgorge the forbidden foods they had been eating, Chief Ishaka thought. He knew this type of situation could not continue without coming to an end someday. He was not in good standing with the monarch, but that did not bother him.

Chief Ishaka attended wakes and burial ceremonies almost every weekend as most adults around did. People were always dying and there were many burials to choose from to attend on weekends. But there was a strange interest that the chief had at such wakes and burials. As a chief, he would make his way to any position he wanted at such ceremonies and so sit at a vantage position to have a full view of the casket. He did not have to wait till mourners were called upon to pay their last respects to the deceased before surveying the coffin's worth.

To the people who knew him close, Chief Ishaka was a man who "remembered the dead." He could retell the lives of dead relatives, friends, and strangers so vividly that he made them come alive again. He was neither a minstrel nor a storyteller as such, but call any deceased person's name and Ishaka would tell you about the person's history and especially about his or her end. In almost every case, the end was unforeseen and had no bearing with the previous years of the person's life. He knew those who died from the wealth they had sought all their lives soon after realizing their dreams. Others, who feared witches and spent thousands of naira fortifying themselves against them with traditional medicines, ended up dying of simple malaria.

"Death now comes easily through many doors," he often said.

To the chief, death baits one to do the wrong things. One of his cousins who had a simple boil and, instead of either taking antibiotics or just leaving it to run its own course, decided to have it surgically removed. He died from the cut. A catechist and a pastor both died in water when they went to fish in the marshes and the villagers saw their end as good riddance for bringing locals to be dipped into baptismal water.

People die as much from the food they eat as from not having food to eat. Water saves and also kills. The doors through which death enters to seize its victims could be strange and fantastic. Where there are no doors, death now creates its own doors to enter wherever it likes to inflict its fatal blow. It burrows its way through rocks and fortifications to spring a surprise at its fated victims. Death has become so magical that it simultaneously comes from all directions to snatch its victim. Where do you run to, you humans who are afraid of death? the chief asked.

Chief Ishaka often took along one of his children, depending on who was available, by persuasion or subtle coercion, when he attended burial ceremonies in order to show him what he considered to be appropriate or inappropriate burials. He thus indirectly suggested the class of casket he wished to be buried in when his time came.

Ishaka was one of the few chiefs with only one wife and blessed with five male children, all of them in school. He understood the importance of education, which, he told the other chiefs, would be the key to success in the future. They derided him as throwing his money away by educating his children that would not have jobs when they completed school. On his part, he chided his colleagues who continued to marry more wives in their old age as if they were lecherous goats on irrepressible heat.

Chief Ishaka once stopped at the Ekakpamre-Warri Road to look at caskets on display by the roadside. This was something new he had not seen before. People in the community used to travel to distant places to buy caskets. Now they were on sale at their doorsteps and they did not need to go far for them. In the array of coffins, he admired one so much that he praised it in front of David, his third son:

"This is the best of the local ones. It is big, solid, and heavy. It is smooth and shiny. It is made of mahogany. It is the ultimate home that one wants to be stuck in forever."

He had seen imported caskets from the United States of America and Great Britain. They were stuffed with velvety and silk linings and were soft like cotton; they were ideal resting places. Ishaka saw them as luxurious vehicles into the afterlife; they were the Cadillac and Mercedes Benz to the next world. With this vehicle, one would have a smooth ride to one's final destination, wherever that might be.

Whenever Ishaka thought about death, he was in a quandary. What happened after death? Did one live another life or come back, born as another human being? How long would one live in death? He could not imagine what everlasting life in death meant.

He planned to visit Ghana in order to see for himself what the standards of coffins had become there. His Ghanaian friend, Mr. Godfrey Aduo, had told him how the art of making coffins had reached an advanced and international standard there. A man or woman worthy to be an ancestor had to depart in a befitting way. That meant that the fisherman had to be buried in a fish-shaped coffin. Each fisherman was given the last respect in the type of fish he caught the most; hence Akoffo was buried in a catfish coffin, just as the catcher of mudfish was interred in a mudfish-shaped one. Godfrey told the chief that in Kumasi, on weekends, in addition to the moving dirges was the wonderful spectacle of different coffins that bore the deceased for burial as black-dressed women sang and danced mournfully. The owner of a poultry farm was buried in a roost; a corn farmer was laid to rest in a corncob; and a teacher had at last dignity in the pencil-shaped coffin with which he departed with a flourish.

Chief Ishaka wished he could be buried in a fan-shaped casket. After all, his title was Adjudju of Agbon, the fan of the kingdom. He blew the heat out of the kingdom that was under continuous assault of the elements. The heat had increased with the gas flares and blowouts that came with the new oil. There will only be comfort after the heat is put out. The chief was thus by virtue of his title the provider of comfort and peace to the community.

When Ishaka was young, he saw coffins on display at Obigbo, a village that straddled both sides of the Warri-Agbor Road. He suffered nightmares from the fright at seeing so many coffins together. Then he wondered how those coffin sellers would pray for their businesses to prosper without wishing people to die. These craftsmen and traders were vultures in their occupation, he had felt then. They prayed for, looked forward to, and benefited from deaths.

But the world was changing, the chief acknowledged. He had changed with the times and now did not fear coffins anymore but in fact admired them. What you cannot escape, you have to embrace, he contended.

Chief Ishaka once visited a very old woman whose children had bought her a coffin when she was seriously ill and they had felt she would not survive the sickness. The old woman had been unconscious for days and woken up only to see the coffin waiting for her body. She laughed cynically and decided to make friends with the coffin, which she asked to be left in her room. She slept in it one night and later asked that it be placed on the rafters of the roof. Once in a while when she fell sick she would ask that it be brought down for her to sleep in. She was still living when Chief Ishaka last asked about her. She had refused to die. Already more than a hundred years old, she seemed to still have a lot of life left in her. The chief wished he could know what magical powers the coffin had to keep the wrinkled face alive.

The Delta Cartel

Since Pere put stealing, robbing, and kidnapping behind him, he felt fine with himself. Gone were the days when he set out in a group of four or five to rob at busy intersections in Warri using the tie-neck style that children played with in the inner streets! This fighting craft many children learnt from their age-mates as they played after school and on weekends.

Pere and his team often chose the Enerhe Junction that milled with people for their exercise. There buses and taxis dropped passengers to continue their journeys to their destinations. Many were workers who passed there to and from work. The crowd provided the atmosphere conducive for him and other area boys to test their stealing skill.

The team mixed freely with others in the crowd. There was no way of knowing who was who in the thronged junction. One of them pushed the person they had suspected of having money or any valuable; then another pushed the target of the attack back, and in the melee Pere or another member of the group sprang the tie-neck hold on the victim who was robbed as he or she struggled to be free from the tight grip of the attackers. Each member of the robbing gang was the others' backup. Once in the grip of the attacker, one felt choked, gasped for air, and struggled for life. It happened so swiftly that the victim had no time to call for help. As soon as the objective of the assault was achieved, the victim received a kick and then was pushed into the crowd while the robbers melted again into the crowd. They stole money, snatched wristwatches, ladies' handbags, and gold necklaces and earrings.

Stories were told of such robberies but nobody was ever caught. The police did not go there, either afraid of the bad boys or bribed by them to keep away. These law enforcement officers received money to keep away from crime scenes; they could do worse things for the sake of money.

That was petty stealing, as Pere saw it. There were a few times they robbed helpless elderly women and he felt uncomfortable when he got home. He shared in the booty but he always had sleepless nights afterwards. His conscience pricked him and he could not see any excuse to justify his participation in such activities. That type of stealing had to stop, he decided. He knew it was wrong to rob the helpless and the weak.

Pere matured and brought his increasing sensitive experience to bear on decisions of his group. The area boys gradually reformed to avoid hurting the helpless - they and the helpless were on the same desperate side of society and so they had to protect them.

Pere passed the area called Angle Ninety in Effurun almost daily and saw a walled compound there but did not one day stop to think about what transpired inside. Tankers carrying all kinds of fuel - petrol, gasoline, and kerosene - parked by the roadside. He simply thought that the tankers were just parked there until driven to a petrol station. Since this place was immediately after a major and busy intersection on the way to the Effurun Refinery, he assumed that the line of tankers was waiting to be loaded.

On the opposite side of the road was the shanty makeshift plank-built settlement of homes, stores, and bukas called Maroko, so named after the slum settlement in Victoria Island in Lagos that was levelled to create a new city for the rich. In this Niger Delta Maroko so much brisk business went on. It was crowded in the evening and at night when people drank, ate, bought all sorts of contraband goods, and prostitutes flaunted themselves before the seeking eye.

Pere got to know the inside story of the fenced compound through a friend of his or rather one of his motor-park-days' colleagues. Owumi had become a driver and he took Pere inside to fill his tank to repay a past kindness when things were really very hard for him. Thanks to the new job, he was doing very well. And he enjoyed his relative prosperity because nobody expected much from him as a driver and yet he knew he made more money a day than a junior civil servant made in a month!

"Who owns this compound?" Pere asked.

"Is it not fuel you want?" Owumi asked back.

"Is this a fuel depot?" Pere asked.

"Have you heard of bunkering?" Owumi asked him in a low tone.

"I don't really know what it is," Pere answered.

Owumi described the process of bunkering to Pere and it looked so simple even though dangerous. He sent his boys to break pipes and from the outflow filled his tanker. He sold some on his way to town and emptied the remainder into underground tanks at petrol stations through special arrangements with trusted dealers.

"The world is not waiting for anybody, and I had to join this business to make ends meet. I could not remain poor and desperate all my life when the means were there to improve my lot. Fortunately I can't complain now," he told Pere.

"You are certainly doing well," Pere responded.

"I thank God for this new way opened to me," Owumi replied.

"I am happy for you," Pere also told him.

Pere could see that his friend, who could barely take two meals a day some years earlier, had put on plenty of weight. The haggard-looking skinny young man now had chubby cheeks, strode with the confidence of one who had no anxieties about his next meal.

"I am putting up a storey building along the Port Harcourt Road. I have to prepare for the future because this open way may not last for ever. I want to rent out the six flats."

"That's a good plan. You must prepare for tomorrow. I envy you," Pere told him.

"It's God's blessing and the way is open for those who see it to follow."

"Is it as simple as that?"

"Until you try it, you won't know," he assured Pere.

"But what of soldiers and police guarding everywhere there are oil pipelines?" Pere asked.

"Police and soja no be Nigerian?" Owumi asked in reply.

Both of them laughed. The import of the question sank into Pere's head.

"You don see goat dey guard cassava leaves? Or you don see pigeon dey guard corn?" Owumi asked Pere.

"I hear you," he replied.

Pere learnt from his friend that many of the rich and notable people in the area were involved in bunkering. It worked like a secret society in which only those involved knew each other. Those who did not belong to the cult of instant wealth were ignorant and moped about the town complaining of economic hardship.

To think of Chief Young Kpeke who owned several estates in Port Harcourt and Warri and also once owned an airline before selling it as a bunkering chieftain made Pere feel it was something he should try his hands at. The chief always dressed in white robes and big coral beads and looked by every measure a very affluent man.

Pere discovered that there were many secrets in town he did not know about. Also Chief Goodluck Ede whose wealth filled so many banks in recent years and was a frequent donor to philanthropic organizations was also in the bunkering business. He had a fleet of the most expensive cars that included Cadillac, Rover, and Jaguar in his palatial mansion in Ometan Street. He had wondered how Chief Ede was able to replenish from his constant donations because he gave out right and left even bigger amounts on subsequent occasions.

"Only the blind are left out," Owumi told him.

And really Pere did not see or know what had been happening around him. You could open your two eyes in the sun and still be blind to the secrets of wealth in the land. He had always believed that only the bold and daring got rich.

Pere also learnt that many of the top military officers were involved in bunkering. The head of the military junta was himself a bunkering chieftain. He had associates who did the job for him to enjoy the huge profits. He had used the bunkering business as a means of favoring loyal officers or buying the loyalty of key ones whose loyalty he needed. Many of the generals had their own tankers taking crude oil to the spot market in Rotterdam. Others tapped the refined oil and shipped their loot to neighbouring poor countries to sell. How else did many of the generals become multimillionaires? To be a favoured general in the Nigerian Army was to be a bunkering chief and a multimillionaire! With the commander-in-chief and his officers involved in bunkering, it had become a semi-official lucrative business despite the many decrees.

"If thief catch thief, wetin e go do?" Owumi asked him.

Of course he will do nothing.

Pere left the compound seriously thinking of joining the bunkering business and having a petrol station. He could now piece together so many things that had seemed unconnected to him. He saw petrol stations springing up everywhere in the country despite the persistent shortage of petrol. He had taken a bus to Maiduguri at the northeastern corner of the country to attend his wife's junior sister's marriage ceremony and, during the long journey, saw firsthand how much the nation's businessmen had fallen in love with petrol stations. From the rainforest coast to the Sahelian end of the country, the favourite business was running a petrol station. Along the roads were not only old and new petrol stations but many others under construction. More were built in towns, where there were many car-owners, but also villages without cars and uninhabited parts of highways also had new petrol stations.

Pere saw petroleum as his own property forcibly taken away from him. He was going to set up a business to reclaim his birthright. Call it illegal business, smuggling, stealing, or bunkering, he did not care what dirty names you called it.

He thought of the mobile police, the army boys, and the foreign planes with military men wielding strange guns and binoculars flying over the airspace. Their presence in the oil-rich area amounted to blatant intimidation and robbery. He would rob the robbers to get back his property. Bell Oil Company or any of the other oil companies did not have more right to the oil than him. The Federal Military Government too in Lagos or Abuja did not have more right to the oil than him. A military decree is an instrument of coercion, exploitation, and oppression and so is invalid whatever Land Use Decree was promulgated to seize lands from its owners, he believed. What was done by force, by its very nature, was illegal and unjust. The oil companies and the military junta did not consult the owners of the land over their oil-prospecting activities. As one has to fight fire with fire, so should the illegality of the outsiders be resisted with whatever means by the insiders.

Pere made more inquiries about bunkering and learnt how multifaceted it was. Every informal business in petroleum products was considered bunkering. Diverting the tankers taking fuel from the refinery to a roadside to sell drums of fuel to hustlers was bunkering. This was done especially when there was fuel scarcity and the petrol station owners were so happy to receive their supplies that they did not check the accuracy of the fuel amount because they knew they would gain by adjusting their fuel pumps to their advantage. Many drivers also made additional tanks which they attached underneath to their vehicles, filled with cheap Nigerian fuel, and travelled to neighboring countries to sell at an exorbitant price. The boldest type of bunkering involved breaking pipelines carrying refined oil to different parts of the country and filling tankers with it.

The reformed area boy who was bent on being a true devotee of Egba started planning by first looking for a business partner. Wealth was there in the Niger Delta; it was there on their farmlands and even in their backyards. Wealth was not gold in the mouth of a python at the unattainable rainbow's end. No, it was not too far away. Though guarded by mobile police and army boys, they were no obstruction to getting the wealth from his own land. The nation's entire army and police force could not monitor the so many pipelines that crisscrossed the forests, villages, and roads in the area. All the planes of the foreign retired marines and mercenaries would not be able to see through the natural green canopy that the forest provided the Niger Delta people.

Besides, it was easy to bribe the guards to turn the other way. These very guards knew what their senior officers were doing under their noses and did not care for the national wealth which did not make their lives better. They would rather get fat tips from the civilian bunkering lords than do their military duty of guarding the pipelines. After all, were they recruited into the Army to guard pipelines or to fight wars? They preferred being posted to Liberia or Sierra Leone, where they could have a free range to loot and rape in the name of peace-keeping than guarding oil pipelines.

Pere knew it would be difficult to find a business partner. Whom would he approach in a society in which everybody wanted to be rich at other people's expense? It did not matter whether it was relatives or friends; sometimes the closer the working partner, the more reasons not to be trusted. He went through a list of people he knew that could be possible business partners. Owumi was already doing very well in the business and so would not be interested in accepting him as part of his business. He needed somebody else who had not only money but good ideas.

In his imaginative wanderings, he came to the Activist. Would he come down the Ivory Tower and agree to be his business partner? They shared common ideas on the oil exploration in their homeland. They wanted the oil to be used to develop the area. Since that was not happening, whatever could be done to hurt the oil companies and the Federal Military Government was fair game. People such as he and the Activist with common objectives could be partners in the bunkering business.

Pere muted the idea to the Activist at a meeting. He was cautious not to sound too pushy. He wanted the Activist to be persuaded by the viability of the project.

"You want the army boys to execute me by firing squad?" the Activist asked Pere.

"God forbid that bad thing! No be so. Nobody go catch us. We know the way," he replied.

"What if they catch us?" the Activist insisted.

"I go tell you how to do am. No be me and you go do am as such," Pere explained.

"Na so you go talk now. When trouble break, you go hide and leave me to suffer."

"Me?" Pere asked, apparently hurt by the Activist's mistrust. "Not me. I no go let you down. I be Egba Boy and we protect our own."

All of a sudden, the Activist saw bunkering as a weapon against the two principal outsiders that were robbing and destroying the people of the Niger Delta.

"You don do business before or na dis one you go take start?" he asked Pere.

"Na one day business dey start. Oga, dis na better business," he answered.

"I no be your oga. I go think of am if you gree say we be both oga for the business," the Activist told Pere.

"Make you think of am well well," Pere advised.

That night the Activist did not sleep till very late. Fortunately, he and Ebi had agreed from the first night of his moving in to have separate bedrooms. It was more exciting when one desiring the other went to his or her bedroom to spend the night. But this was not a night of seeking one's partner; not a night of romance. For the Activist, it was a night of ruminations. Was the desire to hurt one's exploiters and oppressors enough to go into the bunkering business? he asked himself. He thought of the philosophy of ATTACK and assured himself that hurting destroyers of the natural environment was a good thing to do. His thoughts went to Ebi sleeping in the other bedroom. Would she approve of this? From her concern about the rivers, forests, and the ocean, she would like whatever would scale down the activities of the oil companies.

"Egba, guide me to the right path!" he prayed at a point.

The man who had thought hard about some decisions in the past and shown a stoic disposition cried for the first time this night. It was not clear to him whether the tears were of relief or anguish. Not every reasonable act sounds moral, he discovered.

The partnership that became the Delta Cartel was sealed in another meeting.

"Agreed!" the Activist told Pere.

"You are my man," the head of the area boys told him.

"We can go into business."

"I am ready!"

The Activist chose the name to spite the multinational oil

companies and to mimic the powerful OPEC headquartered in Geneva, Switzerland. In addition to that, it was an eye-catching name. Now there was true partnership of the insiders that would break the backbone of the outsiders. No one should take for granted the intelligence of the weak, he told himself.

Both the Activist and Pere then went into a detailed discussion of their proposed business. They would sell fuel and other auto products to cover their real business. They would start in a small way and move gradually by selling only fuel, products of bunkering, and eventually having a petrol station of their own. They would try to buy one from someone selling his or build one from scratch for themselves.

"I can't thank you enough for this wonderful idea," the Activist told Pere.

"Thank you too. You know here it is difficult for two people to agree on anything, not to talk of a joint business," Pere responded.

"It is you that brought the idea of this business. This is great foresight."

"The way is there; somebody showed it to me and I want us to follow it."

The Activist imagined the oil companies suffering heavy losses, and that would please him immensely. Let them bleed to death, he told himself. Similarly, the Federal Military Government would lose much of its oil revenue that had been sustaining the dictatorship. Without money from oil, there would be no incentive for nincompoops to seize power and stay forever in government. Whatever was done to reduce the national wealth undermined the military junta, the Activist believed. He was already gloating over the economic setback of the Federal Military Government even before the plans took shape.

Pere described to him what the business would involve. There were various methods he knew and he explained the more suitable one for them.

"We no go get attachment tanks for motor to drive to Benin Republic or Central African Republic to sell fuel. That na risky business for small money," Pere shifted to pidgin to explain the nitty-gritty side of their plan.

"That na international nonsense," he said. "Na for this our Niger Delta soil we go dey do our business," he further explained.

Pere described how they would recruit a group of boys who would swear to secrecy. Their boys would look out for where oil pipes ran through on the land they were familiar with. The area should be porous, in the sense of not being patrolled by the army or police. They would ascertain whether it was crude or already refined oil from any of the two refineries in Port Harcourt or the one in Effurun running to different storage depots in the country. The boys would change locations as often as possible to confuse the army and police.

"What use will be crude oil that may be difficult to sell anyway?" the Activist asked.

"No, oil is always easy to sell, crude or refined," Pere explained.

He had done his homework on this matter.

"Many army officers and businessmen have their own tankers taking crude oil to foreign countries to sell. There are many avenues to sell crude oil. Where do you think some of the refineries in Ivory Coast, Ghana, and South Africa get their crude oil from? It's our people who sell it to them. There are rumors that some of our military leaders have refineries in those countries. There are Greek and Russian tankers offshore ready to buy crude oil and take to the spot market," Pere explained to the Activist.

For now, Pere told the Activist, the attention should be on already refined oil. The Activist was surprised that Pere, a high school dropout, knew so much about the business already. One should not underestimate anybody. Pere certainly had learnt much from experience, what some would call the school of life. He, the Activist, would contribute his share of the money needed to start. He had been living a modest life and that had left his savings almost intact. He had bought a used car, a Nissan, and it was doing fine. He was not spending much money compared to the many bills he used to settle at month's end while abroad. He was sustaining himself well with his salary, meager as most of his spendthrift colleagues described it. They were equal partners, and so he would contribute half the amount of money needed to start but Pere would do the day-to-day running of the business. He would help when he was free to.

Visiting Auntie Torukpa

Now that she had started a new life with the Activist, Ebi thought it wise for both of them to visit Auntie Torukpa, the only one on her father's side that always remembered to ask of her, and introduce him to her. If they did not see each other for a long time, Torukpa would come to see her. Any time she visited, she brought some plantain and dried fish. Ebi also visited her once in a while and provided her a few luxuries from town. Torukpa did not harass her about marriage and was very proud of her for teaching in the university; all her friends knew that her junior sister, as she called Ebi, taught at Niger Delta State University. Ebi called her Auntie out of respect because they were really cousins.

    She would like to be at Auntie Torukpa's place before she visited and asked about the man living with her. News travelled very fast and one busybody who knew her on campus might tell her, if she did not do so on time. So she decided to go and introduce him to her at her home in Okwagbe.

    Ebi did not explain the purpose of the planned visit to the Activist but only said she wanted to see her Okwagbe aunt whom she had not seen for some months. The Activist felt it would be fun going out of campus. He enjoyed the times they spent outside the campus meeting the real people of the Niger Delta. He was tired of Doc or Prof the campus community used in prefixing each other's name. In fact, they called each other by their ranks. He had felt that the university would be different from the outside society but the same pandering to the ego in town prevailed. There were in state and federal universities professors and vice chancellors who prefixed their names with Chief Professor, after paying huge sums of money to illiterate or half-literate clan heads who called themselves kings or monarchs to offer them traditional titles. Why should one not know the first names of colleagues? If you called them by their first names, they quickly corrected you by saying, "Prof, please!" He wanted to escape the university atmosphere whenever the opportunity availed itself.

The Activist had heard of Okwagbe's fame as not just a crossroads of many river and land routes but also an udje singing and performance community. He wanted to see the place and also to check on how much of the culture of song performance was still there. The festival of songs for which the area was famous had not held for decades, from what he heard, but he still wanted to know more about it. The battle of songs should be exciting from the little he had heard of udje song performance in which two rival groups sang against each other on an appointed day. One year it was one group's turn to perform its songs and the other group to listen and watch; the following year it would be the turn of the group at the receiving end the past year to perform and those who sang previously would then watch.

The Activist also liked rivers and whenever he visited a town, he asked to be shown or taken to the nearby river. There he would dip his legs and wash his hands with the water. If the water was sparkling clean, he washed his face with it. There was something mystical about water and the clean ones invigorated him. He was sure that the big Okwagbe River that he had heard so much about would soothe his mind, body, and soul.

Ebi and the Activist set out for Okwagbe on a Saturday morning. They drove on the Warri-Port Harcourt Road for many kilometers before they branched to the right to the less busy road to the river port town. Rubber trees filled every space in the bush. Rubber tapping overtook palm oil production as the major occupation of the people in the 1950s up to the 1960s when the discovery of petroleum made the time spent in the tedious occupation like time wasted. Many men and women who had been tapping rubber abandoned that means of livelihood to be janitors, messengers, and office boys in the oil companies. The more swampy areas were not favorable for rubber trees; in their places stood imposingly afara, abura, iroko, and mahogany. There were also many palm trees. The entire foliage was deep green.

After crossing a bridge across a small stream, one of the tributaries of the big Okwagbe River, the Activist stopped. He parked the car off the road. He and Ebi went down a small hill to the stream. This herb-dark stream had not been touched by the oil industry's excretions. The Activist pulled off his shoes and socks, rolled up his trousers, and waded into the water. He felt exhilarated. Ebi kicked off her shoes and followed suite.

"This stream is a miracle," Ebi said, "considering that it's still pristine."

"A miracle indeed despite the increase in oil prospecting in the area," the Activist added.

"I bet you it is only a matter of time for the rampaging oil prospecting to catch up with it and pollute its clean water," Ebi told her companion.

"I can see it coming."

"At least we are fortunate to have this experience before it becomes untouchable," said Ebi with the excitement of one witnessing a great spectacle that would soon be unavailable.

They took their time at the stream but soon went back to the car and continued their trip to see Auntie Torukpa.

Okwagbe, at its southernmost side, was the end of the tarred road, which stopped abruptly at the water's edge. That river connected all the peoples of the Niger Delta. The Activist deliberately drove to the road's end and could see the place crowded with traders, buyers, and other travellers trying to take water transport to their separate destinations. At the same time that they were leaving, other people were landing there.

The Activist parked the car. And, accompanied by Ebi, he walked down to the riverbank to perform his ablution ritual. The smell of the fresh fish that were sold by fishermen and women on the riverbank filled the air. Different kinds of boats were being boarded for departure. There was brisk riverside selling and buying of fresh fish, farina, plantain, sweet potatoes, and a variety of fruits and vegetables. Okwagbe brought land and water produce together in one market.

The Okwagbe River's waterfront market that day was a

most lively scene. Many taxis were parked by the road's end. They had brought traders from Warri to buy from the river people what would sustain them in the crowded city of oil workers.

The river itself was full and the currents tempestuous because the rains had been very heavy and persistent lately. The water was muddy and there were weeds, water hyacinths and lilies flowing downstream. Far off, the Activist saw boats coming towards or leaving the town. On the riverside stood signs of Okwagbe's shipping past when ships used to dock to take away palm oil and palm kernels to distant lands. Ebi and the Activist could see the Izon island of Ganagana from the road's end. They could not resist the so many fruits and nuts that young girls and boys hawked. They bought pepper fruits to eat; they also bought fresh corn and sweet potatoes that they would take home. While they liked fish, they did not buy any fresh fish at the beginning of their journey for fear of its rotting fast in the humid atmosphere.

After a taste of the river port's waterfront, Ebi and the Activist went back to the car and drove into the town to see Auntie Torukpa, who was pleasantly surprised to see Ebi and her companion. Fortunately, they had come the day of the traditional week that she did not go to her cassava farm. On edewo, the traditional day of worship, most farmers stayed at home; evil spirits roamed the bush on that day, according to the traditional belief, and no farmer wanted to encounter them.

After her aunt had completed the ritual of welcoming her guests with kola nuts, drinks, and a fifty-naira note, Ebi introduced her companion to Auntie Torukpa, who was happy that they came to see her.

"Both of you match as a couple. Be blessed," she told them.

"Thanks," the Activist responded.

"You chose each other and love will guide you all your life," she told them.

"Amen," Ebi and the Activist responded.

"Your prayers and wishes will be answered."

"Amen."

Auntie Torukpa told them that when she was young, there were many cases in which the young woman and the young man did not choose each other; rather, the choosing was done for them by their parents or relatives, and it was always very hard for the couple in marriage. She went through a similar arrangement and did not quite get used to her husband for the thirty-seven years of their marriage before he died many years ago.

"Both of you are grown-up and know what you are going into. Both of you will be fine," she again said.

"Ebi is a blessing to me," the Activist said.

"She had waited for God to give her a partner and you are surely the one," Auntie Torukpa told him.

"I can't complain about what God has given to me," Ebi told her aunt.

Torukpa was in her early sixties and still looked strong and very agile. On her face was the shadow of her past beauty. The oval face, thin lips, and long eyelashes came from the same stock that made Ebi a charming woman.

"How is America?" Ebi's aunt asked, changing the conversation.

"It's a big place; it is fine but can also be ugly," he answered.

"They say it is like heaven," she further commented.

"I don't know what heaven looks like, but it must be a happy place. Americans have so much but are not half as happy as we are here," he said.

"Let them come and have a taste of our hard life here so that they can better appreciate their life of plenty," Auntie Torukpa said.

Ebi interjected that though she had not been there, it appeared America was different things to different people. She seized the opportunity to move the conversation to something else. She told her aunt that her friend wanted to know about udje dance songs and performance.

"We are the song people," Aunt Torukpa said excitedly. "I wish you told me some days earlier before you came. If you did, I would have looked for singers and performers to entertain you to your fill. Still, we never lack songs. Let me send for Vhophen and see whether he can sing his father's songs; his father was both the leading composer and performer of his quarter."

Auntie Torukpa sent her daughter to go and call Vhophen. While waiting for him, Ebi went to the car to take out the bag containing sardines, corned beef, and biscuits for Auntie Torukpa, who was glad that she brought her the sweet things of town. On days that she wanted to treat herself, she would open a corned beef and take it with biscuits.

The son of the great singer was fortunately at home and answered Torukpa's call. The Activist was very impressed by Vhophen's response; he was impressed by the practice of just walking to somebody at home and asking the person to follow you somewhere and the person would oblige. That readiness to abandon what you were doing to attend to others was admirable. Even if time was money, these people were ready to sacrifice some time for the sake of good human relationship.

The hostess welcomed Vhophen with the bottle of local gin she had first offered to Ebi and the Activist but which they had not touched. After the renowned singer's son had taken a small glass of the gin, Torukpa told him why she had sent for him.

"My niece and her husband want to hear some udje songs. I thought of nowhere else to go for udje songs than to the source. Your father was one of the greatest composers and performers and his songs are so interesting."

"Yes, he certainly was one of the greatest," Vhophen concurred with pride.

"Let them hear some of his best songs, if you don't mind," requested Auntie Torukpa.

"I have given up singing these songs and, in fact, I have forgotten most of them. I am no more into such things. I have changed my life. But I can call some women to sing them for you. Where they falter, I can always assist, but I have stopped singing these songs for some time now," he said.

Vhophen sent Torukpa's daughter, Boma, to call two women that he knew sang his father's songs. The women had often taunted him for inheriting his father's material property but not the songs that made him very famous. Vhophen complained that Uhaghwa, the god of songs, was honoured with these udje songs, and he knew only one God now. He had been converted to one of the new Pentecostal churches that sprang up all over the land and saw his traditional songs as demonic.

The two women arrived. The Activist again internally expressed admiration for their responding so speedily to the call. An older woman called them and the two younger ones put aside their chores to come to her. Call it communal spirit or respect for one's elders, this was the sort of society that made one a real human being. You made sacrifices for others and remained cheerful about everything. He had been learning so much since he returned home.

After the women had sat down, Auntie Torukpa introduced her niece and her husband, as she called the Activist. She then told the two women that her visitors wanted to hear some udje dance songs. The women giggled, a little surprised that such an educated man wanted to hear udje songs. They made faces at Vhophen they knew did not like udje songs. They sang these songs to and from farm and entertained birds and any creatures that had ears.

"No problem," they said; "we are always ready to sing udje songs. We don't need any preparation - singing is not as hard a task as cultivating cassava," Ovwode said, speaking for both herself and her friend, Utoro.

"How did you know these songs, since women did not compose or sing them?" the Activist asked the women.

"My husband was a great singer and long after the performance was abandoned, he used to receive his friend in his parlour every other evening and they would sing the old songs with such joy that you would envy them," Ovwode explained.

Utoro was the wife of her husband's friend. They naturally became friends as their husbands were close.

"They alternated their visits and I also listened and got all the songs of their quarter and those of the opposing side," Utoro said.

Ovwode and Utoro asked Vhophen to tell them what songs they wanted heard, or at least begin one for them to take off from. He scratched his head, as if searching for a song from there. When Vhophen opened his mouth to sing, he could barely go beyond a few seconds before stammering; he had lost memory of his father's talent.

"Don't worry, I think we know the song you mean," the

women chorused.

Then they took up the song. To the Activist's pleasant surprise, Ebi also knew the song and sang along with the two women and Torukpa. The inflections and gestures were so uniform as if they had practiced this beforehand.

"You couldn't grow up here without knowing these songs," Ebi told the Activist at the end of that song.

"Why have you not been singing them to me?" he asked.

"As you can tell, they are men's songs. They emphasize women's frailties and overlook most of the men's. That is why I am not keen on singing them. But I still sing them now because it is important to keep our memory correct, if only to remember our heritage," she explained.

"Yes, I agree with you. We need to reclaim our memory to know our strengths and weaknesses," he said.

"We also have women's songs; songs that only women sing," she explained to her partner.

"And these women's songs must be telling another but complementary story about our people?" he asked.

"Certainly, they do. But we cannot sing to you those songs now," she further explained.

"I understand," the Activist replied.

Ovwode and Utoro together with Ebi and Torukpa sang more udje songs that thrilled the Activist. The body movements that accompanied the singing showed that these songs were really composed for performance. At some stage, Vhophen was so carried away by the spirit of the songs that in spite of his Pentecostal faith he joined the group in singing one of his father's most popular tunes. A rival lead-singer so cared for his throat and voice that he spent all his time and resources to protect and enhance them and in so doing overlooked his overall personal health and soon lost his head, his life!

The Activist could see from the songs how the performance genre laughed at human foibles and follies.

At the end, the Activist and Ebi gave the two women who came to sing four hundred naira in token appreciation of their accepting the impromptu invitation. Vhophen murmured that those songs should be forgotten, and that statement pitched all the other people there against him.

"What's wrong in our people's songs that even made us behave well?" Torukpa asked.

"But you sing and dance to meaningless songs in your church," Ovwode said.

"They sing and dance the most when their pastor is collecting money," Utoro said, provoking loud laughter.

"I really enjoyed the songs. These songs are certainly about us and for us," the Activist told them.

Auntie Torukpa had been up to something all the while. As the song session was on, she had disappeared and reappeared. It was when the flavor of fresh fish pepper-soup assaulted their noses that the visitors realized that she had been preparing food for them. Torukpa brought in the food - pepper soup, yam, and palm oil.

"This is what I could prepare fast enough for you. I hope you will enjoy it."

"We have enjoyed your hospitality and the food will make us enjoy it even more," the Activist said.

"She is an excellent cook. Don't mind her. She is very modest," Ebi said in praise of her aunt.

"You must have learnt from her too," the Activist said.

They consumed their food with much relish. The Activist even asked for more boiled yam and more soup.

"Auntie, what new spices did you use?" Ebi asked.

"I will give you some before you leave," Torukpa replied.

She packed some spices for pepper soup and others for banga and palm oil soups. She asked her daughter to go to the backyard and cut down a bunch of plantain and put it in the boot of her visitors' car. She also went to her kitchen rack, opened it, and took out some fish.

"It's a pity I don't have more fish to give to you, but you will like barracuda and mudfish."

"Thanks, Auntie," both Ebi and the Activist said in appreciation.

As they drove home, the Activist acknowledged that women were the carriers of the community's culture. In Ebi, he was beginning to piece together what he had forgotten about the culture as he was learning new things.

"Why have you not forgotten these songs?" he asked her.

"No, I can't forget them. They are part of me. I know songs of all my peoples, and I am proud of all of them," she said.

What a talent, the Activist realized.

"Why did you not study performance or literature to tap into these materials?" he asked.

"I am happy with what I am doing. Our people are multi-talented. They are very good in pottery and ceramics, and I have much to learn from them in art too," she told him.

"I agree with you. One cannot carry the whole memory of one's people. One has to choose what parts of the memory one needs to bear witness to. Each person's remembrance is tied to other people's memory and everybody should be involved to save the communal memory."

"If the new churches will not strip us naked of our habits," Ebi replied.

"We have to make sure that we don't suffer from communal anomy."

"It will be a great battle. You can see that the custodians have abandoned their responsibility. How are we sure that what they are supposed to be protecting will not be lost with time?" she asked.

"We have to be vigilant about what outsiders bring to us in the form of churches or other things. Some of us will stray from the culture, but as long as many still remember, our heritage will survive," he explained.

"Many of us won't forget our way of life," Ebi told him.

"What I have seen today gladdens my heart. Our culture and everything around make me happy."

"I am happy you find it so. Many other people want either to reject the culture or travel out of it. You have chosen to come back and enjoy it. I appreciate your interest in our culture and people. I am happy that you have not forgotten home," she said.

"Thank you," he responded, as he stretched his right hand to rub her thigh.

Native Intelligence

Tobi Ishaka possessed native intelligence, which he was blessed with in abundance. He had attended the Native Authority Elementary School in colonial times and had been fortunate to make it through Standard Six. With the rigors of colonial education, he accomplished what was comparable to a very good secondary school education of later decades. He could read newspapers and write letters. He made use of his little but sound education in different trading businesses. He started with buying palm kernels and palm oil, which he sold to bigger Nigerian traders who again sold them to European traders for export. He was not doing badly in the palm oil and kernel business before rubber became a major raw material in the world market and he changed to buying and selling rubber sheets because he believed in seizing every opportunity that the times provided. For over two decades rubber tapping would be the major occupation of his people, who produced plenty of rubber sheets and lumps for sale.

Tobi Ishaka bought rubber sheets from individual producers and small buyers and went on to prepare them professionally before selling his tons of sheets to big buyers. He built a large oven house to dry the rubber sheets to the industry standards demanded by the overseas buyers. He taught his clients how to prepare the best grade of rubber sheets, the A1 type, which many had not got the patience and discipline for; most prepared the B-2 grade. He promoted the use of acid instead of fermented cassava liquid to prepare the rubber sheets. Acid made the final product smoother, thinner, and transparent unlike the rough and thick ones of the older process.

After assembling up to twenty tons of sheets, all in their

separate grades, the rubber shipping company in Sapele sent a lorry to collect them for sale to them and eventual shipment overseas. In addition to times of sale, Tobi Ishaka occasionally travelled to the port cities to see the agents themselves to discuss with them in order to learn more about the rubber business. He handled his business in a very professional manner and did not believe in manipulating the scale to his advantage at the expense of his clients, as many other rubber buyers did. He also did not keep a secret of the price of rubber sheets in a business in which prices fluctuated so often. Those who sold rubber sheets to him remained loyal customers for the decades he was in the business.

Tobi Ishaka bought himself a used Mercedes Benz that was in a very good condition. He also took a chieftaincy title. He spent plenty of money on both buying the car and acquiring the chieftaincy title. For a man who had respect for the traditional mores, becoming a chief was the crowning glory of his life. He had looked to the title as a way of contributing to the development of his community, but he soon realized that the council of chiefs lived on corruption. As a man who had worked hard to earn his modest wealth, he had disdain for those who used their chiefly positions as means of making money rather than helping the community.

When in his late fifties, his children advised him to scale down his activities; the rubber buying business was physically exerting. A man who was used to hard work, he felt he was strong enough to continue doing what he had been doing but he still had to listen to his children. That made him to employ two men to work for him and he paid them well. He was in the process of transferring the daily running of the business to his two employees, whom he had trained in the assiduous industry.

Tobi Ishaka had rejoiced when oil was first discovered in his farmland and family land. He expected a transformation of the rural place to a city. He had been to Lagos and seen its beauty in the skyscrapers and roads and had thought that the oil found in the area would be partly used to bring social amenities. After all, the area needed maternity homes, hospitals, post offices, and well-equipped schools. But that joy was short-lived as he saw the national profits from oil taken away; first to develop

Lagos already developed and then to Abuja, the new capital. He saw outsiders occupying all the key positions in the oil companies, while most of their children remained unemployed.

Despite his rather limited education, he was determined to educate his children to have good jobs. He did not believe, as most of the other chiefs did, in marrying many wives, having concubines, and dressing ostentatiously. He saw these as wasteful preoccupations he could not afford to indulge in, since he saw better ways of spending his hard-earned money.

Chief Tobi Ishaka took a long look at the situation in the Niger Delta area and saw no simple solution to the community's problems in the short term. He saw no easy way that the minority groups would seek for a political solution to the revenue sharing formula of the country. The majority groups were rivals and even hostile to each other, but they united on one issue, and that was in ganging up against the minority groups from whose area ninety-five percent of the nation's revenue derived. Once the majority groups ganged together, they possessed the power of a monster. Add their power to that of the military government and the multinational companies, and one could imagine the obscene force that the minority Niger Delta had to contend with. These big powers were not invincible, but it would take so much effort to defeat them, he believed.

Chief Ishaka was also familiar with the wrangling at the chiefs' meetings. Once the companies brought money, there was no way of persuading the chiefs that they were being bribed to deprive their people of economic progress. Those chiefs would forsake their ancestors and people to follow the oil companies for their money. The monarch himself was not a role model for his chiefs or his people because he saw his paramount position as an advantage to cut deals with oil companies that continued to keep him satisfied.

Chief Ishaka sat at home and thought about the situation so many times. He asked himself many questions, but none of the possible answers satisfied him as a solution to the Niger Delta problem. He had to think of long-term strategies to deal with the situation. Education, to him, would solve the problem in the long run, he believed.

He had sent his second son Dennis to the university to study petroleum engineering. He knew that the boy was very good in the sciences and from the beginning had encouraged him to take his studies seriously

Chief Ishaka was elated when his son told him that he had been admitted into the university to study petroleum engineering. That was many years ago.

"Is that not the degree one can use to prospect for oil?" he had asked.

"Yes, Father," the son answered.

"Do it, my son. One day you should find yourself in Bell Oil Company or in any of the other oil companies as an engineer among the white people," he enthused.

He observed that all the engineers were white people. The few Nigerians at the senior staff level were administrators, including the community development officers, who knew nothing about how the oil was extracted from the soil. The foreign engineers used the middle-ranked workers trained at the Petroleum Training Institute at Effurun to do the tedious job without teaching them the full knowledge of drilling. Chief Ishaka felt Nigerian engineers were needed to know how petroleum was drilled. He wondered whether his people or the national government had one day stopped to reflect on what would happen if all the foreign engineers pulled out. Would the situation not be better if an indigene that knew the environment as an engineer drilled for oil in a way that would save the land from the negative excesses of the foreign drillers? Who would empathize more with the fate of crops than the sons and daughters of farmers? Who would protect the creeks, streams, and rivers more than the children of fishermen and women?

"My son, petroleum engineering must be a difficult course, but do it. I will give you all the support that I can and with hard work you will succeed. After the university, you'll gain more experience and you can drill for oil in our family's land," he said.

"That may not be possible, father, because the Federal Military Government has already sold the rights for prospecting oil on our land to the foreigners. They call it oil-prospecting concession. I will not be able to drill for the oil in our own farmland, even if I had the knowledge, unless those concessions are revoked or re-assigned. By the Land Use Decree and the many concessions already sold out, what's in our land has been taken from us and is no longer ours to take back even if we knew how to," he explained.

"We own what is in our land. Don't mind the decrees. The world does not stand still, and soldiers will come and go. Things must change and it is my hope that the world ahead will change to bring into our hands our own destiny," he told his son.

Chief Ishaka considered himself blessed by God and fortunate because his son did extraordinarily well in his university studies. Always at the top of his class, he earned a first class degree, the only one that year in his department. His father was elated. He knew what a first class degree meant and his son was perhaps the only one around who had earned it in any course as far as he could tell.

In his deep reflections about the Niger Delta situation, Chief Ishaka saw the penetration of the oil industry as a major way of wresting the stolen fortune back into his community's hands. His people's satisfaction would give him immeasurable joy. Let the other chiefs fill themselves with tidbits - they were metaphorically eating the leftovers from the companies' tables and so were disgracing themselves. It was true that, apart from the white outsiders, there were also Nigerian outsiders or inlanders and they were from the majority groups. There were still no minority people at the top senior staff level in any of the oil companies.

With his shooting-straight record, when he went to see the General Manager of Bell Oil Company, the Dutchman gave him all the courtesies that a chief deserved. The community development officer had filed many reports on a recalcitrant chief called Tobi Ishaka; so the Bell Oil Company boss knew him before he arrived unannounced.

"What can I do for you, Chief?" the Bell Oil boss asked.

He could not bring himself to pronounce Ishaka because he feared he might mangle the name of a respectable but stubborn chief. Also he did not want to be seen as making a mistake, even if it had to do with the pronunciation of a name.

"I have a problem and a request," the chief told the Bell Oil boss.

"Tell me and let's see what I can do about them."

"I have a son, Dennis. He has not only graduated but has completed the national youth service. He needs a job."

"I can see the problem and the request as one."

"That's why I am here this morning to see you."

"You are welcome."

"I want my son employed. He has the right qualification."

"Your son has a degree in what field?" asked the Dutchman.

"Petroleum engineering," Chief Ishaka replied.

"From which university"

"The University of Lagos," the chief told the Bell Oil boss.

"That's a pretty good university," he complimented.

"What type of degree?" he further asked.

"First Class," Chief Ishaka said with a sense of pride. The two men stared at each other for a moment. Ishaka sat holding his walking stick, his head upright gazing directly at the white man's face.

Meeting one chief's request could go a long way to bring peace to the company's Niger Delta operations, Mr. Van Hoort reasoned. In his mind the Bell Oil executive was considering this matter as a diplomatic issue that in the long run would benefit the company immensely. Once peace reigned, there would be steady production and that would be a great achievement. Nothing paid to the chief's son would compare with the profits from peaceful coexistence with the local community, he reasoned. Mr. Van Hoort saw no better way to achieve the company's goals of steady and peaceful production of oil than to have a recalcitrant chief as their ally.

Mr. Van Hoort also thought of the good publicity that employing one single graduate could generate. This young man was not only Nigerian but also from the community in which Bell Oil had its operations. He would be highlighted as part of Bell Oil's effort to bring in bright young men and women of the Niger Delta area into its great company. In the larger picture, he saw globalization as involving multicultural personnel. The chief's son would wear many hats in the company.

"Chief, I have heard your request. In this company we respect leaders of the community. We also need more personnel of the community in our company. We'll offer your son a senior staff job with immediate effect," Mr. Van Hoort said.

"Thank you very much. I appreciate your kind gesture," the chief told him.

"Let Dennis come in next Monday with his certificate and fill the necessary forms to start work. On our side, we'll prepare an office for him before he arrives."

"I will tell him to be here on Monday. He knows that he has to come to work with his tools, but I'll remind him about what to bring."

"We just want to see his certificate, make a copy of it for our files, and then he can start work."

The chief assured Mr. Van Hoort that Dennis would make him proud.

"I can sense already that he will be a great team player," he told the chief.

"He knows how hard I work."

"No problem, chief. We'll train him to do his very best."

"I will like him to learn fast and make use of his degree," the chief concluded.

"He surely will," the manager said.

When the chief stood to leave, Mr. Van Hoort also stood. The oil executive led the chief to the door, shook his hand, and bowed respectfully.

The chief left contented.

Student Days

Though the relationship between the Activist and Mukoro cooled off for a long time, it had in recent months revived and grown. On campus there were few lecturers to discuss serious and controversial issues with, and Mukoro was one of them. The history lecturer had stopped pestering the Activist to introduce him to former colleagues in the United States. He seemed to have also given up the idea of emigrating, since he received no single positive response to his numerous applications for positions abroad.

The Activist had gone to Mukoro's office and chanced upon father and son engaged in a debate. He left Mukoro and his son to argue for their separate generations.

"In my undergraduate days there were no secret societies; none at all. When you were in school, you were there to learn and to read. Every student was busy attending lectures and tutorials and doing assignments; you spent your time in the classroom and the library. There was no time to think of forming or joining secret societies," Mukoro said.

He was fond of using every opportunity to lecture his son about the good old days when he was an undergraduate at the University of Ibadan.

"There was no time for frivolous activities," he again told his son.

Omagbemi shook his head. He had always held his father's generation responsible for all the bad things happening in the country.

"How could you go through the university without participating in a conclave?" he asked.

"Possible," his father answered. "There were far too many important things to occupy one's time than secret societies," he said.

Mukoro was surprised at the passion with which his son defended his young generation's actions and lifestyle. Why was it that the youths of the day could not argue rationally? He would not leave his son to feel that he was on the right side and the older ones on the wrong side.

"But we demonstrated against imperialists and apartheid; we added our voices to the universal cry against such evils," Dr. Mukoro told him.

"But colonization and apartheid are gone and our internal exploitation remains," the son countered.

"Then why not complete the task started a long time ago?"

"It's because your spoilt generation squandered many opportunities that would have changed the Nigerian society that we are where we are today," the young man retorted.

"We did our best and if you picked up from where we stopped this country would be a far better place than it is today."

"Your best was not good enough. You received so much and gave back nothing. We have to change things."

"How can you say that we gave out nothing?"

"You can see for yourself the state of the nation. If you gave out a little from the much that you received, this country will not be retrogressing."

"You have a right to your personal opinion, but we are not retrogressing. We are developing but we could do much better than we have achieved."

"We are ready to take matters into our own hands and turn things around for the general good. The country needs a revolution."

"Then why misuse youth's energy rather than focus on the general good of society?"

"What's youth meant for, if not to take risks?" Omagbemi asked back.

"You aren't taking worthy risks. You are just indulging in wild activities. One's youth is meant to be conserved for adult days," his father told him.

"Many youths of today may not reach adulthood or old age," Omagbemi said in his characteristic pessimism.

"There you go again. You don't have hope. How can you succeed in whatever you set out to do if you don't even have the least hope of success?"

"We are realists; we don't live in a dream world. We live on this hard earth and know how it feels."

"If being hopeful is to be a dreamer, then so be it. You must have confidence in yourself to succeed; you can't doubt yourself and expect others to believe in you."

Omagbemi attended meetings of his student secret cult all over the country. No place was too far to go. He was never too occupied with his studies not to join in the deliberations of his conclave, as he called their secret meetings. Dr. Mukoro always cited his son's use of the allowance he gave to him to indulge in unnecessary travels as an example of the frivolities he condemned.

"You spend carelessly what you don't work for and yet you say you are responsible. How can that be?

"Why did you have me as your child if you knew you couldn't take care of your parental responsibilities?"

"In my time my father did not pay my school fees; nor did he give me any allowance as I now lavish on you."

"But you had government scholarships all the way through university. Why is it that the country is far richer now than then and yet there are no more scholarships for any of us?" Omagbemi asked.

"Go and ask the military!"

"I am sorry to say that cowards stay at home and point their fingers rather than go out and take action."

"You have to think of something more important to do than attending meetings all over the country in the name of belonging to a Black Axe or White Skull society."

"This is my passion," he told his father.

"We have to control ourselves so that our society does not degenerate into anarchy. Look at what your cult members have done to a female student," Mukoro said.

The news in the print media about the young woman who had been burnt with acid chilled everyone, but did not douse Omagbemi's enthusiasm for his fraternity. She had been kidnapped at night by five male students from the university campus to an unknown location where they held her down and bathed her with acid. The hospital pictures in the national papers were gruesomely graphic.

"If she would not stay with one of us, she might as well die!" Omagbemi defended.

"That's callous."

"At least, we are frank about what we want."

"Must every female student be intimidated to be a girlfriend to one of you?"

"In this world, you use any means necessary to get what you want!"

"That's Malcolm X," his father told him.

"Not really, it was first Machiavelli's idea. I have read *The Prince*. It is one of our bibles in the fraternity," Omagbemi explained to his father.

"What's the difference between the secret society you operate now and that of my father's generation?"

"Ours is a fraternity, not Amarise!" Omagbemi asserted.

"Amarise, as originally conceived, was not a bad society," the father explained.

"Neither is ours," Omagbemi did not hesitate to say. "With time people bring in their fears into whatever they do. They try to take it on the society that denies them opportunities. That's what is happening today. A soldier walks through corpses in a battlefield without being afraid. That's our position. War is war!" Omagbemi declared.

"But whom are you fighting? Why do you fight the same society you are a part of rather than those exploiting you? Why fight other victims rather than the oppressors? It is a big contradiction," his father told him.

The Activist listened to father and son slug it out intellectually without taking sides, even though he belonged to Dr. Mukoro's generation and was definitely on his side. The Activist saw Omagbemi as indirectly assisting the oppressors and exploiters in their strategy to have the people so consumed by their own internal discord that they would forget about their being cheated. The more divided the people were, the easier it would be for the exploiters to realize their goals of high profits. The mouse blows a soothing draught onto the sole even as it bites it! It is after it has done its mischief that the victim of the rabid bite will discover the dangerous infection that can turn into a fatal disease. The Activist acknowledged that there was a lot of energy in the youths that could be redirected into more productive endeavours. It was left for those of his generation to do the redirecting, if these young men would not become nihilists.

Neck-lacing the Traitor

From the second month of his arrival at the university, the Activist started to be invited by many student clubs to make presentations on local, national, and international issues ranging from cultural and social to political ones and he was always ready to address any challenging topic. He spoke to small groups of students and promoted dialogue with them. He was able to reach many, and he always impressed upon them the need for the youths to be the pathfinders of their society because of their energy and talent. The older people could provide wisdom and point out the way, but it was left for the youths to actualize decisions. The young must dream big, he told them, so that they could achieve the seemingly impossible.

There was no neutral ground; either you were on one side or the other, he also told them. According to him, one cannot be with the exploiter and the exploited at the same time. The slave owner and the slave cannot be on the same side. The colonizer and the colonized cannot be on the same side. One must be on the side of humanity. It was cowardly not to choose to take sides. By his sixth month on campus, his message was catching on with many students. He was at last creating a base to work for the change that he sought.

Omagbemi became close to the Activist, who had asked the young man many penetrating questions that gave him so much to think about while alone. The Activist knew that the student would pass on these questions to his mates. Why should students who hardly ate a good meal a day and had no hope of getting a job after graduation spend all their time in secret societies, attacking rival societies and the innocent public rather than reorient their energies against their common foes? Why should the students not have scholarships when their country was one of the major oil-producing and exporting countries in the world? Why should corruption gulp four-fifths of the national revenue rather than education, health, and transportation that would benefit all the citizens of the country? Who was to blame for the Niger Delta people's plight if they kept quiet over what was happening to them? The Activist wanted the state of anomy that prevailed to be transformed into a dynamic one. Things should not remain the same.

Within the nine months of the academic session that marked the Activist's first year of return, the campus atmosphere had changed into a more radical one. Students that used to go and rob bus drivers on the highway were no longer doing so. The secret societies were still there, but instead of engaging in meaningless rituals in the grave hours of the night, they issued statements against the negative policies of the multinational oil companies and the military government. The male student cultists stopped raping female students and asked for work study programs to assist indigent students to make a little money to ease their plight. For once, the student union, often infiltrated by cultists, called on the state and federal governments to award scholarships to all students at the university level.

The vice-chancellor and other senior administrators of the university got reports about the Activist and the radical students and waited for an opportunity to warn him or teach him a lesson. This was not America, they said. He couldn't come to Nigeria to stir up trouble in the university and when there was chaos run back to his second home!

For them, Nigeria was their only home and they would live there whether rotten or not. In fact, many of them loved it the way it was and did not want any changes in the country's affairs. They saw the Activist lecturer as stirring hatred against the oil companies. Had these companies not built a female hostel for the university and were promising to do more for the institution? Every other year, each of the major oil companies invited a don to head their community development office, and that had always been a big boost to them. Sometimes there were as many as three dons on leave as CDOs and they often visited the campus to pay homage to the Vice-Chancellor that nominated them for the position.

What did the Activist want the oil companies to do? Did he want them to share their profits with the poor people because they lived in the Niger Delta? They had seen bore holes and tarred roads in some villages in areas with oil wells. Bell Oil Company was really a development company, and should be congratulated for bringing development to the area. If the villagers vandalized their bore holes and could not get clean water to drink and do their chores, they should blame themselves and not Bell Oil for going back to drinking and using polluted water. If thieves stole cables of transformers and the villagers had no light, it was left for the people to watch their light installations, capture, and punish the thieves and not blame Bell Oil for their problems. If the roads were single-lane and were substandard, they were still better than no roads at all, they argued in defense of Bell Oil and its companions in the oil industry. Were the old bush paths with cockleburs and briars better than the tarred single-lane roads? Was the stream water where they had their bath and also shat better than borehole water?

When there was the blowout at Roko Village, the Activist saw a test case of Bell's callousness that opened an opportunity for attack. The pipes crossing the village burst and caught fire. The pipes had been shoddily laid to the oil installations a long time ago when oil was discovered in the area at a time when oil prices were skyrocketing in the world market because of demand. The pipes were leaking from age because they were also weather beaten. These pipes crossed playgrounds of children, crossed cassava farms of the women, and even went through many parts of the village. Residential homes stood on both sides of pipe lines. When the villagers had protested many years ago about these many pipelines crisscrossing their village, the oil companies bribed their chief twenty miles away in Warri and sent the then community development officer, Professor Kokoba, to tell them that they were safe. The villagers doubted they were safe but there was nothing they could do after their own son they had contributed money to send to study law in England, then a professor, assured them that they were safe.

When there was this outburst of crude oil that easily caught fire, the village was burnt to the ground. It took a whole day of the company doing nothing; it did not even send a fire department team to put out the fire. They knew that there was a blowout and the fire vehicles were stationed at a location less than twenty miles away. Rather, they sat in their offices and issued a statement that the native population was sabotaging their pipelines.

No effort was made to cater for the refugee population of Roko Village. The Activist, Pere and his area boys, and the student union of the university saw an opportunity to demonstrate. They fixed the date for their protest against the oil companies for Friday morning. They would carry placards from one of the oil companies' local headquarters to another.

The administrative offices of these companies were all located in the same presentable area of town.

The oil companies soon heard of the proposed protest. They had ears planted in town and in the university campus. They had dealt with many protests before and felt this would not be difficult to abort. In their meeting on how to handle the impending emergency, they decided to send Bell Oil's community development officer to pacify the student groups. They felt once they could silence the students, others would not go out to protest; after all, they thought, the students were at the vanguard of any violent protest in the area.

Professor Tobore Ede, on a two-year leave from the university, came to campus with the task of pacifying the restless students. He dressed flamboyantly in a flowing robe made of expensive brocade. That robe would cost more than one student's annual school fees; its embroidery alone would take care of a senior student's recommended books for the entire year. He came in, chauffeur-driven; ensconced at the right back seat. As soon as the car stopped, the driver jumped out to open the door for the don to come out. The driver carried his bag after him, as if he were his personal servant.

The professor called the students to a hall and made sure that crates of Coke and cartons of beer were brought to sate their thirst. Alcohol was banned from student meetings and parties on campus, but no administrative official protested against this violation of the university rule.

From the first question, one could tell that the beer and Coke had not doused the fiery spirit of the students.

"Why did Bell Oil not send firefighters to stop the fire?" One student asked.

"My company did its best, but the fire overwhelmed everybody."

"How could the fire overwhelm firefighters that were not there to put it out?"

"I say they tried their best," the don reiterated.

"Why have the displaced villagers not been taken care of?" another student shot at him.

"The villagers set their village on fire because they wanted to extort money from Bell Oil Company. People have become lazy and want an easy way to make money. None of those villagers has a farm as they used to; none of them carries on fishing in waters proverbially rich with all kinds of fresh and salt water fish. The villagers only sit at home drinking illicit gin and playing both draft and eko games," the community development officer proclaimed.

The students were angered by his answers and could not believe what they were hearing. The don took the silence to be approval of his denunciation of his own community. He spoke as if he was not a native of the area.

"The mere fact of oil pipelines passing through their village has made them feel entitled to earn huge sums of money without work. That was why they did it. They are all arsonists," he declared.

The students could tell that he was speaking for his master, Bell Oil. He had shed his own people's accent and was foreign to them. He seemed to be following a script written for him to perform. He had become a dog working for its master.

"Why would the people burn their own homes and lose all they had?" a student asked.

"As I have said, they are lazy and want an easy way to riches," he told them.

"Don't you know that you are insulting our parents?" a voice asked.

"I am telling you the truth," Professor Ede answered.

"Is that Bell Oil Company's truth or the real truth?"

"Are you saying that our parents who work from dawn to dusk are lazy?"

The community development officer wanted to wriggle his way out of a difficult situation and thought of what to say. He adjusted his overflowing robe by throwing the left sleeve onto his shoulder. He wiped his face with a handkerchief. He had not thought of a diplomatic answer when a barrage of other questions was unleashed at him.

"Are you for the people or for the oil exploiters?" a student shouted from a distance.

"Is Bell Oil Company your father or your mother?" another student asked.

By insulting the entire community, the professor had lost the respect the students had for him as their elder. He was like one who spat at his parent's grave.

"Who is that rude student?" the don asked back.

"Answer our questions!" another student shouted.

"I say that is a rude question," the professor replied.

"He is a traitor!" a student shouted with a booming voice.

"Traitor!" echoed and reverberated all over the crowd of students.

The situation suddenly became rowdy and chaotic and, in the commotion that followed, a group of students forced a tire over the don's neck. All of a sudden the ebullient don had become a sacrificial animal that was bound and helpless. The students dragged him outside to the open field, filled the tire with petrol and set him ablaze. They had come prepared to thwart the tricks of Bell Oil Company and its expensively robed community development officer. This incident was the first known case of neck-lacing in the area.

As the fumes and stench of burnt human flesh filled the air, the university was immediately shut down by order of Senate that had no time to meet; the Vice-Chancellor acted on its behalf. All students were asked to leave the campus within an hour or be shot by the soldiers and police that were called in. The university had an unwritten but solemn agreement with the army and police to always come in with weapons whenever there was disquiet. Fortunately, no student was shot dead this time.

The Activist was detained, as a few other lecturers and many students. But there was no case against him and the other lecturers because they were not students and did not go to the meeting in question. Their enemies and rivals on campus wanted to pull a fast one by arguing that some lecturers sent the students to do what they did. If they incited or radicalized the students, they did not need to be at the scene of murder to be condemned for it, their malefactors argued. But the police knew that proving a case of murder by proxy in a university would be difficult to tie to the detained lecturers and so released them as they held the students in custody.

Ebi and the wives of the other detained lecturers had immediately gone to see the Inspector in charge of the case to plead the innocence of their men. One of the wives was the Inspector's sister. Fortunately, the police officer did not need to be given money before they were released the following day. In fact, they had not been detained as such. The lecturers bought cigarettes and kola nuts for the police who allowed them to chat with them at the counter. Though mosquitoes bit them and kept them awake, that was a small price to pay to avoid the label of sleeping in a cell.

Parents of detained students individually or in groups went on the offensive to have their children released. It was a family disgrace to sleep comfortably at home and allow your child to be held in a cell. Family meetings were summoned to gather money to solve the problem. They knew how to deal with the police. With varying amounts of money they succeeded in having their sons and daughters released. In the end, every student detained because of the incident, including those who were not there but the police had rounded up to show they were doing their duty, was released. Very soon there was nobody under arrest or in custody for Professor Tobore Ede's murder case.

But, as happened in such cases, time eased off the brutal memory. After six months of closure, idle students and worried parents became tired of the situation. And soon the university came under pressure from rich parents, including some army and police officers, to reopen.

"Who told you that students killed the community development officer?" some rich parents asked.

"Hooligans from town infiltrated the student gathering to cause the hideous crime," others suggested.

"Professor Tobore Ede was too close to the oil companies," many other lecturers started to say.

"How are we sure that Bell Oil Company itself did not plot this to prevent the proposed mass protest and to gain sympathy from the people it is exploiting?"

The man had died because he was too greedy, others impugned. Why should he insult the entire community, as the students who were there but did not witness his killing said that he did? His case became unsolvable to the police.

All students were fined a huge sum of money to compensate the family of the burnt community development officer and to make repairs in the university resulting from the riot, as it was described. Though times were hard, all the students paid the twelve thousand naira fine imposed on each of them and returned to campus to continue their studies from where they had stopped.

Nothing was paid out of the student levy to the family of Professor Ede after the university authorities assured themselves that it was Bell Oil's responsibility to compensate his family since he was on their assignment and died on active duty for them and not for the university. The surplus from the levy fuelled a civil war among the university administrators who competed for a share of the bonanza.

The practice of picking a development officer ended with the burning to death of Professor Tobore Ede. Press coverage of the blowout and the death of the don brought bad publicity to the oil companies that worked so hard for a good image. They decided to change their strategy of dealing with the local community. The oil companies put their brains together and thought of a new strategy. They knew they could not do without some program that involved the local community. They had learnt from the customs of the Niger Delta people that you had to feed a goat, a cock, or any animal of sacrifice, before slaughtering it! Yes, feed the beast of sacrifice before its slaughter!

Bell Oil and O&G each decided to employ a retired army officer from the rank of colonel and above to be their community liaison officer. They abolished the community development office and in its place set up the new community liaison office (CLO). The new office was the same as the abolished office; it was only the type of person needed that was different. The letterheads changed to reflect the new name. Still, it was only a change of names and also of the insiders the oil companies brought in to do their dirty work for them. They wanted someone who had worn a military uniform instead of an academic gown to calm down his restive people. They knew this would go well with the military government that wanted as many as possible of its serving officers and retired ones to be sated with a chunk of the national cake that oil had brought about.

Within one month of Retired Colonel Samson Dudu assuming the new position, the forgotten refugees from the burnt village of Roko resurfaced and sought a meeting with him. The displaced villagers were expecting the new man, as they called the retired army colonel, to relieve their plight. Colonel Dudu sent word that they should send a delegation of only five people to his office to discuss their plight with him. He could not talk to more than five people at a time and he did not want a mob in his office. The refugees knew they were on the begging side and had to accept his terms and so selected those to represent them. The delegation of five went as arranged.

They arrived before the 10 a.m. they were told to be there. They sat in the reception room while the community liaison officer chatted on the phone with his friends. One must be a woman; he was promising so many things for that evening. After then, he told his secretary who had come in to remind him of the delegation to tell them that he had some urgent matters still to attend to before seeing them. In actual fact, he was watching CNN news in his office. Two and a half hours later, he asked them to come in.

"What do you want Bell Oil Company to do for you?" he asked immediately.

He did not have the courtesy to greet them. He must have

felt he was still in the army from which he was prematurely retired. In the Nigerian Army the officers behaved like gods in their units.

"You know what happened to us. Fortunately none of us died, but we are all homeless and in refugee tents. We have survived till now because of a few generous people that handed us food, but things have become really hard for us. We want to go back to our village. We need assistance to rebuild the village. We can't live elsewhere," the oldest of them explained.

"You must be joking. Do you want my company to build you a new village?" he asked.

"What has happened has happened. We just want to be assisted to go back. Even if we have to live in tents, let them be in our home village from where we can do some farming and take care of ourselves," another explained.

Colonel Dudu stared at them and swung himself in the swivel chair. The air-conditioner wheezed as it blew out cold air. The retired officer had been briefed not to concede to any demands that would cost the company money. This was his real first test as a community liaison officer and he would receive letters of commendation if he did his job well. Doing his job well meant obeying to the letter the dictates of his employers, the masters of Bell Oil Company. He pressed the bell on his table. An attendant rushed in.

"Prepare five cups of tea. Also bring biscuits for these gentlemen!" he ordered.

"Our son, we did not come for tea," the oldest man among them told him.

"That's what I have for you," he told them.

"Are you telling us that you are giving us tea for shelter? Do you know the state we are in?" another member of the delegation asked him.

They rose and walked out on the retired colonel, who felt happy that he conceded nothing to the displaced native community as directed. He felt he had done a magnificent job in remaining steadfast and not allowing any concession to the refugees of Roko village.

The letters of commendation for a job well done did not arrive before the unexpected happened. Only two days after the delegation walked out of his office, Colonel Dudu died from a massive stroke. According to his office attendants, he was sitting comfortably in his big office chair drinking tea and taking some biscuits when the stroke struck him. The company ambulance came within five minutes to rush him to the special hospital in Ugunu but despite all efforts by a team of doctors, the retired colonel could not be saved.

But such was the attraction of Bell Oil Company and its pay that even before the retired colonel was buried, there was lobbying for who would succeed him. Retired Colonel Dudu was buried in a ceremony full of pomp and pageantry attended by beneficiaries, fellow retired military officers, and those who wanted his position. His family was satisfied that it did not have to levy each member to pay a certain amount of money, since Bell Oil Company paid a huge sum to give him a befitting burial. The senior members of the family fought and hurt themselves in the process of sharing what was left of the oil company's compensation for their dead son after his burial.

Within a week of the retired colonel's death, another retired officer, Brigadier Austin Yeri, was appointed to the position of community liaison officer. He had praised the former occupant of his new position during the burial ceremony as an indomitable defender of his people's rights and that his kind would be difficult to come by. He even shed some tears as he broke down momentarily to underscore his grief.

The retired brigadier's townspeople threw a party for him to celebrate his appointment. There was abundance of food and drinks and the gorgeously dressed celebrants danced to traditional music as five different music groups played live. On the following day, Sunday, a special Thanksgiving Mass was said for him. This was a big promotion, even though no pips would be pinned to his agbada robe. The church was not just filled to capacity, but worshippers spilled into the vast mission compound. Blessed are those with good appointments; they never lack followers!

PART TWO

CHANGING TIDES

Pere Ighogboja

Pere Ighogboja was living a good life. From his origins, nobody would have dared to predict that he would live a comfortable life. Many of his kind would have died in a brawl. Others would have died from simple malaria, typhoid, or other diseases after their immunity had been weakened by economic hardship. And still others like him as heads of their area boys would have been assassinated or suffered fatal gunshot wounds in attempts to supplant them. But he who had been uncontrollable in secondary school before he was expelled was not only living a good life, he became a good leader.

Pere had been able to restore dignity to his group, which for decades suffered denigration for what the police accused them of doing. To rise from an agbero, a mere motor park assistant, and to not only lead a difficult group but also to become a rich man in the impoverished area pointed to his stunning success. The shadowy years in which he first joined the area boys and rose through violent means to its leadership had long gone. He had covered up his career in the youth association with some type of work or the other in order to protect himself from not only the police but also from being assassinated by rival factions. He came out of the shadows into limelight; a confident man.

Pere continued to maintain a good relationship with his old friends; he was always humble and did not forget those he had left behind in the race for money. He built a big house that impressed whoever saw it. Now that he was prosperous, he had more friends than when he was a struggling and slovenly dressed man in the motor park. In addition to his initially awkward relationship with the Activist, his wealth had brought him many more friends. These new friends, the sort of rich people who looked out for other rich people to have as friends, came to fraternize with him. Friendship involves sacrifice, and many of Pere's new friends knew he was worth sacrificing for because he could also reciprocate in kind or cash. He was an affable man by nature and his personality drew people to him.

Among his new friends were professionals, businessmen, and academics; people who despised his vocation until recently. Wealth is more effective than the inewheri charm that medicine men prepare for those who seek it to be irresistible. Wealth can transform a poor man to a complete gentleman, rubbing off his rough edges and making him a polished person. Wealth certainly made the head of the area boys an attractive man.

Now Pere's praise-names were chanted with great respect and ardor.

"Egodo r'Oba!"

He was now "The Oba's compound!" to which he responded: "There's no hunger!"

He was also "May God bless you!"

"You have to work hard too!"

They also called him "When an effort turns out good!"

"Then everybody claims credit for it!" he would reply.

And hard he had worked over the years and he continued to work hard still to improve on his current position. For different important people in the community to be his guests in his house gave him much gratification, even though he was a very busy man. In his house low and high people of society met and interacted. Everybody was oblivious of rank and shared the same drinks and other entertainments. Age mattered though, and Pere was able to treat all his guests with respect and warmth.

He was also a family man, who spent much time with his wife and children. They had added a girl, Eloho, to Tonye, their first-born. Tonye was eleven years old and in elementary school; he was his father's idol. Pere took the needs of his family seriously and worked hard to meet them. To the elders, he proved the lie to the view that only boys raised by both parents in a marriage home turned out to be good fathers.

Every old person in the community remembered that he was raised by only his mother and she was a poor and lousy one for that matter. The old attributed Pere's transformation to his destiny and luck. These were things, they said, individuals chose for themselves before they came to the world. Once born, irrespective of the circumstances, every human being lived according to the pre-natal choices - parentage is a medium of coming to the world like a road one takes to a destination! What you do there has nothing to do with how you have come there, the elders explained.

The old used his experience with his wife to philosophize too. To the marriageable young women, good marriage was also an act of fate. Who knew when the beautiful Tosan then rejected seemingly rich and polished suitors for Pere that she was choosing whom God had reserved for her? Her fellow marriageable girls and parents of such daughters felt Tosan was out of her mind when she said she would marry Pere and nobody else.

"How can Tosan throw her beauty at such dirt as that man?"

"The man must have charmed her because there's no explanation for this," they gossiped.

"She will live to regret her choice," other girls had said.

"Does she not know that beauty needs to be maintained to stay beautiful?"

"She doesn't know what money can do?"

"In years to come she will look at the mirror and see a haggard ugly woman in place of her beauty."

"Then it will be too late."

"Her rejections have created opportunities for us though."

"Certainly, she doesn't know what she's doing."

"When our husbands will be driving past her, we'll wave her."

"We'll invite her to our homes to see the comfortable living she rejected."

None of her age-mates understood her choice. They looked forward to laughing at her at some future date for her folly. She would just bite one of her fingers in regret, they thought.

But the future is impenetrable and nobody can look through it to see what's out there. Three of the older and richer men who had made marriage proposals to her that she rejected had died. She would have become a young widow if she had chosen money over love. Two of her other nubile age-mates married but had since become divorcees. Tosan counted herself lucky with her husband. Both Pere and Tosan became a loving and inseparable couple.

The Activist admired Pere immensely for his love of his family. He had noticed that many other men, who claimed to be responsible from their occupations and titles, were virtually negligent of their families. He had been at various burial and wedding ceremonies and seen how people spent money lavishly and stupidly to cut a good image and yet did not take good care of their families at home. He had heard stories of Chief Efekakpo, who "sprayed" money at people at such ceremonies and, for that reason, got invited to every occasion only to return home and complain to his wife about lack of money. Ebisan took matters into her own hands by trashing invitation cards when they came in order to curtail her husband's propensity for lavish spending at traditional ceremonies that made no sense to her, since they could barely survive on their combined incomes. The wife's dogged determination to change his lifestyle succeeded in making a new man of him and he had virtually stopped not only drinking beer but also honouring the frequent invitations to squander his financial resources.

Pere wanted his family to be comfortable. They ate well at home and they looked healthy. His wife dressed well among her fellow housewives. Tosan was very graceful but never ostentatious; her natural beauty shone through whatever dress she put on. Pere provided well for his children at school and planned to send his elder child who was already doing very well in his last year in elementary school to a very good secondary school and then to the university. What he could not achieve, he felt his children should. He would support them to have university degrees and, if possible, be known as doctors. Calling one or both of them Dr. Ighogboja would be so fulfilling to him. He felt that his son that made him spend many years in detention should put to shame those who mocked him for his sake.

Pere presided over the area boys like a democratically elected leader who was responsive to his constituents, even though he fought his way through to the top. He was able to gain the respect of his followers, who deferred to him out of genuine respect rather than out of fear. When his group of area boys discussed issues concerning the community, he allowed everybody who so desired to express his views. He argued persuasively for the side that he took in a debate. He was flexible enough to give up his position or idea if others presented a stronger case for an alternative position. To him a leader should give and take, and so he made every action taken unanimous, and that endeared him to his followers. Such was the case when there was a discussion about what to do with the criminal disregard of the oil companies in polluting the environment. The area boys wanted to take the matter very far so that the military government and Bell Oil Company would be held accountable for their activities in the Niger Delta area.

Pere told his fellow area boys that they needed to have a coalition of interested parties to strengthen their position. He called for an alliance with some academics and student organizations. He had done his homework, since he had both the Activist and Omagbemi in mind. He knew that such an alliance would provide a necessary boost to their activities. If they were really interested in the restoration of the environment and securing control of their resources, these academics and students would make noise, write in the newspapers, and appear on radio and television expressing their views.

"If you add the knowledge of the university teachers to the militancy of the students, including the cultists, we will have a formidable force to move the two mountains of the military government and the multinationals," he explained.

"That is very reasonable," one of them said.

"We surely need allies," another said.

"One broomstick cannot sweep the floor."

"Unity is power," others chorused.

Pere knew their strengths and weaknesses. He knew this was a war that they could not fight alone if they wanted to win. Big wars are won with large armies, alliances, and good strategies; hence he wanted his followers to be ready to have thoughtful allies on their side.

The area boys were preparing to send a petition to both the United Nations in New York and another one to the headquarters of the Anglo-Dutch Bell Oil Company in Amsterdam. They realized that the more groups they were able to involve in the petition, the better their chances of grabbing the attention of the outside world to embarrass their exploiters and tormentors. They would invite the Activist who had experience in such things to coordinate the petition about their local problems to the international body. Theirs was no longer just a local or national issue; it was a purely international and global issue and they needed more sophisticated strategies than they alone could provide to approach it.

The area boys mandated Pere to speak to the Activist and some students about their plan. The young men in the university had a lot of fire in them and would serve as all-weather foot soldiers. The area boys believed that bringing all the different groups together would be a formidable alliance. They were optimistic that the two rugged mountains would soon be moved or at least shaken.

Omagbemi

Omagbemi Mukoro used his student cult membership experience to prepare his way to become the Student Union President of Niger Delta State University. He began to discreetly build up a following after making up his mind to run for a student union position someday. Over the years his interest in politics had grown from mere intellectual and theoretical arguments to that of practical involvement.

"Do something!" his father had always challenged him.

"Don't worry, I will do something when the time comes," he often replied; now hopeful of the future.

"I mean something positive."

"I understand. My politics will be different."

"It must be something beyond what the cult offers."

"Of course the cult is a pathway to the revolution," he assured his father.

"I look forward to seeing the revolution that you talk about."

Omagbemi saw politics as a means of using authority to change things positively, but getting to the position of power was a difficult path and he had to equip himself well to make it. To win an election, he had to use all resources at his disposal.

With so many promises of change, Omagbemi and his cult on campus were able to rally student support for his candidacy of the student union president. He campaigned on bringing peace to the campus, even as he harassed many students. He was a hawk praying for peace, but none of the other candidates was bold enough to challenge him on his double standards.

"We will maintain peace in the campus; enough of strikes and riots. We will make sure that the university is not closed down at random, making us spend six or more years to complete four-year programs. We must dialogue with the government, confront it, if need be, to award scholarships to all indigent students and to create jobs for graduates," he proclaimed.

He knew what his fellow students wanted to hear and he saturated the air with such rhetoric.

"The university should subsidize our food in the cafeteria so that each of us can eat three meals a day. The current situation in which students choose what meals to take and which ones to skip because of high cost is unacceptable. A hungry man is an angry man!" he proclaimed to the delight of his fellow students.

"Our hostels are too congested. We need more hostels built so that we can have space to live like human beings. We should have two students to a room as things used to be so that we can read without disturbing each other," he also suggested.

Omagbemi was young and had not experienced any democratic government in the country and had no political models around to learn from. He was born under military rule, which had continued in one guise or another for more than three decades to direct the affairs of the nation with guns and decrees. But he had prepared himself for politics by reading wide. He had read his history books and knew that Tafawa Balewa had a golden voice that cried for freedom. From his books too he knew Sir Ahmadu Bello as well as Zik of Africa and Chief Obafemi Awolowo, all astute politicians, who put in their best for either their regions or the entire nation. He did some research to know about such political orators as Samuel Akintola, K.O. Mbadiwe, J.S. Tarka, and Aminu Kano that always held their listeners spellbound.

So, despite the decades of military dictatorship, he knew what democracy felt like. It must be something different from a state in which soldiers flogged innocent people with koboko leather thongs; it must be different from the situation in which protesters for basic rights were shot at. In a democracy no leader used decrees to seize your land or property.

His posters carried such slogans as OMAGBEMI REVOLUTION, OMAGBEMI FOR REAL CHANGE, and OMAGBEMI FOR PEACE. The students did not really care about what type of revolution or change he was espousing.

Everybody on campus would like peace to reign instead of anarchy. The students would be happy if they were awarded federal or state scholarships. They would also be very happy if their food was heavily subsidized to the extent that they could take all three meals instead of the selective formulas of 0-1-0, 0-0-1 or 0-1-1 that most of them practiced to skip one or two meals every day. They would surely like to have breakfast, lunch, and dinner; that is how it should be.

The students would be most happy if they had more space in the hostels rather than ten of them squatting in a room meant for two.

"Why should anyone say that the standard of university education is falling when the students are not given the necessary support to perform well in their academic work?" he asked to the delight of his fellow students.

Omagbemi got money from his cult that over the years had built substantial savings out of their night raids on nearby roads. Individual contributions also poured in from those who felt that Omagbemi's big momentum could no longer be stopped by any of his opponents. He also got contributions from some alumni of the university in high positions that were once and still members of the cult as patrons to oil his campaign machine that rolled on like a bulldozer over the other candidates. Omagbemi heavily outspent his opponents, who did not know how to raise capital as he did.

Omagbemi knew the power of pictures and his photograph above OMAGBEMI FOR STUDENT UNION PRESIDENT was posted on walls, trees, and poles. The student union presidential candidate made sure that he posed with groups of young men and women from apparently different ethnic groups to underscore his message of unity and peace. Such unity posters were visible all over the campus. He also promised to buy buses for the student union so that students did not need to take motor bikes to and from town as used to happen and led to many fatal accidents. A student who had lost one of his legs in one of such accidents often hopped beside him to support his campaign for student buses.

Omagbemi's election eve rally was a concert by Daddy Showkey, the popular musician from Ajegunle in Lagos. The sports field venue was crowded and students and others from within the campus and from town danced themselves to delirium. One of the specially-composed songs for the occasion was "Omagbemi Revolution," to which the crowd of youths danced with frenzy. In the song the musician exhorted the students to exercise their rights and change their situation by supporting Omagbemi. His election would fulfill their dream of a comfortable student life, Daddy Showkey sang.

The following day there was no doubt as to who would win the election. Omagbemi who espoused revolution and peace won with a landslide.

After his election as student union president, Omagbemi became very ambitious. The office itself was expanding his political horizon. He now called for a program of making the universities relevant to their immediate communities. He also began to advocate that students should play a vital role in that endeavor. Why were Nigerian universities fenced round? he asked. To him, the university must interact with its environment; it must be open to people and ideas. He did not believe in the Ivory Tower principle that made students and university teachers an exclusive segment of the society in which they operated. "Tear down the fence," he appealed to the university administrators.

Omagbemi sent his general secretary and publicity secretary to look for ways of establishing a community-student entente. He believed that the problems of the neighborhood must serve as catalysts for new problem-solving ideas in the academy. This initiative was at a time when another blowout started to consume a part of the area.

"If you want to help us, appeal to the government and to Bell Oil Company to stop these blowouts that continue to destroy our villages, kill us, and destroy not only our property but our sources of livelihood," some villagers told the student representatives.

The student delegation passed the community's message to the student union. Omagbemi saw an opening to make a point. He needed to mobilize the students to protest against the oil companies endangering the lives of the people with their reckless oil drilling practices. The delegation had observed how unlivable the affected area had become. This was not the sort of place they would like to live in after graduating. Nor was it the sort of place they would like their parents to continue living in. Something must be done to save the people. The community's plea was an SOS they had to act on immediately. There was a cobra on their doorstep and they had to kill it fast before it inflicted a painful death on them with its poison.

Omagbemi set up a committee to plan for a massive demonstration against the oil companies. The student union's publicity secretary was appointed its chairman. They had learnt from the experience of the aborted protest against the oil companies after the destruction of Roko Village by fire. This time they planned to involve the press to promote their activities. They were gearing themselves up for action. To the members of the student union executive, the time for the revolution had at last come. There was excitement in the air.

The protest did not take place. A heavy downpour, as if the sky would collapse, started three days before the proposed protest and lasted for five days. Fortunately, the fires of the blowout were put out by the downpour and not by Bell Oil Company. Omagbemi and his fellow students waited for another opportunity to highlight the callous disregard of the oil companies for the community, and they knew from the frequency of accidents in the oil industry that it would not be long to come.

The Activist

For unknown reasons everybody referred to him as the Activist; his given name and also his family name all forgotten, except in his payroll slip, which nobody else saw. Even those who prepared the pay vouchers did not know his name, which was there but had become a part of the paper work that they took for granted. When he first arrived, his bearded and mustached look gave him a radical demeanor that made him to be called an activist. Though over the years he became clean shaven, which many on campus attributed to his effort to charm rather than scare off Ebi, still from one mouth to another and, reinforced by the proliferating power of gossip and rumor, he got stuck with the name of the Activist.

The Vice-Chancellor of the University, after early suspicions reinforced by rumour mongering and backstabbing by those seeking favours, had no problem with him, since he got reports of the Activist's good teaching. The Activist also contributed to the campus community life with his availability when called upon for public lectures. Students praised him and he did not fool around with the female students as most of his colleagues did. The students looked to him with awe tinged with respect. They prepared for his tests and exams more seriously than they did for the other lecturers' exams that they took for granted. He was meticulous in grading examination papers and submitted grades promptly. Other lecturers, who took weeks and months to submit their students' grades, wondered how he was able to always beat the deadline to submit grades. Some cast aspersions at his American education, which they said was worse than Indian education, both of which were inferior to the British education they thought they received by virtue of Nigeria's colonial heritage.

Such lecturers forgot that they received no British education in the universities which had become shadows of their old selves because of lack of financial resources for adequate maintenance. Those lecturers also forgot that their country could not compare with India in modern technology - the Asian tiger state was having satellites in space; it also had nuclear capabilities, and Bangalore was a flourishing Silicon Valley. As for the American education that they also despised, current American domination of science and technology spoke loud for itself.

The same jealous lecturers made disparaging remarks that the Activist gave only multiple choice questions in exams - doing it the easy American way of examinations! But in reality he gave both essay and multiple choice questions in his examinations. His students did not complain about their grades, since he explained to them why they got the grades he gave to them and they agreed that they got what they deserved. He handed back to his students their corrected scripts after every examination, quite unlike most lecturers that did not give back answer sheets to students in keeping with what they considered to be part of the British education they had received rather than to cover up their crooked grading that favoured and punished students according to their whims and caprices.

The most intriguing thing about the Activist was that he espoused radical ideas, which the university administration found very strange and so could not understand, since he was educated in the United States and not in the former Soviet Union. How somebody who was educated and worked in the headquarters of world capitalism became radical puzzled many administrators. This was more puzzling to comprehend since the Soviet-educated lecturers, alumni of Patrice Lumumba Friendship University, had abandoned their Socialist rhetoric, ideas, and Nkrumah-style togas and were everywhere scampering for money. Since the collapse of the Soviet Union, many of these Socialists had gone into hiding by being more capitalist than American entrepreneurs. They sought money everywhere all the time. They had become ardent devotees of a new god, Capital.

Many of the fallen Marxists had established small businesses on campus, ranging from business centres to restaurants, bukas, and kiosks selling drinks and provisions. Some had gone to the extent of operating commercial copying machines from their offices. And most of the lecturers saw preparing handouts, which they sold at exorbitant prices to students, as a means of making money to buy secondhand Mercedes Benz cars. With such cars, those academics felt they were doing well in the society in which the type of car one drove was a major status symbol. The campus community did not know about the Activist's joint ownership of the Delta Cartel, where many of them fuelled their old cars during the frequent fuel shortages.

The Federal Military Government and Bell Oil Company reinforced the Activist's name. How they got to know him only confirmed that they had spies on campus. After all, once the oil companies stopped recruiting community development officers, they still wanted to maintain some form of relationship with the state university. Bell Oil Company started inviting two senior lecturers or professors each semester to give public lectures and workshops on topics of their own choice in town. It compensated them for the lectures and workshops with five hundred thousand naira each. This half a million naira was definitely a bribe of the upper echelon of the teaching hierarchy. The Activist would not participate in the new programs because he saw through the oil company's subterfuge.

The oil company at its meetings in Amsterdam mentioned the Activist of The Niger Delta State University that was mobilizing the youths, womenfolk, and the elders against oil exploration in the area. According to Bell Oil, such radicals were setting back the hand of the clock of modernization that the company had started. The reports always exaggerated the threats to the oil industry in order to have maximum effect at the meeting. Of course the reports never mentioned what the Activist was acting against - the poisonous methane gas from gas flares, leaking old oil pipes, blowouts, and spillages in the area that had rendered the evergreen wetlands poisoned, the wildlife dead, the aquatic life also dead, and humans in these areas suffering from undiagnosed diseases.

Bell Oil Company and its kindred multinationals were happy when the government started issuing decrees against activists, area boys, and student cultists that had all become a nuisance to their business interests. The government asked the university authorities to stop its academics and students from unnecessary interference in the strategic economic resources of the country. The universities nationwide, very mindful of their academic freedom, did not take kindly to such forays that they believed could gradually erode their traditional freedom. Those working and studying in the university considered themselves to be sacred cows and did not want to lose that status. A general meeting was called to discuss the military government's sinister attempt to erode academic freedom and ended with a resolution condemning the government action as abrasive, unwarranted, demagogic, and unacceptable.

The oil companies had their spies in the Academic Staff Union of Nigerian Universities (ASUNU) and got a feedback on government policies backfiring and not achieving the intended results. They met, as they always did in a clandestine manner, and agreed to look for other ways to drastically reduce the influence of the radical elements on campuses by pumping more money to stuff their mouths, if possible. They set their managers the assignment of looking for creative ways of silencing known and possible critics with huge amounts of local money. It was better to throw away millions of worthless naira, they reasoned, than to lose billions of dollars to protests that blocked oil installations and so reduced the daily output of two and a half million barrels a day. These people did not know how to count; at best after you "tipped" them, they counted the same number twice, the Bell Oil boss told his fellow expatriate staff. All the local population that mattered, they decided, should be befriended with gifts of cash.

Bell Oil Company wrote a letter inviting the Activist to give lectures on American and Nigerian university experiences: a comparative perspective. The topic was specifically tailored to suit him, but the tortoise cannot be caught in a trap! The Activist did not respond; he wanted the oil company to interpret his silence as a refusal to give the lectures. But so persistent were the oil companies in their effort to win over recalcitrant elements in the Niger Delta that they reminded him with another letter. They thought the staggering amount of money he would receive for a public lecture that he did not need to prepare hard for was more than enough to knock him senseless. But he was a sturdy man that however big a bribe was could not overwhelm. He had never been desperate for money and fortunately he was doing very well in his business. He wrote back thanking the Bell Oil representative who had extended him the invitation that he would not be disposed to give such lectures. The matter was closed.

Women of the Niger Delta

Ebi was a unique Niger Delta woman because of her mixed Itsekiri, Izon, and Urhobo descent. She was happy that she was fortunate to be all these fine people in one body. In the campus, she related well with all the groups and always did her best to dispel prejudices against any of the groups.

"We are all the same people," she always insisted among her colleagues.

She could see that the three languages had common words and proverbs based on similar historical experiences and geographical location. In some cases, the gods were the same, only pronounced differently. She thought of Ifri of the Izon that she knew the Urhobo also had as Iphri. Were Egba of the Urhobo and Egbesu of the Izon not the same war god with different names or pronunciations? Was Umalokun not the same for all the riverine groups whether she was Olokun or Mami Wata?

The cry for unity and continued peaceful coexistence was being drowned by calls to tussle for tidbits from the oil companies and the Federal Military Government. The oil companies asked the local people to register as petty contractors so that they could send in bids to supply some basic things - tea, sugar, milk, biscuits, toilet paper, disinfectant, trash bags and baskets, and other things of the sort. Many chiefs rushed to register with the state as general contractors in order to make bids for any supplies. They got more than quadruple returns for what they supplied and they had more money than ever to drink, marry more wives, and throw away at frequent burial and wedding ceremonies.

Many illiterate women were brought to clean toilets; they were taught to vacuum-clean the floors with Hoovers and to pick up dirt from the "unit," as the company workers called their large office complex. Young female graduates, who had been jobless after completing their national service, were recruited to serve tea at ten in the morning and at four o'clock in the afternoon to the staff that closed from work at five. Such ladies, picked for their beauty or other forms of appeal, were paid heavily and they made contacts with the expatriate and Nigerian senior staff that resulted in a busy social life after office hours. This measure benefited all concerned.

The oil companies soon introduced poultry farms, managed by newly recruited men and women to produce abundance of chickens and eggs to serve the tables of the staff and make their faces smooth, round, and shiny. The new workers were freed from poverty and took the job seriously; some of the poultry men came to work in ties and the women in skirt suits.

By virtue of being Bell Oil Company workers, they were heavily paid; the poultry attendant earned more money than a junior lecturer in the university. Still, the poultry workers stole chickens - they strangled and trussed them and then hid them in their bags. They also stole eggs, milk, and toilet paper; some of what they stole they consumed at home and others they gave out as gifts to neighbours and friends to impress them or sold to make some extra money. The establishment knew there was petty stealing going on, but said nothing because the financial loss of the petty theft was too marginal to complain about. Bell Oil Company was too rich to complain about losses that did not show in the company's accounts. It could absorb the workers' greed, if that would make the local population happy and calm.

On its part, the Federal Military Government suddenly issued a statement about revitalizing industries in the Niger Delta. There was excitement in the air that at last change was coming, but the people would see before believing the promised industries. Was the government going to build fishponds, sawmills, or manufacturing industries to engage the former farmers and fishermen and women? Was the government going to build bridges to connect the many islands? After all, oil money had been used to build endless bridges and flyovers in Lagos. The people waited for what

Abuja was up to this time because there had been such promises before but nothing happened. They knew that the witch, for a change, could do some good to whitewash her disgusting image. The liar for a change could tell the truth. Would this be the change to break the jinx of failed promises?

Amidst much publicity, the minister of agriculture and water resources announced the proposed donation of imported fishing nets to riverine communities, another name for the Niger Delta people. The ceremony would take place, as every government initiative, in inland Abuja, the nation's capital. Hundreds of national and international media men and women and their cameras were invited there to capture the show.

The minister had not visited the Niger Delta and so did not know that there was no more fish to catch in many of the creeks, streams, and rivers. The poisons from the blowouts and gas flares had asphyxiated most lives underwater. Traditional rulers from Bori, Bonny, Ughelli, Warri, Yenagoa, and other places with polluted waters were invited for the ceremony. HRH Apo I was happy to be invited because he did not miss any opportunity that promised to bring him money.

The minister welcomed them to the Hilton Hotel not with kola nuts and Gordon Gin but with big brown envelopes stuffed with large denomination naira notes. The chiefs took buffet meals and drinks at the military government's expense. Some had running stomachs after overeating; others were drunk from the inexhaustible bar in every suite. They also indulged in a phoning frenzy at the military government's expense.

The chiefs appeared in their traditional regalia on television singing praises of the Federal Military Government and how the military dictator, a hyena, was a saviour. Their poor people at home, though disgruntled, were helpless in getting rid of the chiefs, since government gazettes legitimized their positions.

Barely two weeks after the fishing net ceremony and after the chiefs had settled down to their normal lives of debauchery and ineptitude, several ethnic clashes broke out in the Niger

Delta. The Itsekiri, Izon, and Urhobo fished and so needed new nets to test whether there was still fish in their waters. Unconfirmed reports said that the Izon were not given any nets at all and that all had gone to the Itsekiri, who not only had many lobbyists and sympathizers in Abuja but also used their beautiful women to get what they wanted. The Izon saw this as another manifestation of their persistent marginalization despite their large population and contribution to the national wealth and felt something should be done once and for all to stop it, if not in Abuja but in the Niger Delta where they lived.

Nobody waited for reports to be confirmed once rumours started flying all over the place. In their response, some Izon youths in a fishing village seized the nets of Itsekiri fishers in their midst. The Itsekiri fishers wanted their nets back and in the ensuing tussle on water one Itsekiri drowned. Once the Itsekiri in Ajamimogha heard that one of them was killed (they did not believe that an Itsekiri man could drown), some of their youths ambushed a group of Izon fishermen and killed them.

Rumour also had it that the Urhobo, whom the Itsekiri and the Izon believed did not know how to fish had received all the nets because one of their retired generals was given the assignment of sharing the nets. A few Urhobo traders that went deep into the riverine areas to sell palm oil and kpokpo garri were beaten and one died. Rumour put the number of dead at thirty.

It was at this same time that the ownership of Warri became a contentious issue. The Itsekiri argued that the town's name was theirs; the Izon people made a similar argument, and the Urhobo did the same. The three groups used their separate languages and history to claim what they had jointly owned or shared in peace!

Mayhem broke out in Warri as had never been experienced before. The air was combustible and nothing was fire resistant because rumour poured into the crowded town different forms of inflammable materials.

On the surface, there were quarters for the three major groups, but in fact no quarter was totally reserved for any group. People of different stocks lived together. In the burning rage that followed, reports of one group killing people of other groups spread. The Izon fought the Itsekiri, the Itsekiri fought the Urhobo, and the Urhobo fought the Itsekiri. At a time nobody knew whom they were fighting. Houses were set ablaze. Flames, of course, leapt from one roof to another indiscriminately. The flames, mindless like the people, covered the whole town with clouds of smoke. Petrol stations owned by Ishan people were razed to the ground in retaliation against the Urhobo. Their languages were so close that they seemed to be speaking the same tongue! Igbo stores were looted in retaliation against the Izon. The Igbo and the Izon were secret bedfellows, according to rumours! The Urhobo heard the Yoruba were assisting the Itsekiri and started fighting them, forgetting that their sons and daughters had been living peacefully among them in Ibadan and Lagos.

At the onset of the burning frenzy, owners of houses boldly scrawled their group's name on their walls; that exposed those houses to fireballs. Those who had earlier felt protected by their ethnic group immediately erased their group's name. The mark of erasure made the particular house to be suspected of belonging to an enemy and that precipitated burning. No group was safe in Warri.

Heinous atrocities took place. Breasts of women and genitals of men of rival groups were hacked off. Pregnant women were disemboweled and the premature babies torn off and thrown into street gutters to die. Izon with Itsekiri wives, Itsekiri women with Izon or Urhobo husbands, and Itsekiri husbands with Izon or Urhobo wives were asked to kill their spouses with machete or poison. If they failed to do so, others of their group proudly volunteered to do it for them.

The situation in Warri became very confused like the people themselves. Many Itsekiri fled to Ughelli, as Urhobo fled to Otumara, and Izon hunkered in Oginibo and Okwagbe.

The Federal Military Government was very cautious in meddling with ethnic rivalries, it proclaimed. It waited for many days for the killings to subside before reacting. There were no policemen or soldiers in the streets to stop the barbarism when it was most savage. Some groups accused others of recruiting soldiers from the local barracks to fight on their sides. Others attributed the professional handling of weapons by one side as proof of army collaboration with the favoured group. A whole week into the killings, when it was getting difficult for the fighters to identify their enemies and targets, they realized that they might be killing their own men and women as others; there was a lull in the bloodletting. It was then the Federal Military Government found a window of opportunity to wade in to stop the carnage. It decided to use all the powers at its disposal to stop what it described as mayhem. It dispatched soldiers and tanks to patrol the town. A curfew was imposed from dusk till dawn and anybody that broke it was shot at sight.

The soldiers in charge of security harassed people, extorted money, raped women, robbed, and shot dead those who resisted the extortion and robbery and described them as saboteurs of peace.

"Stop!" they shouted at pedestrians from a distance.

"Hands up!" they also ordered.

"Stand there!" thundered the soldiers.

"Double up and pass!" they shouted at oncoming pedestrians, who threw their hands into the air once they saw soldiers at checkpoints.

Woe betide the pedestrian who did not obey military orders. To prove they meant business, the checkpoint soldiers shot a deaf man with his dog for not throwing his hands up in order to keep peace!

You broke the peace, according to them, if you did not succumb to their wishes and personal orders. You were a saboteur if you did not enrich them. You were a saboteur if you had the ill luck of passing by their checkpoints when their moods were sour. The soldiers erected sandbags with the cement bags they seized from dealers. They were in charge of law and order in town and nobody could question their methods. Drunken soldiers in sunlight plucked down those they claimed broke the night curfew! The town lost another hundred people or more in one week from the military intervention.

The tense situation abated somewhat when the soldiers were replaced by policemen, who turned out to be equally corrupt but not as reckless with their guns. The policemen were issued a specific number of bullets or cartridges which they must account for at the end of their working day. They preferred to sell their ammunitions to armed robbers than waste them on innocent people or shoot into the air as the soldiers did with impunity. So they sold ammunitions to different groups involved in the mayhem at an exorbitant price. On a few occasions they sold their guns and reported that they had been stolen.

The police brought down the sandbags that the soldiers had erected and threw a nail-studded plank or a log across many sections of every major road. Nothing on wheels could pass without stopping at the checkpoints to do the bidding of the police. Beside this, on every major street in town, they placed a big drum. There every passing car, bus, or motor bike dropped twenty naira. Some car drivers who panicked when they saw the police with guns had no time to look for a twenty-naira note and so threw in one hundred or two hundred naira to be free from police trouble.

From morning to night the drums got filled many times, fulfilling the police mantra: drop by drop the big drum gets filled! The policemen shared the loot and went to spend their proceeds on pool houses where they betted on football in Australia and England. After the betting, they went on to take pepper soup with beer and to fondle young ladies that wanted a slice of the cake they saw with them. Only young ladies and prostitutes were friends of the police who helped to spread HIV/AIDS infection to them for onward transmission to others in town.

In the midst of the crisis people came from as far away as Aba, Abeokuta, Kano, and Yola to buy body parts to prepare money-doubling and other strong medicines; they thanked their God for meeting their difficult needs. The secret market of body parts under Otokutu Bridge outside town flourished as never before.

Bell Oil Company and other oil companies were happy that there was no room for protests in the undeclared state of emergency. Their workers continued to pump oil to Escravos into super-tankers. A few of the workers died in the period of ethnic clashes, especially those that could not get to their camps, safe havens, when the killing started. Other workers came to work with machete cuts; a few with bullet wounds, and others just dazed by the loss of family members or friends. They could not afford to lose such lucrative jobs that made them live very well among a poor population. But Bell Oil Company was happy that the oil continued to flow without any interruption. Business was not affected, they reported to their head office in Europe.

The refugee problem was enormous. The Red Cross fed a stream of refugees from different quarters. In the Red Cross camps were now quartered Itsekiri, Izon, and Urhobo refugees under the same roof or tent; the refugees not only ate the same bread but drank the same water offered them by the outside charities.

In the refugee tents, everybody spoke either English or pidgin and nobody spoke Itsekiri, Izon, or Urhobo. In the unsanitary environment of the tent, Wilberforce and Yemi established an intimate relationship. Neither the Izon man nor the Itsekiri woman asked about the other's ethnic group.

"Thanks," Efe told Ebitan, after she offered him food.

"You need it more than I. I have already eaten," the Itsekiri woman told the Urhobo man.

"I hope your wound is healing," Omare, an Itsekiri, told Cecelia, an Izon woman who had looked at him with tenderness.

At night, the murmuring and moaning in the dark among men and women were neither in Itsekiri, Izon, or Urhobo. There was love in their distress. Some conceptions of more mixed children would come from the refugee camp experience.

The older women and many young educated ones had begun to think deeply about not only their plight but also that of their men, children, and their collective future. They saw clearer than the men whose vision had been impaired by their killings. Men had displayed blood as a badge of courage, unlike the women who had recoiled from it. To the women, all the groups in Warri were losers because the state and federal governments did not think the self-destruction horrible enough for any assistance or compensation to the surviving victims. The Red Cross put you in a tent but did not help you to build your destroyed home. You were responsible for your health bills if you did not want to die from the wounds sustained; you were responsible for your fate. If your store was burnt, you bore the loss on your own. Every victim of the violence was on his or her own.

Mrs. Timi Taylor took the initiative to start the reconciliation effort. She had a mixed Itsekiri father and an Urhobo mother. She invited Ebi and others to a meeting in Warri. It was a gathering of representative women of the area. Women farmers, fishers, traders, priestesses, chiefs, lawyers, lecturers, doctors, and women of other occupations that the organizer could think of were summoned.

"We all witnessed what happened recently; many survivors are still nursing their wounds and tallying their losses. We have become so senseless that we turn our machetes and guns against our brothers, sisters, fathers, mothers, and relatives. What evil spirit has possessed us to be so bloodthirsty?" she asked the gathering of women.

Her audience listened attentively. It was thoughtful of her to invite only the women.

"I have called you my fellow sisters to discuss the many issues that pertain to us in the ongoing oil exploration in our area. Let us not pretend and say we don't know what fueled the crisis in Warri and neighbouring areas. It was oil that caused the bloody conflagration that we have just survived. Before oil was discovered in the area, every fisherman and woman could afford to buy for themselves as many nets as they needed. When did a proud people start to fight over charity?"

The women nodded in approval to her remarks. Their fellow women and men had been fishing from the beginning of time and they had always produced the tools they used in fishing. They made or bought scooping nets, cone nets, and ariri nets and with them caught the fish they not only consumed but also sold. It was a shame that they had to fight over nets that those who knew nothing about fishing had given them.

"The oil wealth is intoxicating the Federal Military Government and the oil companies and they are hurting the Niger Delta people in their lack of sobriety. But there is so much that we coastal people can do for permanent peace in our area," Mrs. Taylor told the gathering.

"But we must start by sharing whatever is adversely affecting our womanhood," she added.

Umutor was sixty-one years old but was athletic and did not reflect her age. She used to fish in all the rivers and streams around Oginibo but now did some petty farming. She raised her right hand and stood up to talk.

"I am Umutor and I came this morning from Oginibo. I knew this was going to be a great meeting and missing a day's work is no problem. After all, there is not much to show for the hard work because of our soil and rivers. Thank you, Timi, for calling us women together. We have before now been divided into wives and daughters in our separate villages and towns, but this is the first time we are meeting as women. Thank you," she said.

"Thank you too, Umutor," Mrs. Taylor responded.

Umutor was not done. She continued standing. She was tall and slim. She coughed lightly to clear her throat and draw attention.

"I don't know what is happening elsewhere, but in the Oginibo area the women are finding it difficult to conceive. This is a recent problem. You can see that I have given out my best, but I am concerned about our young ones. Are they not of the same stock as their mothers that delivered so many children? A mother does not proclaim the number of children she has but our mothers were really fertile," she told her fellow women.

Umutor touched a sensitive cord in the women. She opened a floodgate of complaints that had been closed. Many of the older women itched to talk.

"I am Titi; I come from Gbaregolor," another woman introduced herself.

"What our sister Umutor has said is very true. But there is much more happening to us women in recent years. Our pregnant women are delivering so many malformed babies.

What used to be a rarity is now commonplace. What has happened to the handsomeness of our men and the beauty of our women? Where has our gracefulness gone that our babies no longer inherit it from the womb as was done for ages?" she asked the humming audience.

Reports of mothers stifling malformed babies had increased. Some mothers of such babies did it themselves; others, who lacked the courage for such murder, took the highly malformed infants to their uncles to put to everlasting sleep.

"I come from Ekpan and my name is Matije. You have not heard all that is wrong with us. What affects our men also affects us women," she said, then paused to allow the idea she was attempting to convey to sink into the heads of her listeners.

Many women nodded and others giggled. Matije continued.

"Your husband may look well, but many of our men are now sick. Newly married young women complain openly about the weakness of their men; we older women see for ourselves what is happening. To be blunt about it, our husbands are losing their manhood at a very early age. How can old men be stronger than younger men?" Matije asked to the women's applause.

"I am Maomi. I am from Ajagbodudu. Let me tell you what we have observed in our area. Our young girls of ten are now menstruating. Is menstruation not meant to signal the beginning of a sex life? How can these ten-year-old girls cope with men? At the same time many women now reach their menopause before forty in the same area where women used to conceive even when over fifty," she explained.

Mrs. Taylor nodded. She signalled that she also wanted to contribute to the litany of woes that the Niger Delta women were suffering from.

"Our mothers did not complain of any burning inside their bodies. I don't know whether those of you that are past childbearing like me feel it, but I live daily with this new condition. It is as if a fire is blazing inside me. I have heard others complain of the same burning that our educated sisters call hot flushes. Where did those flushes hide before oil came into our lives? Imagine me roasting in the harmattan cold! The discomfort of being a woman has definitely increased with the discovery of oil in our backyard," she announced.

"What witches are causing us these problems?" Matije asked.

All their problems centered on the oil that was discovered in the area. The older women narrated what life was before Bell Oil Company arrived. That was not too long ago, according to them, before 1958. They once lived in a paradise that had disappeared with the oil boom. They remembered how men dressed in white overalls and helmets came in open jeeps and pickups with long hoses to invade the area. These strange men cleared paths through the bush and rolled out coiled hoses along their way. At some point, they set up a blast that shook the ground that made them jump up in jubilation. That was when they struck oil somewhere in the area. They marked the point that would later become an oil well.

Of the compensation Bell Oil Company paid for destroying farms, none of the older women wanted to talk about it. It was a rip off, because the company's supervisors took much of the money and paid the people a mere pittance. The supervisors built mansions, bought cars, and married more wives from their corrupt enrichments.

The Bell Oil field workers came from the town and seduced them with money. The women had not seen so much money lavished on them before, and these men really spent so much on them. The single women became girlfriends and concubines to the workers, who brought dresses, provisions, and money to them from town. These strangers were so charming that even many married women easily fell for them. Yes, married women ran after the men from the town to flirt and make love! These townspeople did not care about sleeping with other people's wives, unlike the rural men, who still held to strong moral values and considered such an act a taboo. Young wives, especially those who were yet to have children, went even further; they eloped with their oil-company lovers. The sexual deals that took place were unprecedented.

Now the women had come to meet forty years later. Nobody was deceived about the aftermath of oil found in the area. They had sat on this oil for centuries and lived happily without drilling it. What the gods gave to them, a gift wrapped in green foliage or dark soil, did not need to be opened. Outsiders from overseas and from towns came to them to blow up the earth to check where oil was. They disturbed not only human peace but also the peace of the gods. Mami Wata and all the water gods and goddesses had abandoned their waters and taken away their fortune.

Pipes had been laid across groves, villages, and towns, intruding into the private spaces of animal, plant, and human populations. All the storks, kingfishers, weaverbirds, sunbirds, and many others had disappeared. The herbs and flowers were almost gone and only the old remembered them by their names. Simple herbs that cured many ailments had disappeared with the coming of oil. Now the human population was suffering from ill health because of the disappearance of the sources of their medicines. In addition to losing curatives for known ailments, new sicknesses had come in without known cures. The people saw for themselves what came from the oil prospecting that they had once glorified as the beginning of a prosperous age.

The women discussed how to make their environment safe from pollution and attract real development. Bell Oil, the other oil companies, and the Federal Military Government could make as much wealth as they wanted from the area, but let them be mindful that people had always lived there and were still living there. The communities of the oil-producing areas wanted to breathe fresh and clean air; they wanted to drink clean water; they also wanted to swim and fish in their streams and rivers. They did not want to eat fish that harboured poisons in them. They wanted to farm their own crops to be self-reliant on food. They wanted to live a healthy life. And they wanted the damage already done to the environment to be treated seriously. Let the profiteers spend a fraction of their wealth to restore the environment, they demanded.

Mrs. Timi Taylor asked for a coordinating committee to be set up to run the new association's affairs and also to mobilize and to recruit other women into it. They must ride on the wave of current enthusiasm to achieve some concrete results, she told them. The women's gathering elected Mrs. Timi Taylor as its president and Ebi Emasheyi as the secretary. An executive committee was also put in place for the Women of the Delta Forum (WODEFOR).

The women primed themselves for action. They would look for ways to talk to the oil companies to persuade them to arrest the deteriorating environmental situation in the Niger Delta. They would also address the military government about their concerns. They knew that would be a difficult task because the soldiers in government did not respect women. They saw women as only sex mates and would be pushed hard for a meaningful discussion, but they would do their possible best.

If the talks with the oil companies and the military government failed, they would look for unconventional ways to compel them to act. They would start with persuasion but if that failed, they would have to confront those ruining them and their environment with the power they possessed. Bell Oil Company and the Federal Military Government might be mountains, but the women knew they had precedents in their customs of defeating tyrants. What would compel the oil companies and the military government to act remained a secret they would keep till they wielded the weapon. Let the oil bosses and the military chiefs not continue to take women for granted! They would be surprised at the power that women could wield when driven to the wall, Mrs Taylor said. Ebi realized there was much to do for the women to succeed.

Man and Woman

Now that Ebi and the Activist were living together, they behaved as if neither of them could stay alone for any length of time without the other. Each had no doubt bewitched the other.

"How did your meeting go, my Mami Wata?"

"It was great. Things went much better than I expected."

"What happened?"

"So much commitment I have never seen in our women before now. We certainly have woken from slumber."

"Women have always wielded more power than men who often intimidated them not to exercise their natural talent."

"Just like the common people who, despite their number and power, succumb to needless exploitation from their lords."

"Ebi, you're on fire today."

"I certainly am. You need to see our women narrate their experiences and see their resolve and you'll be proud of them."

"I have always been proud of you."

"We want all of us to be appreciated. Honey, don't single me out from my sisters."

"You know I respect you all."

"That's what we want from all men."

"Your work is clearly cut out for you."

"Yes, I will do much travelling to make WODEFOR grow."

"What's that?"

"Our newly formed association is called Women of the Delta Forum, WODEFOR for short."

"You have my support one hundred and ten percent."

"I need it now to be strong enough to do my duty."

"You're already strong!"

"Okay, I need to be stronger."

"You wan be Dick Tiger or Hogan Bassey?" the Activist asked.

"Make you no worry," Ebi replied. "I no go knock you down. No be that power I want."

"I for fear-o."

"I want to be me, Ebi, and nobody else."

"I was just joking."

Ebi went in to change into a cotton blouse and shorts and came back to meet the Activist in the sitting room.

"You are glowing," the Activist complimented.

"Thanks. And you too," Ebi replied.

They embraced each other and fell into the couch. They were happy and contented. They clasped each other and kissed. How time changed people! The old maid and the old bachelor had been transformed into a new youthfulness that only deep love could bring about. Now they were partners in a relationship that was more than that of husband and wife, also more than that of friends or companions and yet all of them in one.

For some days Ebi had been thinking of her monthly visitor that had not come. There was a certain regularity to it which had not been disrupted since they started living together. When she was single, she was never anxious about its coming sooner or later. Now that she was in this intimate relationship, she could not trust things would remain the same anymore. She was now anxious but wanted to be doubly sure that her visitor would not come this time. She would cherish motherhood if thrust upon her. She wanted another week or more to pass before announcing the good news to her partner.

Each of them came home as soon as class or whatever official engagement was over. While Ebi prepared the traditional dishes that the Activist loved to eat, once in a while he prepared omelette for their breakfast. It was a special recipe that the Activist refused to divulge to Ebi. He felt that once she knew it, he could no longer boast of being the only one with that special culinary skill. Now she had to wait for him to prepare it and he loved that. Ebi had stopped asking him to teach her; she just told him when she wanted to have omelette, which he prepared with pleasure. Whatever he could do to relieve and impress Ebi, he did with delight.

Another week passed. The monthly visitor did not arrive and Ebi started to feel some signals flashing in her body. All the signs pointed to a new experience. She was sure she had conceived. She waited till bedtime before telling the Activist.

"It appears I'm pregnant."

"What a joy!"

The Activist had noticed that while Ebi's body was generally warmer than normal the past week, she did not complain of fever. He also saw a new glow on her face. In addition, she was eating more than normal. Ebi's good news confirmed these changes he had observed in her.

He held her to himself in a tight embrace.

"Let's celebrate it," he told her.

He lifted her nightgown and rubbed his hand on her stomach, then placed his ear on the navel as if listening to the new life there.

"You were a bachelor for too long! It's too early to hear anything," she told him.

"You tell me this as if you have done this before."

"We women know these things intuitively. We both may be doing this late, but a woman knows her body very well."

"You are really a blessing to me. I have never doubted that you are Mami Wata. I love you."

"I love you too," she told him.

"You are bringing good fortune to my life."

"You have done the same to mine too."

"I am so happy that we are going to be parents soon."

"It will be a great pleasure, even though it will be a big challenge to both of us."

"Sweetie, we'll deal with it."

The two companions were very excited about this development in their relationship; they had conjoined into a new being.

Ebi, who had waited for an opportunity all the while they had lived together, found the right time to tell the Activist the Udoma story.

"You have always been selfless and caring," the Activist told her.

"I did what I could to help the couple," she explained.

"Not many women in your position then would do that."

"I am happy I have conceived without being anxious about it."

"Blessed is the womb that needs no fees or sacrifices to bring forth a new life," the Activist intoned, laughing.

"Let's value what has come to us effortlessly," Ebi said.

"We certainly must."

"I never all the while ever thought about it."

"Blessed is the union that is consummated in an offspring," the Activist again chanted.

"This is a great gift we must cherish."

"It is a welcome gift."

"You are the best," the Activist told her.

"You too; thanks," she responded.

The partners pulled off their clothes to feel each other's warm body that had become a comforter. They longed for each other as never before.

Two months had passed since Ebi announced the good news. The Activist then decided to get married to Ebi. Ebi had been pleasantly surprised that the Activist brought up the idea. She had felt fine with their arrangement of living together. After all, they were virtually husband and wife.

Though satisfied with the informal relationship, the Activist felt they had to make accommodation with their customs. And so he suggested their marrying to Ebi one evening after one of Ebi's sumptuous dinners.

"How?" she asked.

"Some form of marriage that we can do that will not compromise our love," he explained.

"If it is going to be a marriage, don't you think it has to be in church, court registry, or according to native law and custom?" she asked.

"The past week or so I have thought about it. I can't marry in the church I don't attend. As for the registry, it is a joke. I don't feel the state should be involved in this. I like our traditions, but they have to change with the times. I believe their excesses should be curtailed," the Activist told her.

"And that means?" she asked.

"We have to marry not only for our sake but also for the sake of the unborn," he told her.

"I will be happy if it is possible. But what do we do if you reject the many known ways in which marriage takes place?"

"Let's be creative about it. We don't need to go to your family home. We can bring a few people from Okwagbe to represent your people. At the same time, I can invite two to three from my family to come and be witnesses," he explained.

"And where do we do this?" she asked.

"The venue will not be a problem," he assured her.

"I can ask Torukpa to play the role of my mother," she told him.

"I think that will be most appropriate. She's really your mother now."

The marriage ceremony took only three weeks to arrange. In a ceremony that took place without any publicity, the Activist and Ebi were able to achieve a traditional marriage on campus witnessed only by just a few colleagues that they knew would pass the word to others. The ceremony did not take place in Ebi's flat. Rather the Activist secured a lounge beside the University Club that conveniently took the twelve or so people that would be witnesses to the sanctifying of their union.

It was casual but graceful and dignified. Ebi and the Activist put on simple traditional dresses made from the same white jacquard material; Ebi wore a wrapper, blouse, and head-tie and the Activist a jumper and shirt. Poko and Dafe represented the Activist's family, while Torukpa was her mother. Ejenavi, a close paternal cousin, also came from Okwagbe. Dr. Mukoro and Dr. Otite were invited to the ceremony as were Pere Ighogboja, Tosan, and Omagbemi. Two of Ebi's old prayer group members were also there.

The simple and rather brief ceremony was conducted in the traditional way. Ejenavi, by virtue of representing Ebi's family, addressed Torukpa.

"The man of learning has informed us that he is interested in our daughter and wants to marry her. We can't tell him about our decision until we hear from you. We want to know whether you accept him to be husband of your daughter."

"I accept," Torukpa told the gathering.

Then Ejenavi called Ebi to come forward, and addressed her.

"Our Doctor has told us he loves you and wants to marry you. Your mother has agreed that he should marry you. So has the Emasheyi family that I represent. Do you agree to be his wife?"

"Yes, I agree," Ebi said softly.

There was applause for the couple. Ejenavi, as custom demanded, prayed over a piece of kola nut and a small glass of Gordon gin that their lives be blessed with children, good health, prosperity, and all the good things of life. The Activist bit from the lobe of kola nut and gave the remaining part to Ebi and both chewed and swallowed. Then again the Activist drank half the small glass of gin and passed the other half to Ebi to drink.

"You are now husband and wife," Ejenavi pronounced.

The Activist and Ebi embraced, as their relatives and friends applauded wildly. After this, drinks were served. The food that had been kept in coolers was also served. Everybody joked about the belated marriage but felt it was necessary. Before members of the University Club began to come in, the marriage ceremony had ended.

Members of the university community were not surprised when they heard after the marriage had taken place. After all, things would not have happened that way if he was not the Activist and Ebi Emasheyi was not the desperate one.

"Do you expect yam tubers to bring forth leaves of cassava?" one of the women asked.

"Aren't you happy that they married, if that is what one can call what they did?" another asked.

The Nude Protest

What Pere and the other area boys first conceived and brought to the attention of like-minded lecturers and students of the Niger Delta State University caught on with those who heard about it. Later the newly formed women's association threw its support behind the idea of sending a delegation to the United Nations and mobilizing opinion in North America and Europe to curtail the excesses of the oil companies in the Niger Delta area.

Their plan could not have come at a more auspicious time. The United Nations Organization was organizing a conference on oil exploration and local communities after receiving persistent complaints from communities in Africa, Asia, and Latin America about Western oil companies and their operations in those areas. Bell Oil International, O&G, Brotal, Sina, and others were going to attend to defend their prospecting methods and more importantly to prove that they developed areas in which they operated.

For months Pere, the Activist, and Omagbemi worked hard to assemble materials to make a case against the oil companies. The Activist knew the impact of pictures on Westerners and made sure that they hired an experienced professional photographer to have coloured photos of their exhibits to present in the court of world opinion. As the coalition grew larger, Pere withdrew to the background, happy that the idea spawned in their meeting had gained universal acceptance among their people.

"The god of restitution is on our side. It's a matter of time and we'll get back what's being taken away from us."

"Many thanks for this great idea," the Activist told Pere.

The Activist did not want to be in the delegation either,

even though he was pressed hard to be a member. He told the organizers that the materials were already there and they did not need one who had returned from the United States to be in the delegation. Let those who had known the soil all their lives do this for all of them.

"We thank you for your great contribution to this work," Mrs. Taylor told the Activist at the meeting to select the delegates.

The Niger Delta delegation comprised of three men and two women: Chief Tobi Ishaka, Mr. Omagbemi Mukoro, Dr. Biriye Otite, a senior lecturer with specialization in ecology, Mrs. Timi Taylor, and Ebi Emasheyi. Ebi had kept her family name after the traditional marriage and the Activist had no problem with that. The delegates formulated a strategy to draw attention to the helpless situation of the Niger Delta communities.

Members of the Niger Delta delegation arrived at the airport prepared - they had all got their respective visas to enter both The Netherlands and the United States. The time came for them to go through immigration formalities in preparation for the KLM flight to Amsterdam. They followed the line and, travelling together, gave all their passports to the same immigration official for stamping.

"Are you travelling together?" the immigration official asked.

"Yes."

He peered into the computer screen for several minutes. His eyeglasses were big and looked old. He typed in one name after another. He shook his head; a gesture that the travellers could not interpret.

"Who's your leader?" he then asked.

"Dr. Biriye Otite."

"What delegation is this?"

"We are Niger Delta people."

"Were you cleared by the Federal Military Government to have this delegation?"

They were silent.

"Did the Government clear you to travel abroad?" the immigration official asked again.

"Do we need clearance to travel?" Chief Ishaka asked, on behalf of the delegates.

"Of course, you do. You need clearance to form a delegation. And you also need government clearance to travel abroad. Did your foreign sponsors not tell you what you needed to do?"

The questions had become cynical.

"We have no foreign sponsors," Dr. Biriye answered for the delegation.

"Tell me you have no foreign backers. You will tell my boss that. Leave your passports and other travel documents with me. Please go into that hall there," as he pointed to what looked like an interrogation room, "and see the chief of airport security."

There Dr. Otite was taken aside as the head of the delegation that was going out to embarrass the Federal Military Government.

"Are you still a lecturer at Niger Delta State University?" the rotund chief of security asked.

"He is," both Chief Ishaka and Mrs. Taylor answered for him.

"Shut your mouths! I am addressing a saboteur," the Michelin man in charge of airport security yelled at them despite his blatantly junior age.

He breathed loud and with some difficulty. He called on one of his male agents, Idris, to take aside the university lecturer. Then he called another female agent, Miriam, to take the two ladies away into a room for searching.

"You never know what women nowadays carry in their bodies. Looks can be very deceptive," he said laughing and exposing his kola nut-stained teeth.

Mrs. Taylor and Ebi looked at Miriam disdainfully. Mrs. Taylor was in front. The two women feigned not hearing Miriam when she ordered them to stand astride a line. As the female agent stretched her hands towards Mrs. Taylor, she shouted at her:

"Take your hands off me! Who are you? Have you no respect for your mother?"

"Na oga send me-o!"

"Who cares about who sent you?" Mrs. Taylor asked.

"Make una sit here. I go tell am say nothing dey with una."

After about five minutes, the women rejoined the men in the larger hall.

"Officer, the man you are torturing and humiliating is our son we chose to be our leader. You might as well take me and leave him alone," Chief Ishaka told the airport security chief.

The elderly chief could no longer contain his rage. An overzealous Idris had pushed Dr. Otite with the butt of his gun and asked him to frog-jump. When the university lecturer hesitated to obey the orders, the agent pointed the gun at his head. It was at this time that the chief stepped forward to intervene.

The airport chief of security thought of what to do next for a moment. He looked at Chief Ishaka and the matriarchal Mrs. Taylor.

"You people cannot travel. I have orders from above to seize your passports. Idris, let go the doctor and let them go back home."

When the members of the delegation returned from Lagos and reported how they were stopped from flying out, those who knew about the trip were so incensed that they wanted their people to take matters into their own hands and block all roads leading to oil installations. But the leaders, mindful of their peaceful heritage, advised that that would provide the Federal Military Government its desired excuse to send in troops to massacre them as it had done without provocation before. If the soldiers and policemen had shot at people in their homes and streets in their normal routines, what would the brute forces not do when given the excuse of blocking oil installations and stopping the nation from increasing its foreign reserve?

Within days of the aborted overseas trip of the oil community's delegation, federal secret service agents descended on Niger Delta State for what they described as a major security operation. They raided offices and homes of the delegates and confiscated documents, coloured pictures and maps, slides, and videocassettes taken of sites of oil pollution. The agents were surprised at the tomes of documents, especially the photos and videocassettes of different parts of the Niger Delta, in the suspects' possession; they treated all the members of the delegation as suspects in a grand plot. To them it was a big scoop because the documents they seized would have definitely put the Federal Military Government and Bell Oil Company in a bad light to the rest of the world. Pictures, they knew, do not lie. Here they could see what had become of wetlands, aviaries, and farmlands as well as of the community. There were pictures of impoverished people in dugouts paddling towards the ocean to have a catch since there were no fish in nearby creeks and rivers and the few shoals in nearby waters were not safe for human consumption. Coloured pictures of lakes and streams with green water, no doubt the chlorine and other chemicals used by the companies, told the people's sad story. There were also pictures of children sitting beside gas flaring sites and innocently inhaling poisonous gas, and of pregnant women sitting in front of their homes with blowouts less than a hundred yards away imperilling not only their lives but also lives of the unborn.

"Did these people not know that this could compromise the security of the country?" the agents asked.

The delegates reported their sad experiences to the community and there was an outrage, which was further incensed by the search and seizure of related and unrelated documents from offices and homes of the delegates. The people felt bitter that the government could stoop so low to achieve its aims of keeping the outside world ignorant of its collaboration with Bell Oil and the other oil companies. If it were not afraid, why did it not allow the people to present their case to the world? It was left for the Federal Military Government to counter their presentation and it had the ministers of information, petroleum resources, and foreign affairs to do that simple job. But it was afraid that it had no case and so had to resort to repressive methods.

The oil companies heaved a heavy sigh of relief. The possible embarrassment that would have needed hundreds of millions of dollars in public relations campaign to counter had been averted. They lauded the foresight of the government in stopping the delegation from flying out.

They had frantically set in motion committees to answer any queries they were expecting after the conference from their headquarters in Europe and the United States. They had been spared a big headache, if not a more serious affliction.

This was why they preferred governments run by strongmen in Africa, Asia, and Latin America to democracies whose presidents were never in full control of the affairs of their nations. Their executive directors wanted to do something special for the president and his cabinet ministers who ensured this great relief.

In pursuit of showing their appreciation, the oil companies met secretly to discuss buying a new executive jet to replace the ageing one being used by the president. The military leader had been unable to commit a hundred million dollars out of the billions he had received from the oil companies in taxes and kickbacks the past year to buying a new aircraft. These African military leaders so much loved money that they ignored their personal security, the oil bosses wondered. How would a president that received billions of dollars from oil taxes alone be flying a rickety plane that could crash any moment? They could not understand the mind of the African, but they knew well that he smiled when he saw money. They knew the president was stashing a great percentage of his nation's earnings in banks abroad, but that was Nigeria's problem and not theirs.

But much as the military strongman was not thoughtful enough about his personal safety, it was in the oil companies' interest to protect him. He might feel safe among his people because of his huge army that he often bragged about as the largest in Africa, but the plane he flew was a worse safety hazard to him than his oppressed people. Instead of buying him a brand new plane, they thought of sending one of their bigger jets to Holland to be refurbished and painted with Nigeria's national colours and donated to the president to add to his executive fleet. That would be his Independence Day surprise and gift. He would feel much appreciated, they reasoned, and he would definitely reciprocate in ways that would further benefit Bell Oil and other oil companies many times over their expenses.

An oil blowout, exacerbated by a pipe leakage and fuelled by gas flares, threw Ekakpamre and its people into an unprecedented state of anxiety. Many oil wells dotted their old farmlands now abandoned because they had become either a part of a security zone, fenced oil installations, or a wasteland. From those wells surface pipes carried crude oil to flow stations. The blaze was savage. At first children ran out to watch it but soon their parents ran to physically drag them from endangering their lives. With strong winds blowing, anybody nearby could be engulfed by the flames.

Bell Oil knew very well that there was a blowout but did not ask its fire-fighting team to put out the fire. The Uto River was literally burning. Evergreen plants, dry leaves, and shrubs that stood by the river all became combustible materials. The poisonous methane gas fumes engulfed plants, wildlife, and humans around for days. Houses in the riverside town were threatened. If nothing was done to put out the fire, the townspeople stood the chance of losing many of their homes. The residents would not seek refuge outside the town for fear of losing all they had. Policemen or soldiers drafted to the scene would, instead of putting out the fire and protecting lives and property, loot the homes. Ekakpamre residents had learnt from experience and from stories of other victims of frequent oil blowouts. The people's frantic efforts to douse the blaze with sand and water was of no effect. In fact, the little water from wells they threw at the flames made things worse. They suddenly realized that water could fuel fire.

The residents found themselves helpless before this monstrous fire. They were all black from the sooth of smoke and ashes. There were many premature births because some pregnant women went into sudden labour. Babies coughed relentlessly. The old wheezed. Eyes itched and those already with poor eyesight had their problems worsened by the fire and smoke. No one was safe from the fuming blaze.

Omagbemi saw for himself the callousness of both the oil company whose pipes caused the problem and the Federal Military Government that was supposed to protect its citizens against natural or man-made disasters. For several days of this strange phenomenon of a river in flames, the local community was left helpless. The student union president mobilized his fellow students. This was a decisive moment. They had to help the community and be counted as friends or stay out and be counted as collaborators with the outsiders. Omagbemi chose the path of entente and friendship with the people and called for a massive protest against the multinational arsonists, as he described the oil companies and their callous practices that allowed so many fires to rage unchecked in the area.

The student protest would be remembered not for putting out the fire consuming the Uto River and also threatening the lives of Ekakpamre people but for its brutal suppression by mobile policemen that Bell Oil Company asked to be sent to secure their installations. The head of the mobile police unit was paid a huge monthly stipend from a secret fund by Bell Oil Company and he reciprocated the kind gesture in ways that pleased his payers.

The students carried green leaves and branches to signify the peaceful nature of their protest. They wore white headbands, also as a sign of peace. They wanted to draw attention to the plight of the Ekakpamre community so that either the oil company or the military government could do something immediately. Would they wait till a whole town was razed to the ground before acting? Or did they want the people dead so as to have no obstacle to appropriating their land? Was the Roko Village experience of the previous year not bad enough? A riverfront had burnt out; now it was a river.

Bell Oil Company received information about the planned protest. It called on the Federal Military Government to stop student cultists and anarchist youths from vandalizing their installations. It put out a press release even before the protest march started that the current protest had made them cut back oil production in Nigeria. The company's press officer added that the Federal Military Government would lose sixteen million dollars daily for these wanton acts of hooliganism. The company certainly knew the red flag with which to taunt the Abuja bull!

Bell Oil's statement was transmitted to Supreme Headquarters through secret channels before anybody else heard it. The Federal Military Government was thrown into an unprecedented panic. How would it survive without earning those dollars from oil? Would the oil companies not see this as a sign of weakness and so collaborate with foreign intelligence to undermine it to install a new strongman that would do their bidding? It had to act swiftly and decisively. The government promptly gave orders to troops stationed in Warri to stop the protest with immediate effect.

Within the first five minutes of the peaceful march starting from the riverside area most affected by the blowout, bursts of gunfire from soldiers that had earlier that day at half light dug trenches and taken position in them broke out. Amidst the crowd of villagers, Egba Boys, students, and others that joined out of curiosity, several protesters were shot dead. In the stampede following the shootings, hundreds of demonstrators were hurt. The war god of the military and the oil companies received sufficient sacrifice of human blood! The corpses of the dead and many wounded who could not run but fell down littered the landscape. Blood splattered on the soil and on leaves. The carnage was there in the sun.

In their statement the police denied shooting at anybody. They only shot into the air and later shot in self-defense, they wrote in their official report of the incident. The military government swiftly issued a statement commending the police and army for bringing a quick solution to the problem in the Niger Delta. According to the government statement, the FMG could not stand by and allow social miscreants and misfits to sabotage a strategic sector of the country's economy and, bearing in mind the national security interests involved, had to solve the problem swiftly.

The national media - radio, television, and print - were all quiet. It did not matter whether they were state-owned or private; they did not compete for such news because the journalists were also under the company's pay from that secret fund earmarked for the oil-producing communities! They only published the government bulletin and showed no picture of the carnage for the nation or the world to see.

Everywhere there was mourning for the dead. It did not matter whether the dead were relatives or not; the community mourned for all the dead. Women wore black clothes and left their hair unmade. Men, young and old, had their hair shaved to express their grief. Many younger men wore black headbands. Dirges and wails were heard everywhere. The army collected the dead into their vans and took them to bury secretly. The military officers in charge of this operation felt that nobody would ever find out the site behind their barracks, where some of their wives farmed. The community would know where the seized bodies of their relatives had been dumped but would not dare speak out for fear of reprisal.

The women were now very aware of the threat of oil fire to their lives. In recent times they had observed that the oil companies were capable of breaking their own old pipes or leaving leaks to worsen so as to blame the local communities for sabotage. The more the oil companies accused the local communities and projected their loss in millions or billions of dollars, the more the Federal Military Government listened to their call for protection. The community could not understand this love between the oil companies and the FMG that led the government to kill its own people to protect foreigners duping it of billions of dollars. To the women, the unending blaze could be one of the oil companies' tactics to draw in the Federal Military Government to provide them free security rather than pay for it.

The women leaders held a meeting and agreed to use their naked strength against the tyrants. They would do this in a most dramatic way by seizing a flow station and an oil-loading facility and then stripping there in protest. Only women who had reached their menopause would take part, according to the plan. This was in keeping with traditional practice of cursing the oppressor.

Bell Oil and the FMG were worse than any tyrant that had reared his head among them. The Bell Oil boss was Ogiso, the legendary tyrant that had unleashed unspeakable tyranny upon the people. The head of the FMG was also Ogiso. The women felt their people had endured enough of tyranny and now they had to use their last means of power, a nude march, to defend themselves.

Ebi sent out a circular that both she and Mrs. Taylor had

signed describing the uncommon action they needed to carry out to save the land, as she expressed it. She described those to be involved and how those not directly involved should give them moral and logistical support.

"We need to act now before it is too late. We have all seen how each day matters get worse. Our lives cannot be one long story of being victimized. We have to put a stop to being victimized in order for us to live happy and contented lives. It is a fight for survival. No matter what happens, we shall be victorious because our cause is just," Ebi wrote.

Mrs. Taylor was a charismatic leader and she travelled all over the Niger Delta talking to the women's groups about the plan. There was no scarcity of women to volunteer for such a noble cause. Ebi made arrangements for buses to bring in the potential women protesters to a point, where they would take boats to the venues of the proposed action. She knew how important logistics would be to the success of this nude protest and planned the minute details of bringing protesters to the protest sites.

The oil companies and their home media soon heard about the planned nude protest. The import of such stripping by women was something that intrigued Bell Oil. The foreign bosses at first dismissed it as mere theatrics by old women who wanted self-promotion. But it soon sank into their heads that the spectacle of old women displaying their shrivelled breasts and bottoms on television screens all over the world would be no laughing matter.

Rather than allow these women to make laughing stocks of their bodies, Bell Oil Company took the side of caution. "You never can foretell the consequence of their stupid action," the company leaders reasoned. They wanted to protect their jobs and also their shareholders' interests. They could foresee calls from shareholders asking why they allowed such a shameful act to happen and that could cost them their jobs.

The oil company's senior executives therefore called their Nigerian subordinates for a meeting. Left out were the very few Nigerian senior staff members. The foreign bosses invited to the meeting those who would like to impress them with the hope of receiving promotion in return.

"What's going on? What are the old women up to?" Mr. John Pritchard, a senior manager, asked.

"What do you mean?" Mr. Dele Oyenuga asked back.

"Don't tell me you've not heard what's going on! Your old women are preparing to strip in front of television cameras in protest at our installations," the Dutch Van Geon explained.

"Kai!" Malam Gusau exclaimed with disgust at the possibility of that obscene display.

"It must be a serious matter. Very serious," said Mr. Peter Okadike.

"For God's sake, explain!" shouted Mr. Pritchard.

"Tell us the meaning of all these!" Van Geon demanded.

"Women's nude protest is the worst curse possible in the traditional society. It's a curse invoked when all measures to seek redress or justice have failed. And those cursed always died within days," Peter Okadike explained.

"Is that a threat?" Mr. Pritchard asked.

"No, sir, I am only telling you the meaning of the women's nude protest," he said in self-defense.

"These people are ingrates," Mr. Pritchard further commented.

"Let's leave that for now," Van Geon told his colleague.

Tea and biscuits were served to the Nigerians invited to the meeting for their service. The expatriate staff looked at them as they drank tea and ate the biscuits. There was silence and from the body language of the expatriates the Nigerians knew they were being hurried. Even before some had taken all their tea and biscuits the American Dale Richards told the Nigerians: "Thanks, guys; we appreciate your frank counsel. You can leave."

Once the Nigerian advisers were out, the foreigners burst out laughing at the bunch of superstitious men that they had believed were enlightened Christians but were really heathens.

"When will these people leave behind their voodoo beliefs?" Mr. Pritchard asked.

"Old habits die hard," Van Geon sighed.

"All the schooling and Christianizing of many decades have done little to change the people and their ways," Mr. Beesley lamented.

Mr. Beesley was British and felt most competent of the expatriates to comment on people that his small but powerful nation had colonized for over a half century. He gave a deep sigh of exasperation. Mr. Pritchard and Van Geon chuckled.

Still, they had got the information they needed from their local subordinates and believed the situation was more serious than the laughable antics of old women. So the company strategists decided to take action dramatic enough to steal the thunder from these women. How could a crowd of old native women sabotage a global company of Bell Oil's standing? they asked themselves.

Some of the foreign correspondents, who had heard about the impending protest, already made arrangements to be embedded with Bell Oil Company which had many helicopters. But many other correspondents were too excited about the prospect of naked mothers and grandmothers that they chose not to be stuck with the multinationals, however comfortable that would be. Rather, they wanted to witness and report a prizewinning event; they wanted to be in the midst of the protesting women, nude or not, and see things from close quarters.

The main foreign media around, the BBC and CNN, before the event even started that day, in order to excite their waking home audiences, reported that nude elderly women of the Niger Delta were preparing a major assault on oil installations. They knew that their home people woke with their hearts thumping in anticipation of how the stock market would perform that day. Oil was the most important product that could affect investments and stocks. In less than one hour, the whole world heard about a mass of Niger Delta women stripping at a super-tanker-loading station in protest at their mistreatment by Bell Oil Company and the Federal Military Government.

Within minutes of the CNN International news report, Bell Oil sent firefighters to go and stop the burning river that had blazed for twelve days! By the time the squadron of firefighters scrambled to Ekakpamre, the Uto River had burnt itself out because the local community's effort had paid off as the fire did not spread into the town.

The Federal Military Government heard the news of the women's planned protest. It had earlier received confidential briefings from Bell Oil.

The head of the military junta was a very superstitious general and did not know what to do with these elderly women. If they were men, he would have given orders that they should be shot. But these were not just women but old women, who should be treated with respect. However, under no circumstances should they be allowed to embarrass the whole nation. After telling the chief of Bell Oil to take all necessary measures to prevent the women from stripping, the dark-goggled general asked his security advisers to contact Bell Oil Company with immediate effect and together formulate a common strategy to resolve the sensational problem on their hands.

Meanwhile the women had gathered at designated points to be bussed to the flow station and the oil-shipping terminal. Both Mrs. Taylor's and Ebi's efforts had paid off. Bringing the women volunteers to the gathering points had been easily accomplished.

The foreign press photographers realized that obscenity laws in their home countries with nude beaches, pornographic magazines and videos, and strip clubs, forbade showing naked women on network stations, but they wanted to bear witness to keep the photos in their archives. Who knows, these photos could be auctioned at Christie's or Sotheby's the way stolen ivory, masks, and terracotta figures from the Niger Delta were now being auctioned for fantastic amounts of dollars.

True to their plan, the Niger Delta women got to the flow station they had earmarked for the nude protest. Their boats landed at both the flow station and the nearby island tanker-loading station. They had dared the waves in boats to the island port where slaves used to be taken away from the Bight of Benin in the Slave Coast. Bell Oil Company had easily built a modern jetty, exactly where slave ships used to dock and the port was as busy as it used to be hundreds of years ago with slave cargo.

The women were set for action. The Nigerian workers who

had heard of the planned women's nude protest either did not show up for work or slipped out before the women arrived. They were not ready to commit a taboo seeing women old enough to be their mothers or grandmothers naked! The gatemen were so embarrassed that they did not resist when they saw a stream of elderly women pouring in from boats. From the stare in the women's eyes, the gatemen knew the women meant business and so ran away. The women took over both facilities without any resistance from the guards.

The assembling women had not fully readied themselves in the formation they had planned before helicopters appeared in the horizon and started to land noisily. This distracted the old women for a few minutes. The younger women who would hold the clothes after the older ones undressed stood ready for their assignment. Every eye gazed at the landing helicopters. After coming down from the helicopters at both stations and with bullhorns and loudspeakers, well-groomed black men on behalf of the oil company told the women that they were ready to discuss their demands.

"No-oo!" the women chorused, after Mrs. Timi Taylor.

The air was tense with anticipation of what would happen next. The media people had now converged there; they did not want to waste their films before the main event.

Everybody held his or her breath. Who would start the stripping and what would follow? The journalists were set to cover the spectacle they had been waiting for like a big bonanza. The women began murmuring among themselves. The pressmen and women knew the time for the great spectacle had come.

It happened so fast simultaneously. The world was denied the spectacle of a naked parade of old women before the oil terminal and the nearby flow station. Mask-wearing Navy personnel with the assistance of retired marines kept by Bell Oil Company in their own coordinated plan overwhelmed the island with tear gas and a type of gas nobody knew its name but it made people dizzy and mindless. Every exposed person was dazed and the women and pressmen became drowsy and sleepy.

After the troops made sure that they had seized every

camera and record of the happening, they loaded the women and journalists into big speed boats, which suddenly emerged at the oil terminal. They had been waiting at a safe distance in the thick fog and had been signaled to dock for the human cargo that awaited them.

In the boats the women gradually regained consciousness and were at a loss as to where they were. They discovered that they were being taken to Warri to be released but they were too dazed to think clearly. The women and press personnel would complain that their pockets had been ransacked and their money and jewellry stolen by the Navy men. A few women were raped in their drowsy state in the boats. As usual, no national paper reported the incident that would remain a shame in the legacy of the cooperation between the oil companies and the FMG.

The sudden abortion of the nude protest threw the women into shock that took them several days to recover from. Those raped had nobody to complain to, since the police and the army saw rape as male entertainment and not as a violation of a woman's sovereign body and a criminal act. In all their planning before the assembly at the flow station and terminal, it did not occur to the women that the oil companies and the FMG were capable of not only stifling but also brutalizing them.

A week after, the women made a head count of the participants in the aborted protest and made sure that nobody was missing. It was after then that WODEFOR called a news conference to issue a statement on what had happened. The executive committee members were all present to underscore their unity and the importance of the occasion.

As Secretary of WODEFOR, Ebi read the opening statement.

"Only those who ordered and carried out our violation know what they deserve. God and our ancestors are not sleeping, they were witnesses! Let those who assaulted us know the crime they have committed. Let Bell Oil and the Federal Military Government stop killing us slowly. We cannot sit and watch our land made unlivable by outsiders. We will continue to fight to hand over the land, waters, and air of our birth to our children in a livable state."

Mrs. Taylor then took over to talk about the water, air, and soil that had all been contaminated by the oil exploration; she repeated all the known atrocities of the devils, as she now called Bell Oil and the other oil companies. She said she wanted to let the world know that the women of the Niger Delta would not give up their struggle until positive changes came. She invoked the patron goddess of women, Umalokun, to avenge the rape and humiliation of women during the protest.

The news of Mr. Van Hoort's heart attack and death a week later would not have had much significance on its own and might have been seen as natural if nothing else of national importance happened. After all, heart attacks happen to adults; more so to busy executives such as Mr. Van Hoort who had passed middle age. Exactly two weeks after the aborted nude protest, the death of the head of the FMG, General Mustapha Ali Dongo, in weird circumstances, meant the women's stripping protest that was thought aborted had worked. Is it not the religion of the oil lords, the people asked, that says that one can sin by action as well as by intent and thought? The women's thoughtfully planned action was fulfilled cosmically - they brought down tyrants that their men failed to remove. The two tyrants that tormented the Niger Delta people were gone!

Both Bell Oil Company and the Federal Military Government picked new leaders almost at the same time to replace their deceased ones. The new Bell Oil boss, Mr. Klaus Bilt, was sent from the headquarters in Amsterdam. He was a veteran of the oil industry and had served in Indonesia for seven years before being posted back to the international headquarters only to be sent to head the Nigerian operations. In a press conference, covered by national and international media, the new oil boss promised to make changes in the way Bell Oil Company worked in Nigeria. He did not explain any specific changes he planned to carry out in the company's area of operations.

The people wanted to see changes before believing him. Was he not a bear like Mr. Van Hoort and were they Niger

Delta people not lambs? The powerful multinational lord again promising the helpless people what the bear would promise to the lambs!

The Federal Military Government could not remain headless for more than a few hours. Another head was bound to spring from somewhere in the barracks or corridors of power. Those generals and other officers who had been in the same craft with their late captain met behind closed doors. No officer trusted the other and the rivalry would have gone on for days to cause a stalemate or a bloody clash. But a compromise solution won the day. An interim administration was established comprising of civilians and military officers in a diarchy arrangement charged with preparation for full democratic elections.

The interim head of state, a retired public relations manager of Bell Oil and now an Ife chief, promised to set up a development agency to tackle the perennial problems of the Niger Delta. But making promises was in the tradition of whoever occupied Aso Rock in Abuja, as their predecessors in Dodan Barracks in Lagos had done. It was part of the inauguration ritual, always mouthed to fulfill an oath nobody in the nation expected to be respected. Would this fox treat the chickens differently?

The week following his inauguration the interim leader, Chief Jacob Oleitan, received the October surprise. Mr. Bilt presented him a new aircraft - a special executive Boeing 737. The relationship between Bell Oil Company and the Federal Government must not be allowed to suffer because of the death of their leaders. The two new leaders embraced and their picture was on television that evening before Chief Oleitan made the Independence Eve broadcast.

Rising Tide

When the tide comes in, the coastal river's bank gets flooded with the abundance of the sea and releases sand-wrecked boats into freedom. The goddess of wealth lavishes her favourites with unimagined fortune and she has many favourites among humans. Wealth comes in many ways to someone; sometimes quietly and in trickles and at other times blatantly. When someone is destined to be rich, according to the elders, whatever the person's enterprise becomes like a magic soap; put a little in your hand and it will so foam that you will wash and wash so much with it.

Pere and the Activist easily recruited five area boys for their bunkering business. They bought a used pickup and twenty empty drums to start with. They then made sure that their assistants had the basic tools for their operation. They gave the boys enough money to go to the tools shop to buy the types of knives, axes, and other tools they needed to cut the oil pipes. These were in preparation for a tanker or tankers that would haul their loot to petrol stations because one could not do serious bunkering business without a tanker or several tankers at one's disposal.

The workers and their Delta Cartel employers had an unwritten but binding agreement. The workers, if caught, should never disclose their backers. The employers should, if it became necessary, use any means possible to free their workers if caught. That meant bribing the police or soldiers with whatever amount of money it would take to secure their freedom. The major part of the gentleman's contract was trust. All were sure that there would be no problem since the boys knew the terrain more than the military and police patrols that drove jeeps around looking for women and bribes rather than guarding the pipelines. Pere had learnt that some of the police and soldiers were deliberately lured out of their watch to sleep with paid women in order to provide the chance for easy bunkering.

How would you send out rhinos, just because they had horns, to ferret out antelopes from the forest? Or how would crocodiles and alligators rid the wetlands of snakes? The patrols might be armed but the area boys knew their home terrain and could always elude the guards.

Pere and the Activist took a patient path in their new business. After their accord, they waited for an opportunity, which soon came. Pere had seen a broken-down tanker on the road and had asked several of his boys to find out the owner and what was being done to tow it away from the road before it caused a major accident. He also wanted to know what arrangements were being made for its repair. In just one day his boys identified the owner, whose business was not doing well. Police and army boys had extorted every penny of his profit and he was looking into other safer areas of business to invest in. The oil business, according to him, was not as lucrative as it appeared to those outside it. Pere and the Activist bought the broken-down tanker from its owner, who desperately needed money. They got a towing truck to take it to a mechanic's workshop to have it repaired. Once out of the mechanic's workshop, the tanker drove smoothly and was ready for the oil-lifting business.

Drop by drop an ocean would eventually be created with patience. The industrious ant through persistence builds a monumental hill with simple grains of sand. The Delta Cartel's petrol station started small between two villages on the Warri-Agbor Road. Location is a major factor in the success or failure of a business. The Activist and Pere knew this and so wanted their petrol station in a rather remote area but on the highway. They calculated this to be the best site for their business, which did not need to be too visible.

The Delta Cartel did not need plenty of money to start as the petrol stations in Warri or Port Harcourt that had increasingly combined provision stores, pharmacies, petrol stations, and other businesses in one. Many had beautiful architectural designs, often storied buildings, and had a spacious office for the director on the top floor. With two underground tanks for petrol and one for diesel in place of eight in the township and one surface tank for kerosene in place of three in town, the business partners implemented their plans without too much financial strain or sweat either.

The business partners mustered their resources together and did not need to borrow any money from the banks. That saved them from loan officers, who often exploited desperate customers by proposing to be accepted as partners in a business they had not worked to bring about as a condition for granting the loan.

The Activist behaved like a seasoned economist and advised on cutting costs without losing quality. It was a delicate balance that he achieved with personal experience. He had been living a modest life since he returned from the United States and nobody outside his home knew he had much money. He always lamented the way most of his colleagues lavished the little money they had on needless luxuries. They spent money at marriage and funeral ceremonies and also bought highly expensive clothes for the occasions to impress. He could not bring himself to understand why his colleagues "sprayed" their hard-earned money on other people. Taking out their female students to hotels in town also cost these university teachers plenty of money because flirtation is often expensive.

Pere personally ran many errands to avoid paying out money to professional contractors to build the station. Once the two partners had agreed on the plan, it was left for Pere to implement. He assumed the role of the contractor and oversaw the building of the structure. The station had two pumps for petrol and one each for diesel and kerosene. The partners believed that those who needed their products would come there and join the queue for as long as it took to get to his or her turn to fill their car, bus or lorry tanks. And the women who wanted kerosene to cook would queue all the time it took to get to their turn to buy the needed cooking fuel. Being on the highway that robbers paraded, the appearance of modesty or insignificance would protect their investment and the workers from attack.

Though the Activist was co-owner and co-director, Pere acted as the visible director of the outfit. He employed the workers and inspected and checked sales on a daily basis. He measured the fuel remaining in each tank and gauged how long it would last before fresh supplies came in. He knew when more of each type of fuel was needed.

The Activist came in several times a week and sat with Pere to discuss their joint business as they talked jovially. Even some of the ground staff did not know that he had half the shares of the business in which they worked. Pere and the Activist played draft and eko game as they planned the next step in their business.

Within three months, the business partners were astounded by the progress they had made within such a short time. Theirs was a private business, officially called independent marketer, and they supplied themselves the different types of fuel they sold. They bought engine oil though, the Super-V, Brotal, and Sina brands of oil, brake fluids, distilled water, and other products that motorists needed to keep their engines running.

The frequent strikes of the refinery workers turned the Delta Cartel into a multi-million naira business within a short time. In a protracted strike by oil workers to force the military to cede power to civilians, oil became very scarce. A senior military member of the interim government had seized power, abrogated the diarchy, and promised to hand over power as soon as possible. In a major oil-producing country, everything revolves around oil; hence the strike to press the upstart general to give up power to civilians. Why did he have to seize power when arrangements were already being made for democratic elections? The public supported the strike to embarrass the dictator.

The Delta Cartel petrol station made sure it did not sell a drop of any fuel once there was going to be a strike of oil workers. For two weeks before the strike the station continued to hoard all brands of fuel. All supplies were emptied into drums and the whole bush around hid the hundreds of drums of different types of fuel. With the underground tanks untouched and the bush filled with drums, the Delta Cartel prepared well for the impending strike. After all, as the Activist joked, it was not raining when Noah built the ark!

Once the strike started, the respective prices of petrol, diesel, and kerosene more than quadrupled. Officially, there was no fuel for sale. The capital lettered sign of NO FUEL swung at the station's closed gate. Other handwritten signs of "No Petrol," "No Kerosene," and "No Diesel" were placed in front of the station too. There was no supply, according to the boys and girls who waved off any driver attempting to come down to open the gate for entry.

"You no dey see? No fuel!"

"Which time fuel go come?"

"I don't know. When Oga come we go know," the girl would say.

"If you like, make you go see-am or come later," another attendant would say.

"I fit see am for office?"

"No, come for night!"

That was an indication that fuel was being hoarded. The real business took place at night. The fuel sold only at night to the rich people who could not bear any discomfort in their opulent lives. These people could not afford to walk; their legs could not carry them anywhere outside their homes. They needed to drive even if only to show off as others trekked. Those who came at night to buy fuel could not afford to live in darkness or suffer the constant humidity of the Niger Delta weather. They had to buy fuel for their generators to power their air-conditioners. The rich needed water in their baths and showers and their boreholes did not work without electricity, which fuel in their generators made available. At night the town coughed persistently as the generators exhaled toxic dark fumes. No one would be counted among the privileged in Warri without a generator whose noise prevented people from sleeping soundly but pleased its owner for being counted among the rich in the neighborhood.

The electricity company soon joined the strike and turned the whole nation into a blackout state. There were no negotiations going on to end the strike and a sense of desperation seized everybody. Fuel prices rose to ten times their normal prices. Nobody, including the journalists, cared to ask questions about rumours that the independent marketers paid the top officials of the electricity corporation tons of money in order to prolong the strike for them to maximize their profits. To further intensify the strike, importers of generators in the country, in order to maximize their already brisk profits, also bribed the senior officials of the electricity company not to negotiate with the government. With the heavy bribes shared among the negotiating team, the national electricity providers became resistant to negotiations and, even when they started, set impossible terms for the government to meet. The reluctant negotiations soon broke down and the strike continued; every night black with pockets of light and fumes exhaled by generators of the rich in town.

In recent times Pere had delegated authority to more assistants and he closed early most days to spend more time at the Delta Cartel. The area boys strongly supported the nationwide strike to bring down the military government. At night Pere, heavily guarded by four armed area boys, went to the lonely roadside station to direct the business. Oil had become an elixir that was sought desperately. Without kerosene, many townspeople could not cook because there was no more firewood and they were ready to buy a four-litre gallon for half a month's salary. How they got money to spend only God knew. But it was a country in which everybody knew that everybody else spent more than his or her salary. Nobody asked the other where they made their money despite the poor economy. Every person made money on the side, just as both Pere and the Activist were doing in a grand style. People complained of poor pay or no jobs, but they lived on, spending lavishly from what they did not earn at work. Men were buying fuel to seduce women. And many sophisticated women refused making love except in an air-conditioned room that only the rich could afford in the desperate times. Who offered fuel received much in return in a new kind of trade by barter. The saying in town changed from "Money for hand, back for ground!" to "Fuel for jerry-can, back for ground!"

By the end of the strike and other fuel scarcities artificially created, the two business partners saw the wisdom in doing what others were doing openly without the public not really knowing what was involved. People talked about bunkering, but how many knew what it meant? How many dared to do it? Almost all the time the police and army boys surrendered to wads of naira notes and did not put up a fight. The bold survive; the weak die. Pere felt vindicated by his philosophy of life.

    The two business partners had their own plans for the wealth that was foaming bigger and bigger. The magic soap was foaming beyond their wildest dreams. Both were surprised at the dedication of their "boys" in the field. They treated them very well, paying them heavily and taking their personal needs as theirs. All the assistants had started building personal houses and had become the envy of other area boys, but they did not disclose the nature of their assistantship to Pere. They were all happy in the Cartel.

Pere was interested in owning property. He did not believe in building or buying houses for rent though. From his experience in Warri over the years, he was not ready for the task of dealing with stubborn tenants. Some people rented flats they could not afford by borrowing money to pay for the first year and after then defaulted on rent payments and even physically threatened landlords. Many defaulting tenants deliberately went to court and it took six months to one year to evict a rent-defaulting tenant. That was a long time to lose money, Pere thought.

    Pere liked hotels. Hotels were the new enterprises after petrol stations. He bought a large piece of land in Warri and started the first phase of a hotel complex. He wanted to implement his giant plan of a big hotel complex in phases rather than build the entire hotel at once. He had learnt from the mistakes of other local entrepreneurs. Whenever he drove past the uncompleted mammoth complex on Airport Road, he shook his head. The owner had planned too big and could not for the past twenty years complete the project despite having already sunk in hundreds of millions of naira. The owner of the cement block behemoth must be saying, "Had I known, I would have started small and built upon it little by little!"

    Pere wanted profit from the business to be used to expand it.

He knew people would always need hotel accommodation in Warri. It was a central town, a place for rest on the Lagos-Eastern route. Being also the headquarters of many oil companies, including Bell Oil, it was a big commercial centre. Wherever there were jobs and industries, hotels would thrive, he believed.

But he would soon find out as an hotelier that money flowed from two main sources that he had not thought about in all his planning. There was so much flirtation going on and men would bring women as some women brought men to pay for rooms for a fling of several hours for which they were ready to pay whatever he charged. From late afternoon through midnight was particularly busy on weekdays. Weekends brought so many customers from morning through night. It was as if lovemaking was the main weekend pastime of the people, who so much liked clandestine and illicit sex that they came to the hotel prepared to pay for the pleasure.

Of course all the flirts had prepared alibis for their regular partners, and with so many social and cultural associations, Pentecostal all-night prayer vigils, and wake-keepings and burials, there were as many opportunities to flirt as the people wished. To keep themselves from being seen together entering and leaving the hotel, some lovers came and left singly - they often gave themselves intervals of a quarter of an hour and in some cases the men later caught up with the women on the road and pretended to give them a ride.

The hotelier also made plenty of money from beers such as Gulder, Skol, Sparkling, Star, Rock, Guinness Stout, and malt drinks in the sexual escapades. The customers seemed to believe that the drinks enhanced their sexual prowess and enjoyment and so drank and drank to refuel their sex drives. The more they drank and slept, the heavier the bills they had to pay when they got out of their revelries.

Hoteliers also engaged in other deals. Their proprietors sought government agencies and company facilitators that brought their workers to stay for months. It was a particularly good deal for newly employed workers, who stayed there for a month and often extended their temporary residency to three months. Government and companies paid whatever was charged but whoever did the booking was given a big tip by the hotelier.

Pere smiled at his success when he was able to get newly recruited Bell Oil Company workers or those posted to Warri to stay in his hotel. The mobile police that the company paid to protect its offices also stayed in Moonshine Hotel. So did the mobile police patrolling the oil pipelines. They brought women for drinks and sex orgies and often missed their patrol beats because of frequent hangovers.

Pere deliberately overcharged Bell Oil Company while making it look like a special bargain for the company. He also made the company to think that its guests were treated in a very special way. After all, the company lifted more barrels of oil than it declared and underpaid taxes, even as it proclaimed its development mission in the area. "Cunning man die, cunning man bury am!" he reflected.

Preparing food for Bell Oil workers also netted monthly hundreds of thousands of naira that the multibillion-dollar company did not question and regularly settled. The Nigerian liaison between the oil company and the hotel did the arrangements and got a big tip from the hotelier. The first Bell Oil official to do the transaction resigned after a year, when transferred to a non-lucrative position in the company, to start his own business - running a hotel!

Pere's hotel gradually grew big and occupied a very large area of a street's end. He planted flowers and trees to provide shade for his customers. He placed love seats where companions could sit and talk and drink if they were tired of being indoors. Once one visited Moonshine Hotel, one came back because of the privacy it afforded and its quiet and cool atmosphere.

With the profits that came in, Pere planned ahead and opened another hotel in Port Harcourt, which he saw as not different from Warri. Its residents shared the same sharp appetite for clandestine sex that hotels helped to fill. Of course there were the usual wedding parties, social and cultural associations' meetings, and the weekend parties for which there was payment for the space and purchase of drinks. Pere had been able to corner the needs of his people: fuel and sex.

Business could not be better.

The Activist was no longer a mere visiting professor. He had already been confirmed as a full professor and nobody was surprised at his simple but cultured living. He had been given what the university described as a "professorial house" in the exclusive senior staff section of the campus and he and Ebi had bidden goodbye to Ebi's two-bedroom flat.

As the Delta people often say, money does not hide its impact on people - it always shows! It was not only the salary of a professor that changed the Activist's life. The business by the side that the campus people did not know about lifted him. Bunkering would be the magic soap whose foam he would use to wash and wash so much laundry to look like new.

When money started to come in thousands and then millions of naira from the Cartel, the Activist did not buy a new car, as many on campus in his situation would have done. Rather he bought what he considered to be very fine paintings and artworks to decorate his house. He traveled to Lagos to art galleries and bought the best he could find. He had works of Bruce Onobrakpeya, Demas Nwoko, Dele Jegede, Lamidi Fakeye, Nike, and other famous Nigerian artists. Ebi's freshly designed pots added diversity to the collection. She arranged things in a very beautiful manner and their house became the story on campus. She believed many of their campus visitors came to really see for themselves what the American activist and the old maid had become as husband and wife at home.

Ebi achieved double success. She had not only got her Ph.D. in art but also given birth. She and her spouse had been blessed with a girl they named Ufuoma because she had brought them peace and fulfillment. The parents took care of Ufuoma to the point of spoiling her, but that did not bother them because they felt that the girl was lucky. As soon as the girl started talking, she was registered in a private kindergarten school, the one that very few could afford and there she learnt with children of Bell Oil and other oil company workers. To the Activist, this was a major form of counter-penetration as the private schools around should not be for outsiders alone but, being the best, should be attended also by Niger

Delta children.

With his wealth, the Activist thought far ahead. He liked wealth but from the beginning wanted wealth to be of use to him to enhance humanity. He wanted to rob the oil companies and the Federal Military Government to spite them for their indifference to the suffering of the Niger Delta people. He felt a sense of fulfillment that the Delta Cartel had worked magically. How things had changed! He had lived on a shoestring in the United States, and only six years after his return to Nigeria, he was a multi-millionaire that few hardly noticed. He knew he could do much to influence happenings in the country. He was not going to sponsor a military coup against the upstart general because he was by principle against military governments. He was not going to risk his life to promote decadence. He thought of better things to do with his money.

He had his eyes set on controlling a segment of the media to influence or affect public opinion. He had seen how the concerns of the Niger Delta people had gone unreported. If he controlled a media house, that would not happen. The people needed allies in the media and he would provide one for them in whatever he chose to invest in.

The interim military government had begun to loosen its grip on media houses. It announced that individuals could get licenses to establish television and radio stations and newspapers. Many people who nursed political ambition were already establishing television or radio stations in preparation for partisan politics. The military leader often reminded his subjects that he would soon lift the ban on party politics. This he repeated to forestall a counter coup against him and to deflect attacks of foreign leaders aimed at him.

The Activist chose establishing a newspaper, which he knew that, though capital intensive, he could run efficiently. It could start small and be run more as a regional newspaper than a full-fledged national paper. He did not have the pickups or other means of transportation that would set out overnight to fan out all over the country to deliver the newspaper. He would aim to circulate the paper in the South-South, Lagos, and the Abuja areas. With time the philosophy of the paper and the good reportage he hoped to encourage would win it readers nationwide when there would be infrastructures set in place for mass production and wide circulation. After all, there were newspapers springing up all over the country and each was trying to establish a niche of its own.

The Patriot started with old-fashioned printing machines that were gradually replaced by more modern ones and then, with time, state-of-the-art equipment. Old daguerreotype printers gave way to big computers that were soon replaced by smarter smaller computers that were updated with the latest programs. With desktop publishing programs, the newspaper became easier to bring out regularly.

And so *The Patriot* started as a weekly with good reportage of events in the Niger Delta. Whatever of significance happened in Port Harcourt, Bori, Nembe, Bonny, Yenagoa, Oleh, Ughelli, Sapele, Umutu, Ogwashi-Uku, and Warri, among so many places, got reported. It was as if those who had been silenced all along suddenly got a voice of their own and that made a difference. The paper was a big hit at the Niger Delta State University campus, Warri, and the entire Niger Delta. It reported news; it analyzed local, national, and international news. It gave space to the folklore of the people, and that made them to know more about what united them rather than what divided them that outsiders harped upon. The newspaper was patriotic, pro-people, and for justice and fairness. As the readership increased, it became a daily without Saturday and Sunday editions.

After thoughtful discussion, Ebi, now Dr. Emasheyi, agreed to retire early from the university to manage the newspaper on a fulltime basis. She was appointed the manager/publisher of *The Patriot*. She felt she would be in a position to better promote the interests of the Niger Delta women in such a strategic appointment. She would do a bi-weekly column, "Women Matters" together with managing the paper.

The Activist was on the Board of Directors. With Omagbemi Mukoro unemployed for two years after graduation and national service, he became the logical choice for the paper's editor-in-chief. The Activist had over the years got to know how intelligent and energetic he was and felt he should be the one to run the opinion matters of the paper. The motto of the paper was "Justice and Humanity for the People."

For the first time people of the Niger Delta freely exercised their public voice. Incidents in the area that used to go unreported started to appear in black-and-white to be read and kept as a witness of their experiences. The paper produced annals of local events, a book of the major experiences of the people. It detailed how the people fared in the previous year and that edition became an unofficial ombudsman of government and corporate activities in the Niger Delta area.

Of course the oil companies were not happy that *The Patriot's* editorial policy took the side of the community rather than theirs. They protested as usual to the Interim Federal Military Government (IFMG) that in the changing dispensation could only vaguely ask that all newspapers should exercise caution in their publications. *The Patriot* carefully researched news and set up mechanisms to check and recheck its authenticity. It avoided libelling anybody or group and so was not worried by what it published. It became the avenue to wage the local community's agitation for control of its natural resources. The paper did not mind being called the champion of resource control. It showed in coloured and black-and-white photographs the damage done to the environment.

The only frogs seen were deformed - one-eyed or one-legged. Blind turtles were caught on land. Deformed babies were not left out of the pictures. What had not been seen before was exposed in *The Patriot*. For its close monitoring of the eco system of the area, the paper soon won the Green Peace Reporting Award which came with a cash prize of ten thousand dollars. The paper's reporting put the oil companies, especially Bell Oil, and the Federal Government on the defensive.

The Patriot gradually built up the resources and wherewithal to publish Saturday and Sunday editions. These weekend editions balanced entertainment with news. There was a detachable four-page supplement on Friday that announced the social and cultural events of that weekend - burials, weddings, and other parties. Many rich people bought spaces to congratulate their friends, relatives, and loved ones on their birthdays, promotions, or conferment of chieftaincy titles that took place all-year round. Others who did not know what else to do with their money spent hundreds of thousands of naira to remember their parents that died out of neglect twenty or more years ago! Even after the fees for such self-promotion was raised, the paper continued to be filled.

One of the bizarre stories that the Saturday edition of the paper carried was an incident at the Moonshine Hotel, Pere's hotel complex. While avoiding the frivolous, the paper had to tell the truth and report things as they happened. A sex scandal blew up at the hotel and led to injuries; it of course brought in the police, who extorted money from the two parties involved.

An elderly rich man's young wife, one of four, had taken a young lover and they always drove to Moonshine Hotel to take a room for several hours. She was a beauty, the main consideration for the rich man's decision to marry her in the first place. She had made up her mind to endure the old man so as to live well on his money while still satisfying her sexual appetite with the younger men she fancied. The young lecturer took his rendezvous with this beauty as a regular thing and they made arrangements to be coming to the hotel to make love. The frequenting of the hotel caught the attention of those who knew the rich chief; they brought his wife's secret affair to his ear. He soon set traps all over the place and it did not take long before one of them caught both tight. The chief barged into the secret lovers while they were naked in bed.

The Patriot reported what happened. The old chief and the wife's young lover exchanged blows that led to the old chief losing several teeth. Police came in and arrested both men and only released them after their paying heavily to close the case because of its embarrassment. The chief's wife did not accompany him to their marital home but went straight to her parents' home. Gossip later spread that, within two weeks of the shameful incident at Moonshine Hotel, she travelled to Italy to join the growing number of sex entertainers there from Nigeria. The young lecturer endured finger-pointing for some weeks but on a campus where sex scandals happened so often his case was soon forgotten.

Omagbemi soon had to approve the publication of a similar incident also on a weekend issue. A married professor had been putting pressure on a female student who was the wife of a junior lecturer on campus. Since the woman felt that if she resisted him, he would flunk her however hard she studied, she decided to appear to go along with his plans to go to a hotel in town and make love. The professor gave her money to pay for a room in a hotel that he had indicated to her. The female student told her husband and gave him clues as to where she would be and he should open the door at the crucial time.

When Professor Don Odili came in and went straight to meet his student, a lecturer's wife, he was in very high spirits. That was what he liked about Nigerian universities; the teacher's ability to do whatever he wanted to do with female students. He could and would sleep with the women he fancied. He had tried it several times in the two years he had returned from Britain and succeeded all the times. He wanted change; after all, change was the spice of life. The female students, including this one he now fancied, were much younger than his middle-aged wife who had become boring.

The twenty-eight-year-old woman coaxed Professor Odili to remove his clothes and delayed him from touching her too intimately.

"It takes me time to warm up," she told him.

"That's okay with me."

"It really takes me a long time to be in the mood."

Don't worry, we are already here. A few more minutes won't spoil the fun."

"Thanks for being so considerate."

"You are welcome."

The professor, who spoke with the accent of an Englishman, thought he was in for the treat of his life. She had deliberately left the door unlocked.

"I am already heating up."

"Slow down, don't rush."

As the learned don's erection reached an uncontrollable state, the woman coughed out loud as a signal. Her husband pushed open the door. Don Odili thought it was one of the housekeepers not polite enough to knock before mistakenly opening the door. But behold, the husband of the woman he was trying to rape standing before him! The lecherous don was pushed out naked. He did not put up any resistance.

Outside he was a pitiable figure and only an embarrassed but sympathetic housekeeper threw a towel at him to cover his manhood.

"Oh my God, is this a ghost? What am I seeing? I am finished!" he exclaimed.

"Yes, you are finished, crook!" the woman's husband replied.

"Please, forgive me," he pleaded.

Instantly the enormity of what he had done dawned on him. How would he get home and face his own wife and the university community after the news of his action spread? Was he not the professor who spoke so loudly about discipline on campus?

Of course he had to still drive home to meet his wife and the university community. Within a week of his shame, unable to handle the embarrassment and the legal repercussions of his action, he was out of the university. Rumour later said he went to his home state to teach in a college of education.

A day after reporting the incident which drew much interest and gossip on campus, *The Patriot* ran an editorial on sexual harassment and indiscretion on the university campus where AIDS was spreading at an alarming rate. It warned university teachers to maintain self-control so that they would be role models rather than goats on heat.

The editorial on Wednesday was reinforced in the following Saturday issue of the paper by Dr. Ebi Emasheyi's "Women Matters" column on "Women's Right to Say No Out and Loud." She wrote that every woman was a sovereign body and should keep herself inviolate by repelling every physical assault by any man. Female students should report unwanted moves from their teachers to the university authorities. Regulations should be put in place to protect female students. At the same time the institution should create checks and balances to avoid frivolous accusations from either side. The paper generated intense discussion on campus that made teachers and students not to cross impermissible lines in their relationships.

It gladdened Ebi's heart that Niger Delta State University soon set up a committee of students and teachers to address the issue of romantic relationships between students and teachers. The committee was asked to define sexual harassment and rape and to recommend punishment for violators.

Ishaka's Bell Oil Son

Dennis Ishaka was doing very well in Bell Oil Company as far as his position and salary were concerned. From the moment he took up the appointment brokered by his father, Mr. Van Hoort and his inner circle of the senior staff decided to make the young and smart Dennis Ishaka to share in all the luxuries, privileges, and benefits of the company, but not in its technical expertise and experience. Allowing him to acquire technical drilling experience would be suicidal for the expatriate staff and business. Let those who want technology from others for free wait till the next world, the oil boss thought.

Dennis was given an impressive quarter in the Ugunu site, a transplanted European high-class township in the Niger Delta forest. The entire site was fenced with a concrete wall on top of which were razor-sharp wires which were electrified in case any intruder wanted to test either his climbing skill or his shock-resistance capacity. The company meant business and would not allow any monkey tricks to rob the residents. It made its senior service workers safe in their residences so that they could sleep comfortably and dream uninterrupted by hoodlums or robbers.

Eucalyptus, bougainvillea, crotons, hibiscus, rhododendrons, and whistling pines adorned the complex in special patterns. There were already enough local trees outside and the landscapers had to give these specially selected plants and flowers room in the European enclave called Ugunu. The lawns were mowed regularly in the rain as in the sun. Bell Oil would not compromise the beauty of its unit no matter the weather.

Several gardeners drove mowers and kept the entire place manicured and trimmed. Some other workers swept the roads and picked up trash from the streets. Trash drums stood at different locations to ensure that the streets were maintained and kept clean. Bold signs admonished residents against littering and violators were threatened with heavy fines. This town was neither Warri nor Lagos, slum cities; rather it was Ugunu, a model European township in the heart of Africa.

Ugunu residents had their own electric plants that catered for them constantly. Those living there knew nothing of power outage that plagued the rest of the country. The facility's high-powered generators took off automatically the moment the National Electric Power Authority's light went off. Sometimes, it kicked off once the national grid's voltage turned into a dull yellowish flicker, the power too low to carry the many appliances and gadgets that made living at Ugunu a comfortable experience. The township's residents could not also rely on the water corporation and so had boreholes that provided them adequate and constant supply of water.

Behind the tall concrete fence, local villagers still fetched water from the Ugunu River, brown from chemicals of oil exploration, for bathing and cooking needs. At night the villagers saw from a distance the ever-glowing light in the Bell Oil residential enclave. Bright floodlights shone from electric poles over the concrete wall to ensure that any intruder would be caught before any serious attempt was made to infiltrate the complex.

Parks and swimming pools were there for relaxation. The workers at Ugunu had a mini Disneyland for their children to play in after school, on weekends, and during vacations. They had a club in a large compound for their relaxation and entertainment. Though cinema houses outside Ugunu had transformed into new Pentecostal churches, the Bell Oil Senior Staff Club had a big screen that showed some of the latest movies in North America and Europe. The food and drinks were heavily subsidized by the company to increase the morale and subsequently the productivity of workers. The single men and women among them did not need to cook to eat, with good food at such a very affordable price. The residents played tennis, badminton, squash, ping-pong, dart, chess, and whatever game white people played at home. There was no draught; there was also no eko game - those who wanted such games could drive out and play in the slum quarters of Warri!

Dennis was unmarried and yet got allocated to him a big five-bedroom house and behind it a boy's quarter. Two uniformed guards kept watch over the house night and day. The guards on duty also opened and closed the cast-iron gate. To show the importance of his position, Dennis had a uniformed driver permanently assigned to him. His official car, a Saab, was imported and that made him look very distinguished among drivers of locally assembled Peugeot cars.

Since he had not joined the company for long, Dennis was doing extremely well by Bell Oil standards. The first time his father came to visit him, the chief was dumbfounded. He could not believe that his son, a young graduate, had within six months been transformed into an *oyibo* despite his black skin. The gate men allowed him into the compound on his self-identification but still had to press the bell for the son to accept to see his own father. That was the instruction in the whole site - you had to know who came to visit you before allowing the person in. There was a device in the house through which Dennis could look out and see who wanted to visit him. He ran down to receive his father.

Chief Tobi Ishaka was impressed by his son's progress but had certain misgivings.

"I thought you were going to be in the rigs and oil wells dirtying yourself and learning how oil is extracted from the soil. This place may be beautiful but is too far from the field," he told his son.

"This is where they placed me. I hope with time they will send me to the oilfield. I am still relatively new here but the Nigerians who have been here for many years say that I am lucky to be in this place," he explained to his father.

"Be careful. You have to look straight at where you are going. Don't let them make you forget your goal," the chief preached to his son.

"I know, father;" he answered.

Dennis wanted his father to feel good about him and his job and so did not share with him the special way he was being treated. He was grateful that his father made this position possible. A degree in petroleum engineering had taken some of his course mates to teach physics and chemistry in secondary schools. Those were the lucky ones, because many others were still unemployed and were ready to be managers of petrol stations if the opportunity was there for them. He was very fortunate that his father's foresight and forcefulness had brought this about.

Dennis's bosses placed him where he would not need to soil or hurt his hands. Those who worked in the office had hands soft like ripe bananas, unlike the chapped and calloused hands of field workers. He did not need to wear a uniform or a protective helmet to do his work - he was far away from the rigs and the flow stations. Rather, he was expected to put on a suit as a senior administrative officer. He was placed in the corporate hospitality section of the company and was one of the officers that received important visitors that came to see them. These visitors included international oil importers, foreign dignitaries, presidents, ministers, state governors, and other visitors classified as very important personalities.

Dennis sat in his regal chair before a big desk from eight to five. Many days or weeks passed without any very important visitor that he had to welcome or take to the General Manager and then give a tour of the administrative headquarters. Such days or weeks, he spent his time reading about the company. Old bulletins were available and he kept himself busy reading the projects of the company worldwide. From his reading he learnt how big and global the company really was. The Niger Delta was just one of so many areas around the world where Bell Oil did its oil prospecting, drilling, and shipping business.

Dennis Ishaka sat in that office for three years and expected a transfer, which eventually came. He had expected to be posted to the rigs and be a supervisor or something else there, but the company's policymakers made him to understand that he was too important to the company to be sent to the muddy mangrove waters of oil rigs, where workers had to contend with mosquitoes, iguanas, crocodiles, pythons, and inclement swampy weather. They did not want to endanger the chief's son's life by exposing him to malaria and the bite of the iguana!

Rather, they needed him to help the corporate hospitality section more and so posted him to Amsterdam, the company's international headquarters. This was an enviable posting and he should consider himself very lucky to be the first Nigerian employee from the Niger Delta to be so elevated.

"You'll enjoy Amsterdam," Mr. Bilt assured him.

The General Manager had been at the global headquarters and so knew firsthand what it felt like to be there.

"Thanks," Dennis responded.

"Amsterdam will change your life; you won't regret working there," the Bell Oil boss further told Dennis.

"I have never been there, but it surely should be an interesting place," he told his boss.

"Congratulations!"

"Thanks for everything."

The company gave Dennis a great sendoff party, to which his father was invited but he feigned having malaria fever and did not attend. Bell Oil's treatment of his son had not changed with the death of Mr. Van Hoort and his replacement by Mr. Bilt. He did not know what to make of his son's transfer to Amsterdam. Was he being further removed from the drilling fields or where he could at last crack the puzzle of drilling? But time was running fast before his knowledge of petroleum engineering started to rust. How long did Dennis have to be in the company before learning what ought to be his orientation course there? he asked himself.

Already his fellow chiefs had known that his son was a big man in Bell Oil Company and taunted him with his known anti-Bell Oil stance in discussions in their council. The other chiefs felt he was now on their side, but he did not care about their thoughts and suspicions. He still refused to share in the payoffs to the monarch and his chiefs from the oil companies. The end result of his son someday successfully prospecting for oil from their own lands was what mattered to him.

The Nigerian employees of Bell Oil Company gave Dennis another sendoff party. There was much to eat and drink. Invitees consumed different types of pepper soup prepared with fish, ox tail, goat meat, and an assortment of offal. Jollof rice, banga soup, pounded yam, and eba were also served.

There was abundance of palm wine, beer, hard liquor, wine, and bottled fruit juices. Some of the female guests stuffed their handbags with fried goat meat and small bottles of Guinness Stout to take home. It was their way of getting something from Bell Oil that made so much money from their land, such people believed. A local band, Tony Bees, played highlife music, often interspersing its own original compositions with popular Rex Lawson's and Sally Young's songs, and people crowded the floor and danced to their hearts' content.

At a point about the middle of the party, the chairman of the occasion drew everybody's attention to why they were there and giving a party to their illustrious son, who had been posted to the company's international headquarters in Amsterdam.

"This party is for you, Dennis. We are proud of you. You are one of the very few Nigerians here who sit in the same room with the white men," he said.

All at the party listened attentively. No praise was enough for Dennis Ishaka, the rising Nigerian star in Bell Oil Company. What a lucky man he was! After a pause, the chairman of the occasion continued.

"You are going to Amsterdam, the global headquarters of our company. There's no other Nigerian we know of in that huge and tall office building whose pictures we see.

You will be our eyes and ears there. Don't forget those of us you are leaving behind; always have us on your mind."

At this there was a loud applause. They were giving him this honour so that he would speak for them when the chance arose at the global headquarters. But the chairman was not done with his speech.

"Many of us are supposed to be senior staff, but we are in the dark about the workings of this company. You are privileged to know that. We know though that the local decisions of Bell Oil Company are really taken in Amsterdam. Our General Manager takes directives from abroad. All he does here is just to implement what has been decided in the big company's world headquarters. Speak about us when there; write about us when there; above all let them there know that we are here," he concluded.

Another loud applause rocked the party hall.

The master of ceremony whose role had been usurped by the chairman took the microphone.

"Thank you, Mr. Chairman. Thank you, everybody! Let's hear Mr. Dennis Ishaka," he said, and walked to hand over the microphone to the guest of honor.

"Thank you, everybody, from the bottom of my heart. You know the whole company gave me a sendoff party last week. I am not saying I didn't enjoy it, but no party can beat this one. Thank you and thank you for this party that will be the envy of any party anywhere," he said, and paused as people roared and clapped.

"When your own people see it fit to honour you, it is a great moment. Let me assure you that my progress will be your progress, and I will always remember you and this day."

Everybody, including the chairman, stood and gave Dennis a standing ovation. It was an enjoyable party that left all satisfied.

Dennis had four weeks within which to report in Amsterdam. In addition to the two major parties, there were other small parties, some taking place in the company's clubhouse and others at his friends' homes in Warri. The Activist and Dr. Mukoro invited Dennis to the University Club and shared pepper soup and drinks with him. The Activist did not fail to impress on Dennis the irony of the situation - while he had come home because he was tired of living abroad, he, Dennis, was being sent abroad!

"You must always remember home because your peace and happiness are connected to your people's plight," the Activist explained to him.

"Thanks for your advice," Dennis said.

"I just wanted you to know what you are going into. If you are not careful outside, you will miss your road, as we say, and you know what that means. It's not all rose-coloured there as we hear about foreign places. I am happy though that yours is a mere transfer and you may be brought back any time you have completed your assignment."

"From the look of things, I may not stay there for long. But who knows?"

"Be guided by the love of your people," the Activist concluded.

At the global headquarters, appropriately named Bell Oil International Headquarters, Dennis was given a magnificent office. In the forty-storey building, his office was located on the thirty-ninth floor to show how important the company regarded him. The office was specially equipped with beautiful furniture and all the state-of-the-art gadgets and appurtenances available in developed countries. There were screens for display as if he would be expected to make presentations in his office. Art works for which Holland is famous, especially drawings and paintings of ships and portraits, and works of their masters, including Van Gogh's, adorned the walls. The chief's son's name was already emblazoned on a polished mahogany wood tablet and placed at the head of his desk: DENNIS ISHAKA, ESQ. CORPORATE HOSPITALITY MANAGER, INTERNATIONAL HEADQUARTERS.

Dennis wondered if his country's president's office that so attracted many military officers to stage coups and risk their lives was as luxurious and impressive as his at Bell Oil International. Special pens were stuck into pen holders. The special brown Formica made the table to shine smoothly and reflectively. The office floor was rugged and yet a specially designed Persian rug covered the center. There was a separate chair arrangement in a corner of the big office, where Dennis would receive visitors or have discussion with his staff. The whole office smelt so fresh and surreal in its elevation. Through the windows Dennis could look down at canals and roads crisscrossing the city.

Within weeks of Dennis assuming his new appointment in Amsterdam, the first international bulletin from the corporate division came out. It was colourfully produced and glossy. There he was on so many pages. The editors of the bulletin made sure they included many of the pictures of his arrival and welcoming to his new post, photographed smiling and shaking hands with his new colleagues. There was a flattering profile of him, which he had not submitted. The company really knew much more about him than he had thought. He was the son of an important chief in the African Niger Delta who had risen close to the highest possible position in the company. His degree in petroleum engineering from a highly rated Nigerian university made him the sort of smart young men and women that the company needed to compete globally in the next phase of technological competition in the oil industry. His enviable position, the profile continued, showed how Bell Oil was a truly international company that had diversity of personnel and employed indigenes of local communities where they operated into the company's top hierarchy.

Six months in Amsterdam, Dennis Ishaka, Esq. was even freer than he was at his desk in Nigeria. The company supplied him English-language newspapers and magazines; so he had regular supply of *The International Herald-Tribune, The Wall Street Journal, The Financial Times* of London, *Time Magazine*, and a host of others. Reading these papers occupied most of his workday. He also received foreign visitors and was photographed with them for the company's different press releases and bulletins. He was a black spot in a sea of white, and Bell Oil International's policy-makers liked it so. He had learnt that his rank of a manager was common at the headquarters and that the real head was called a chief executive officer.

His immediate boss, Mr. Kasperman, advised him to visit museums, galleries, and other interesting places in Amsterdam. He also asked him to have a social life.

"This place is dull and cold. You will go nuts if you have no company and just stay at home."

"I am fine. I find the place exciting and I am fully occupied," Dennis replied.

"You will certainly not find the place fine for too long when the winter arrives. You need to have company to keep yourself busy. In any case, if you can handle it, do so but if I were in your position and single and from so far away, I would make friends to keep myself busy. The Dutch are very hospitable people and our women know how to treat strangers very well," Mr. Kasperman counselled and explained.

"Thanks," Dennis replied.

Dennis felt that his Dutch colleagues pitied him for reasons he could not understand. Couldn't he live alone in Amsterdam? Why were they so keen for him to have a female partner? None of them had said it directly, but he was mature enough to understand what they meant.

Dennis wrote to his father about his experience so far at the global headquarters of Bell Oil. He was fine in health, but he could not say the same of his spirit. He detailed the courtesies done to him, but he was having little or no work and felt underutilized. When he thought about what he had heard concerning white people who worked very hard, he knew that there was something wrong in his not having much work to do in the office. He who came on transfer with so much zeal to roll up his sleeves and do whatever hard work he would be asked to do was rather idle. He was already tired of having nothing to do not only with petroleum engineering but also with his time. He knew now that he was being left out of both the production and trade secrets of Bell Oil International. He also reported what Mr. Kasperman told him about having a social life and that he had noticed the seductive lady, a blonde, they had now assigned to him as his assistant but who only served him tea in the office.

Chief Tobi Ishaka was not impressed by the European life of his son. This was not the career he had dreamt for him. Dennis was being made a socialite rather than a practical petroleum engineer. He was being transformed into a bureaucrat instead of the engineer he was supposed to be. Chief Ishaka felt he did not need to be a learned man and an engineer to discern the tricks being played on his son.

The chief had two points to emphasize in his reply to his son. He was mature enough to marry and he needed a woman to be stable. He should take his leave, come home, and marry before a Dutch woman stole into his bed and ruined him. He was not against marrying people from other places and cultures, which his people were used to in the Niger Delta. However, marrying a continent away while on transfer in a job could make Dennis to forget his own home and priorities. There were so many young ladies in the Niger Delta to marry from and they would be happy to have him as a husband. "Many men in high positions are brought down by women for lack of self-control. Other men with high potentials are distracted from their courses by women. The best weapon against a weakness is countering it. Marriage will wipe out the opportunity for women to tempt and distract you; at least marriage will reduce it drastically. Take heed!" he wrote.

The chief added that the longer he kept away from the oil rigs and the nitty-gritty task of oil drilling, the more he would forget about where he was going. He did not want his engineering degree to rust in distant Amsterdam. There was work for him in the Niger Delta, where Bell Oil continued to discover more oil wells every month. "You are still not doing the job for which Mr. Van Hoort employed you. My understanding was that you would use your graduate degree to work to understand in practical terms how to prospect for and drill oil. I want you to know how to drill the oil that may still be in our farmlands or lands; I want you to do it. Why should people from far away come and map where underground we have oil, extract and take it away? I have told you so many times and I say it again. I want you to possess the witchcraft of the white man. I want you to acquire his technical craft to know what is deep down inside the bowels of the earth here. The way the white man lives at home, from what I have heard, is another matter. I don't want you to be seduced by his luxuries and women. Take heed!" he again warned.

Dennis was supposed to be the head of his section but the decisions were always taken for him and announced as his. He was aware his email was monitored, like what happened to everybody else. It was for public use but only for private correspondence that did not violate any laws; a subtle warning that the company read their messages. He did not use the email to write about his frustrations to his father and friends in Nigeria.

His assistant tried to engage him in a conversation whenever she came in. She wore a fine skirt suit that fitted her wasp-waist figure very well. She was thin and tall and with her blonde hair and high heels a typical Dutch postcard beauty. She almost had no other work than serving him tea and she served nobody else tea. She was his personal assistant in a job that was not defined to him. She was not his messenger and so he could not send her on errands, which she might have willingly carried out.

"I am Erika," she had introduced herself.

"Thanks. I am Dennis as you already know," Dennis had replied.

"What's the meaning of I-sha-kah?" she asked.

"What's the meaning of Erika?" Dennis asked back.

"Oh, it's just a simple Dutch name!" she explained.

"Oh! I thought European names had something to do with their history or culture," he told her.

"Not mine. I don't even know what it means, if our names have meaning," she responded.

Dennis succeeded in deflecting her from prying into the meaning of his father's name, which he had not even cared to ask about and so did not know. Erika was the latest in asking for the meaning of his family name. He would always ask for the meaning of their names too.

"But what a fine-sounding name I-sha-ka is! Sounds like Shaka. Are you a Zulu?"

"No, Erika; the Zulu people don't live in Nigeria; they live in South Africa."

"How would I know that without your explanation? Thanks for this knowledge."

"You are welcome."

"You must forgive me for my ignorance. But what is your tribe?"

"Tell me yours first before I tell you mine."

"We have no tribes in Holland."

"We are a people, not tribes, in Africa."

"But all the books I read about Africa talk about tribes."

"Who wrote those books?" he asked.

"I don't know, but do your people write books too?"

Dennis saw no need continuing the conversation with her; he did not want to be too familiar with one designated as his office assistant but only serving him tea. He told her "Excuse me; I have to do some work." And that freed him for that moment.

But Erika and the senior management of the company knew that Dennis had nothing doing except reading newspapers. Erika flaunted herself at him every workday. She had long legs and wore high heel boots with which she took seductive steps in the office. She wore a different designer brand of pantyhose almost every day to work, and she made sure that Dennis saw her legs. In recent times once in the big office, where she virtually had a small desk in a corner, she kicked off her boots and also took off her jacket. With her big breasts half-exposed and with provocative perfumes, she came close to Dennis.

"Can I whisper some secret into your ears?"

"What secret?"

"When you hear it, you will know it's a big secret."

"Okay!" Dennis said out of curiosity.

And she came close to whisper into his ears so that the young African could inhale the perfumed body of a Dutch woman at her prime.

"There is no secret as such," she laughed.

"Sure, there's no secret? Has the secret disappeared?"

"Okay, I-sha-ka, what do you do after work and on weekends?"

"Erika, Ishaka is my surname, not my first name," he said to correct her from calling his name so informally.

"Should I call you Dennis or Mr. I-sha-ka?"

"Better one of them."

"Thanks, Dennis. Aren't you bored? I can show you many places. I have lived in this city for many years and I love it."

"I am not bored. I am only homesick at times," Dennis told her.

The admission of homesickness opened to Erika a new front to tenderly assault him with her body. Was being lonely or homesick not the same thing? She wondered.

"Do you know I know how to massage? I can massage you. I can also take you out. Can I come and pick you up for an evening out?"

"I am already occupied this evening," he lamely said.

"I'll come for you tomorrow or some other time then. You'll have a good time if you allow me to treat you," she told him with a warm smile.

Suddenly the words in his father's letter began to ring in his head:

"Take heed!"

Erika had for six months, before Dennis arrived, had a Jamaican boyfriend who had to leave Holland because of immigration problems. His dreadlocks and accent aroused her sexually, according to her, and she was virtually cooped up with him after work. She had planned to visit Kingston, Jamaica, with him and learn more about Rasta and reggae in their founding homes before his sudden departure. Dennis was clean-shaven and had his hair cut low but Erika hoped he with his accent would be another Marvin who would always bring her so much excitement.

Erika had gleaned from their conversations in the office where Dennis lived in the city and knew how to get to his flat without being directed. She believed in researching about what she needed to know and did not ask too many questions about what she wanted. One Saturday morning she came to see Dennis. He was surprised that she came without either being invited or letting him know beforehand as was customary in the society. She came dressed casually but beautifully like one going out to have fun. She apologized for not calling him before coming but said she was going somewhere out of town and thought it would be great to see him first before leaving.

"Dennis, if you don't mind, could you accompany me on this fun drive? I just want to have a pleasure drive to The Hague, perhaps get as far as to Rotterdam and then return late in the afternoon."

"Will that not take more than a half day's drive?"

"Not really. I just want to be out of town to shake off the week's hard work blues."

"You relax by driving out of town instead of resting at home?"

"Yes, Dennis. It has been a tough week. I want to recharge for the next week."

Dennis wondered what hard work she did in the office to recharge for. He had nothing doing that morning.

"Don't be scared; I'll bring you back," she assured him with a smile.

"I'm not scared!"

"Good. I thought you were scared of being seen with a Dutch lady."

"Come on, Erika; that's not one of my worries."

"What worries do you have then?"

"I'm joking. I don't have any worries really. I'll go with you."

"You'll love the trip."

"It will be a sort of excursion for me."

"You'll live to remember it."

Erika and Dennis entered the car for the pleasure drive. She was excited and saw an opportunity to show off the beauty of her country. For long Dennis knew Holland through Peak milk. This was the brand of milk he preferred for his tea, cereals, and Quaker Oats. He used the powdered milk as well as the canned liquid one; they were both made in Holland. He had read about the cows, the canals, and the dikes that held back the ocean from pouring into the land that was below sea level. But now he had the opportunity of having a Dutch woman present the country to him. He could see the large number of people riding bicycles. He also thought about the complexity of the country.

"Why is your country called both Holland and The Netherlands?"

"Our country is called The Netherlands because most of it is below sea level. It is divided into the low and high countries. I am Friesian and come from the group spread across the seaside."

"What's your country's official name?"

"I will say The Netherlands, but it is also Holland."

Traffic was brisk but orderly. Every driver kept to their side of the road and nobody was in a hurry to overtake others. Not once did Dennis hear any driver blaring horns. They drove past lakes and rivers that were still fresh and beautiful as they must have been thousands of years ago. People swam in the lakes and fished in the rivers. According to Erika, some types of boats that emitted dangerous fumes were banned from the waters.

Erika stopped at a park off the main highway to take a walk. Rabbits, squirrels, deer, and different types of birds were not scared by walkers around. Many of the trees must be hundreds of years old and yet looked fresh. A stream flowed through the park; it was shallow but its water was silvery clean. Dennis was surprised at the pristine beauty of the waters compared to what had happened to the creeks, streams, and rivers of the Niger Delta. Dutch forests were still fresh despite the centuries the trees had grown, unlike the dying forests of his native Niger Delta. After about thirty minutes in the rest area, the two went back to the car to continue their fun drive.

Erika and Dennis took lunch in a restaurant at The Hague, which the Nigerian associated with the World Court. They took chicken sandwich. Erika had a few bites and left the rest. Dennis was not surprised that she was thin. He devoured his sandwich and still did not feel quite filled, but he knew he would take a snack as soon as he was back to his flat.

"Dennis, I have not told you this before but I have to because I want you to know me as I want to know you," she told him.

"What do you want to tell me?"

"I want to introduce myself. I don't think you know my background as such."

"Tell me about yourself."

"I studied Public Communications at the University of Leiden. I took a minor in Business Administration. I entered Bell Oil International with the hope of building up its global image. In two years I have been moved from office to office and now I am your assistant."

"What offices were you in before mine?"

"So many, but no need to list them. Every office has been in this same building. You can see that I was not happy until they made me your special assistant."

"So you are happy now?"

"Yes. At least I like you. You don't give me any problem though I won't mind your problem."

"Why do you so much trust that I can't give you any problem?"

"I didn't like the men in whose offices I had worked; they all wanted me and I didn't like them."

Dennis was surprised and did not know what to make of her. Was she relieved to be with him or she was saying these things for him to trust her?

When in the early evening they came home exhausted, Erika decided to rest before going back to her flat.

"I didn't know it would be so exhausting," she told Dennis.

"Being out for so many hours is bound to take its toll."

"Goodness, I have to rest a bit before I leave you."

"Take your time."

After Dennis allowed her to go to his bed rather than nap clumsily on one of the sofas, he knew he was in for something he had not planned for. She was in no hurry to leave. Was she taking him literally when he said that she should take her time?

Erika ended up passing the night in the same bed with Dennis. They had moaned and cried in excitement many times until they were too exhausted to continue lovemaking and both fell into deep sleep. It was upon waking that Dennis realized that he had violated what he knew was a basic work ethic, not sleeping with one working directly under him.

Debating in his mind what to do about Erika occupied his mind the following days. Should he ask that she be transferred from his office? He realized that he had no say in her being assigned to assist him in the first place. However, if her role as an assistant was limited to serving him tea, did he really need somebody to prepare and serve him tea? But now that she had passed the night at his and she was even getting closer to him, would she not be angry to reveal their intimacy?

The following week Erika became more provocative in the office and attempted to kiss him, but Dennis withdrew from her.

"This is an office. Please let's leave that to sometime later," he told her.

"But what stops us from kissing. There's nobody watching us and this is nobody's business," she responded.

"Do you know there may be cameras in this office monitoring the goings-on here?" he asked.

"This is an oil company and not a spying agency," she retorted.

Dennis knew he was in a quandary. Still the affairs of Bell Oil International went on. Time passed. He could not believe that more than a year passed so fast in Amsterdam. By the beginning of his second year, there was an annual report and he had to sign as the African representative of Bell Oil International Headquarters. He had become Erika's companion and they frequented restaurants, clubs, and movie houses. He observed in the clubs how drugs were so prevalent and so easy to get. Erika admitted she had tried ecstasy and cocaine in high school and in her first year in the university but had become totally clean.

With time Dennis started to be genuinely interested in Erika. She was comforting and warm in a cold climate. He learnt much about Dutch lifestyle from her, but that made him yearn more for home. He thought about his father and the warning, but he could no longer leave this woman alone. He could not say no to her beautiful body that he wanted almost daily. This thought troubled him at night before he fell asleep in her arms. She had become his preoccupation.

Ishaka's Funeral

When Chief Ishaka suddenly died, the wailing in his compound was uncontrollable. Family, relatives, and friends wept profusely not just because he died with the many more possible years to still live aborted, but because of the very nature of his death in a ghastly accident that everyone would pray to be spared from. He was relatively old but not quite old in his late sixties. He was agile and still maintained his erect tall figure. His hair was shorter as would be expected of his age but not gray. He would have gone without a walking stick for another ten years or more at the rate at which he carried himself before the sudden end. In the community, he was yet to be counted among the very old.

Chief Ishaka on that inauspicious evening was returning home from the council of chiefs' meeting. It had been a contentious meeting in which the monarch, fearing for his life, wanted measures to be taken against the area boys who had sent him threatening letters about his cozy relationship with Bell Oil Company. Of course he denied having received money on behalf of the oil-producing community from Bell Oil but he was scared because of the precedent already set. Area boys of Eni, a neighbouring clan, had beheaded their traditional ruler after accusing him of keeping for himself what O&G Company gave to the entire community. The news had sent shockwaves all over the oil-producing area.

"In cases like this," Chief Ishaka had declared, "let Your Royal Highness make a public statement accepting or denying the accusation. Either it is true or it is false," he declared.

"Our royal father should make a public statement on what? When has it happened that hooligans should force the hands of our king?" Chief Oke, a favourite of the monarch, asked.

"Our royal father is guided by our ancestors and gods and not by demands of petty thieves," Chief Odede declared.

"A father can be held accountable for his actions by his children. All I am saying is that our king should come out clean, say it is a lie or it is true," Chief Ishaka stubbornly reiterated.

"Chief Ishaka, on behalf of His Royal Highness and his august council of chiefs, I demand you withdraw those words," Chief Fatakpa said.

"I respect our royal father, but my withdrawing words I have spoken will not help in this matter. I stand by my words," Chief Ishaka told the gathering.

The king and most in the council were visibly annoyed that Chief Ishaka did not withdraw his statement. In his throne, HRH Apo I waved his fly whisk to draw attention.

"Does Adjudju r'Agbon know the implication of his words? Is he accusing Oborame of theft?" he asked.

Oborame was one of his many royal names that evoked mystical power. He was also called Ogbimi, Dumagba, and Kodokodo by his subjects. He had opened the floodgate of attacks against Chief Ishaka.

"Yes, Chief Ishaka is paying area boys to drag the honourable name of our king into disrepute!" Chief Fatakpa said.

"He is inciting hooligans against the king and his council!" Chief Oke added.

"How dare you cast doubts on the integrity of the traditional institution of which you are also a member?" Chief Tebele asked.

"You of all people?" the monarch asked rhetorically.

"You argue with us here about money and yet your son sends you so much money," another chief, who wanted to be seen as defending the monarch, stated.

"Let's sanction him for insulting our king, his exalted office, and also all of us. He enjoys Bell Oil the most of all of us. His son overseas is one of the highest paid black men in the world," Chief Odede declared.

"If he so hates this council, he should leave it. He came in open-eyed; he should know that he is no longer welcome in this sacred institution," Chief Tebele declared.

The royal father waved his flywhisk again to maintain order. Never before in his thirty-year reign had he seen such acrimonious debate. Chief Ishaka was not ready to lay the matter to rest. He wanted the relationship between the oil companies and the council of chiefs to be resolved once and for all. Why should money bags be brought to the king and his chiefs instead of that money to be used to develop the community? he asked himself.

The arguments went on and on without either side winning. The day was far gone and many of the chiefs were hungry, having stayed far beyond the time they had expected to leave for home. Since the matter was not resolved, another meeting was fixed for the next weekend to thrash it out.

It was during Chief Ishaka's drive home at dusk that his 1983 model Mercedes Benz 230 ran into a "luxurious" passenger bus colliding with a super-size petrol tanker that sparked an inferno all around. Where petrol is involved in an accident is always a dangerous scene. By the time the flames had burnt themselves out, there was not even a single bone taken from the accident scene that could be ascribed to a name. Flesh, bone, and blood all had fuelled the blaze. With over forty people involved, the remnant bones could not be identified. Most of the skulls succumbed to the fire and many of those left disintegrated into ashes when picked up.

Wailing in Chief Ishaka's compound went on for days. Those close to him that had heard him speak about the type of burial he wanted knew that his hope had been foiled by an act of fate.

"An old man dies at home in his bed," he used to say.

Chief Ishaka did not fancy dying even in the hospital. That, to him, reduced the dignity of the person, but he had over the years accepted the near certainty that his corpse would have to be kept in a morgue while arrangements were being made for a befitting burial.

Burials now needed months to arrange to be successful; it took time to bring the family from different work places together and also to procure all the necessary things for a praiseworthy burial. Every dignified burial involved a cortege stretching from the hospital to the burial site. The line of cars reflected the deceased person's status and popularity.

Chief Ishaka had expected to live till very old age. After all, he was taking the precautions for long life. He had met that death-free woman at a time when she was critically ill and could not ask her for the secret she had found in the coffin.

"I came to greet you," was all he could tell her.

"Thank you for remembering that I am still alive," she told him.

"Our ancestors will continue to protect you."

"Ise!" she intoned.

Chief Ishaka's family members were at first confused about how he should be buried.

The children surely had a big problem on their hands. How would they bury their father whose body was not there? Would the assembled body parts be reconstructed into their father's figure for display? What were they going to bury? Should they place an order for an artistic coffin from Ghana as he would have liked or import one of those beautiful caskets from Europe or North America? He would have approved of either as a suitable getaway craft to the afterlife. What would they put into the craft of their choice that their father would have approved of? For a man without body but only ashen bones to display at the wake, it was a difficult consideration for his children and the elders of the family

The deceased chief had to go in style but in a conventional manner with pallbearers, a cortege of wailers, and an unending convoy of fine cars that his chiefly title entitled him to. He had to be brought from a hospital or a clinic in a keening ambulance. How would they manage to bring his bodiless remains from a clinic or hospital in a dignifying ambulance? They would arrange things, make up things, and invent new ways to bury the bodiless dead.

The people who had felt pity for the chief for dying in that accident that took away his body did not take into consideration the ingenuity of the human mind when challenged by difficult circumstances. Some elderly sympathizers consoled the Ishaka family that a burial's main objective was to give peace to the spirit of the deceased in its new abode. If the chief heard that, it would have given him sufficient consolation to forget about his corpse.

The children did not let their father down. Everything was coordinated between the children at home and the one abroad by telephone. There was much expected of Dennis by virtue of his working abroad and earning foreign currency that made the high status of wealth easy to attain back in Nigeria. The son working in Bell Oil International Headquarters was given the assignment of buying the coffin or casket that he considered most befitting. Based on his instinct, he decided to buy an American casket, which he expected to be far more expensive than the artistic one from Ghana. He wanted to spend dollars to show the worth of what he bought.

Dennis flew from Amsterdam to the United States to personally make his choice. The casket was expensive but he knew a parent's funeral took place only once and he had to do it in a memorable way. Among his people, one can borrow in order to make a grand impression. He did not borrow but he was ready to spend as much as possible to bury his father and make a lasting impression. Nothing would be too much to spend in burying his father who personally made his job in Bell Oil Company possible. He had saved enough money to spend a big fraction without feeling financially depleted.

At the last moment, Dennis changed his mind on the American casket which he had already bought and flown as cargo to Lagos to await collection. Instead of flying to Lagos straightaway from the United States, he flew first class to Accra to place an express order for a casket from the great artists of Ghana. With money available, the work moved very fast and in just two days the custom-made casket was ready for collection. It was the biggest fan he had ever seen. He marveled at the creativity of the craftsmen, who sculpted the magnificent fan of a coffin.

Dennis flew with the Ghanaian coffin to Lagos, where he collected the American one and had both of them taken to the Niger Delta. They had two caskets there to choose from for the burial of one bodiless dead.

Erika flew from Amsterdam to attend Dennis's father's funeral. When the sad news first came to Dennis in

Amsterdam, he felt devastated because he knew he had not yet fulfilled his father's dream, which made him to cry about his personal failure. Erika consoled him in the office and at home. She took over running his flat, preparing his meals, and stroking his head as it lay on her thighs. She had wanted to accompany Dennis home, but he had given the excuse of flying to the United States to buy a casket to keep her from accompanying him home.

"If it will be okay with you, contact me when I should be back in Nigeria and let me know whether you can make it," he had told her.

"I surely will like to come and see your place and be by you," she replied.

"I'll appreciate that but don't let it be a bother. My home is very far away," he told her.

"No place is too far away to reach if you know it. After all, you came from there. I really want to be by you."

"We'll see."

"We surely will in the Niger Delta," she told him.

Deep inside him Dennis knew that his father would not have approved of Erika coming to his funeral. Was she his wife? Who was she to him? Was she what he joined Bell Oil Company for? He knew Erika to have a certain stubbornness that made her do what she wanted and she persisted until she got her wish. He did not know that all the time they had become intimate that Erika had again gleaned so much information from him that she knew so much that she did not need to ask from him the direction to get to his family compound.

Dennis deliberately did not want to call her from the United States.

When he arrived in Lagos, he still did not call her and felt that without his talking to her, she would not think of coming to attend his father's funeral. He did not want her to remind him of his failure to achieve what his father had wished for from him. He still knew nothing of drilling oil.

Erika was not the one who stopped at what she wanted to do because she lacked cooperation. She believed in herself and achieving what she wanted. She found her way to Warri and then came to the compound without anybody accompanying her. Dennis was very surprised but had to be a good host once she arrived.

There was a debate among Chief Ishaka's children about which of the casket or coffin to be used for the burial. They chose the Ghanaian fan-shaped coffin over the American casket, which one of the children said he would sell to those who would need it - men and women were dying at such a fast rate and their children so much wanted to impress that within days it would be out of their custody at a fantastic price.

At Chief Ishaka's funeral, the family prepared food that more than went round every mouth present. Though there were family members and friends expected to be there and invited guests, the burial of an important person like Chief Ishaka brought everybody who could attend. Those uninvited might not get seats of honour in front positions with fancy tables, but they were welcomed and served food and drinks that were more than plentiful. The family slaughtered three cows, five goats, and so many chickens. Jollof rice and a variety of traditional dishes were served. People had more than enough of fried chicken and beef with Guinness Stout, Gulder beer, and an assortment of other drinks. As happened in such lavish burials, many women stuffed their handbags with fried meat and small bottles of Guinness Stout. The women sang. The chiefs, who had put behind their misunderstanding with Ishaka because one does not quarrel with the dead, came in their white regalia. Anybody who attended the celebration of Chief Ishaka's life at his burial had his or her fill of enjoyment.

The Activist, who had stopped going to funerals because of the waste he saw in them, had to waive his self-prohibition and attended the chief's funeral. Chief Ishaka had been his ally, a true insider, as he called him. He, Ebi, and some other members of the university community and *The Patriot* saw somebody in their society that, without much formal education, projected sterling qualities of integrity, dignity, and humanity. Pere and Tosan also came to pay their respects to the late chief. The mourners and all gathered did not fall short of encomiums for him. *The Patriot* profiled him on a weekend issue and there was much about their father the children would be proud of in the tributes paid to him.

Dennis had joined the association of Nigerian senior staff oil workers who contributed five hundred naira every month towards funerals and weddings. Whoever was bereaved or involved in a wedding was assisted with a hundred thousand naira. Nobody wanted to be bereaved but everybody looked forward to the next ceremony, an occasion to flaunt their high-status positions, drink, impress the poor, and flirt. Many love deals were struck at such ceremonies. Though he had been away, Dennis was accorded the honor of a current member of the association; hence members came to spend and make his father's burial a memorable event.

All in attendance admired the new-style coffin that was closed forobvious reasons. Ishaka made a dignified entry into the other world. He no doubt would be smiling and nodding his head as he watched his own burial from the other world. He would be pleased with his children's effort to give him a dignified entry into the hassle-free world. If he saw Erika always beside Dennis, as if she would be lost without clinging to him, he would shake his head at his son's missed opportunity and misdirection.

So the burial would have given him mixed feelings. He would be happy about the ceremony, but there was a dream of his which had been deferred or destroyed inadvertently that would be disconcerting to him. The pain to him would be that only his son Dennis and he knew about it. It was a secret that would have been exposed only after Dennis not only discovered oil in their farmland or family's land, but also used the white man's witchcraft to drill it for export. That would have been a first not only in the Niger Delta but also in Nigeria and West Africa.

The presence of Erika rubbing her body on his son like a cat would have caused him a heart-ache. The Niger Delta sun had tanned her into an olive oil complexion that she liked. She had lost her pale-white ghostly look and now glowed in a charming way. But to the departed chief watching from beyond, the farmlands were still there, but the knowledge he expected from Dennis had been blown away by Bell Oil Company and a Dutch blonde.

Erika asked many questions about the customs. Were people mourning or partying at the burial? Why should the children wear expensive clothes and beads when they were in mourning? Why did they have to spend so much money in a funeral when the living among them needed money to live much better? Why was a burial so drawn-out that it lasted a whole week? Dennis could only tell her that he grew up to meet such customs and that they had been there and would probably continue to be so for a long time to come. There had been changes, according to Dennis, but such changes only made burials more expensive as each burial was compared to previous ones. The competitive spirit of the people was more acted out in burials than in other endeavours.

Erika's arrival at the Ishaka family compound had at first caused a stir. Young and old wondered who she was and rumour and gossip spread the news that she was Dennis's wife. Children stared at her; the young unmarried women around were rude to her out of jealousy. Within days the community grew accustomed to her and she moved freely as if she had long been a part of the community.

While still there, before the seven-day burial ceremony was over, Erika told Dennis that she had missed her period and she was sure what they had been planting playfully and excitedly for months in Amsterdam and since her arrival in the Niger Delta had started to sprout. Dennis could feel his heart beating in reaction to the news. He was apprehensive but he had to be the good host he had made every effort to be since her arrival.

He spent the following nights imagining Erika big with their child serving him tea in his office in Amsterdam. The CEO might not be surprised and would not ask any questions. That was one of the virtues of the Dutch, their being so liberal that they did not poke their noses into somebody else's business. The company hierarchy might not even care or they might just feel satisfied that they had accomplished their objective of keeping the young African at the company's global headquarters fully occupied. Mr. Kasperman would be happy about the turn of events.

As Erika's immediate supervisor, he would be the one to

approve her maternity leave. Would she stay at her flat or move to his? The week of mourning in Amsterdam had virtually cooped Erika at his and he knew that she would not move home again to her former home. They had become inseparable. With all the kisses, massaging, and fondling, how could any of them live alone again? How was he going to handle it? He did not know how to answer the questions he had asked himself but believed time would solve the problem. Now that the burial ceremony was over, his mind was focused on returning to Bell Oil International Headquarters.

Activist Governor

The Activist had political ambition all along and bid his time as to when to join the fray for elective office. The public was very skeptical about the upstart general at the helm of the IFMG. He was making promises like his predecessors did for decades about handing over power to elected representatives of the people. These military officers had found power so sweet like a berry that they had all reneged on their public pronouncements. So many times had many individuals been lured into politics preparatory to democratic elections only for the military to abort their efforts. One general aborted three preparations for general elections; the last after he decreed two national parties, built party headquarters for them in every local government area of the federation, and paid for the campaign of the two presidential candidates! Another general even allowed elections to take place and annulled the results once it was clear that his preferred presidential candidate was losing woefully; the apparent winner of the elections was picked up and would die under military guard in detention. Very few people now took seriously any plan for the military to hand over power to democratically elected civilians.

But the current general was under siege and afraid of a counter coup any moment and so was being forced by circumstances to really relinquish power. Reports flew around of his sleeping at different locations every night for fear of being picked up or attacked while asleep in a known place. Even the leopard asleep is easy to capture or kill! The scared general invited marabouts from all over the West African region to make him charms; they also performed sacrifices to ward off evil spirits and humans that threatened his life. The general felt insecure despite his huge army and the rings of defense that the marabouts drew around him. He had begun to use doubles to avoid assassination by rivals and enemies. He rarely left his home and office and had not visited any part of the country outside the capital, and that only after the road had been cleared for at least three hours. This time the promised elections might be different from the past tricks of the military to gain respite for their juntas and consolidate themselves in power, the Activist thought.

With money at his disposal and the staunch support of the Delta Cartel, the Activist knew he could win a political race in the area. *The Patriot* was so popular that the prospective voters would lean towards whomever the paper endorsed. He had learnt from experience in the United States how the media manipulated public opinion to support a particular candidate they endorsed and he had anticipated the paper would play a crucial role in his political career. Fortunately, the paper was very popular in the State and was selling well outside too. With a good campaign organization, the Activist was sure to have a free medium to present his case to be governor of Niger Delta State or one of the three senators representing the State at Abuja.

The opportune time came. The new military head of state continued to be subjected to acerbic criticism from abroad. He was virtually ostracized in international gatherings. He was not allowed to visit Europe or North America and some foreign leaders had made this view known to him. In Africa he was treated like a leper; no other leader wanted him close, not to talk of shaking his hands. Even his foreign minister was not allowed to attend meetings of his African peers. In the new spirit of African self-criticism and development, the leaders of the continent embraced democracy in their path of economic development and poured scorn at any military government in the new century. After military rule had ended in South America and Asia, why should Africa be the last bastion of military rule? The leader was called many ugly names, including the Pariah of Africa and the Butcher of Abuja.

The general who had thought that seizing power would lead to enjoyment found ruling to be a form of self-torture. The presidential mansion, Aso Rock, instead of the paradise he had expected became hell to him. Only he knew the extent of the discomfort of the palace. He now realized that it was only from a distance that Aso Rock was a paradise. Get in and you were trapped as he was. He had to fight his way out alive. He received reports that soured the otherwise sweet berry of power he had planned to continue consuming. He was under constant threat of assassination and realized too late that being at the head of the government was not worth it. As a general who had made money from constructing new barracks all over the country, he had enjoyed his life much better as a quartermaster general than now as the president. Then he also wielded sufficient power to almost make happen what he wanted. Now things had changed. He was under perennial siege and he prayed for time to save his head.

The leopard of state wanted to change its spots and transform itself into a lamb or a dove, something the rest of the world would accept and play with. He no longer used his officer's uniform but wore embroidered robes to deceive people as if he were a civilian head of government. But he knew that his makeup was not enough to save him for too long. He set up a two-year plan for the military's withdrawal from government.

The ruling council created an election commission with the responsibility of arranging elections at local, state, and federal levels. The few people who could speak out questioned the independence of the electoral commission, but the general promised that he was serious in his determination to hand over power to civilians. He wore dark goggles day and night and no astute political scientist or diviner could read his mind to tell whether he was sincere or lying like his uniformed kind.

The Activist debated in his mind as to whether he should run for a federal senatorial seat or for his State's governorship. He reflected on the position that he would be most effective in. How effective would he be among over one hundred senators in Abuja, where the interest was in sharing oil money and not dealing with the problems of the country? He would just be a lone voice in the wilderness and the strong howling winds of the savannah would drown him from being heard. He knew from experience that those who went to Abuja forgot the people who sent them there and filled their own pockets with the money supposed to be used to fund projects that would benefit the people. Abuja had become a capital city of thieves that the Activist would not want to identify with.

"What do you think, Ebi?"

"It's one thing talking politics as you've been doing but it'll be another thing getting involved practically."

"Somebody has to get involved to change the state of things," he explained.

"All I can say is that it's dangerous, but I will support whatever you choose to do."

"I will appreciate your support as always in this."

"Of course I will support you wholeheartedly. Your dream is also my dream; your life is also my life. Count on me more than a hundred percent," she assured the Activist.

"You have given me what I need to declare my candidacy for whatever office I seek," he said as he embraced Ebi.

"You will win. I am sure of our success," she reassured him.

"Thanks. Good to know that you believe in my capacity to win. I know that with your help, I'll win whatever position I run for," the Activist told her.

After several nights of soul searching, the Activist made up his mind. He came down to fighting the gubernatorial race in the state where he had been very active. He knew Niger Delta State very well and wanted to so change it as to make it a model state in the nation. It would be a great opportunity, if elected, for him to show accountability to his own people. He wanted to make a difference at the state level rather than go to the federal capital and be frustrated by an assembly of greedy men and women.

In an unexpected declaration from the electoral commission, no parties were allowed to be formed for the promised elections. All of a sudden the manoeuvring about political parties that had consumed the nation for almost a year came to a sudden end. The doubters of the upstart general and his commitment to handing over power to elected civilians increased. But the hounded leader made a prime time broadcast to reassure the entire nation that the elections would hold as scheduled.

Time was short and there was no time to cry against the

electoral commission's decision. This was more so as it was the imposed umpire of the game and it could disqualify any candidate it wanted out of the elections. No candidate could appeal against the electoral commission's decisions. The electoral commission had declared that each candidate was to run on his or her own recognition and that was accepted by the potential candidates as law. Still every candidate that passed the screening exercise had to have an emblem; this was necessary as the mostly non-literate rural population had to be given the chance to participate in the democratic process.

Twelve candidates were cleared to run for the governor's office in Niger Delta State. The Activist had feared that he might be disqualified but was fortunate that international observers had said they would only monitor the elections if everybody who wanted to run for an office and met the published criteria was allowed. The general wanted international legitimacy to relieve him of his burden and his wishes were passed down to his appointed electoral commission members.

The Activist worked very hard to run an effective campaign. He took leave of absence from the university to devote his time fully to the electioneering campaign. He did not want his attention to be divided between work and politics but wanted his heart, head, and soul to be in his campaign. He was surprised that the Vice-Chancellor had no problem approving his move and even wished him good luck.

"You have been a great pillar of Niger Delta State University. I know you will win and make this state the dream of all other states."

"With your support and of others on campus and the entire state, I hope to win the election."

"I have no doubt about your success and you will even be a greater pillar of the university as our governor. Shall I call you Your Excellency?"

"Not yet, but I will do my best to win. Should I be elected, I will make improving higher education one of my cardinal pursuits."

"God be with you," the Vice-Chancellor prayed.

"Thanks," the Activist responded.

The Activist brought together his resources in the Delta Cartel, *The Patriot*, and relationship with the Egba boys, the students, and the university to wage a vigorous campaign. Pere threw behind him the support of the youths who respected him for his fight on their behalf. He made available his hotel vehicles to the Activist's campaign.

Ebi, of course as Dr. Emasheyi, campaigned for him and her special favourable disposition brought Itsekiri, Izon, and Urhobo together on the Activist's side. Already known as a women's leader, she presented her husband to the women as the one who would best serve their interests.

"He understands the plight of women and has consistently been sensitive to women and their problems. He is a different kind of man from the chauvinists around. He is a new man and I love him. Vote for him and he will make all of us proud," Ebi campaigned.

The other candidates had not thought of the power of women in elections and other matters and so made no special effort to court the women's votes.

The Activist created avenues to speak to different groups and to shake hands with individuals.

"I need your vote to be Governor of our proud state," he told those men and women whose hands he shook.

His opponents who felt they knew the state better than him because they had always lived there and did not spend twenty-five years outside only went round dropping moneybags at the feet of chiefs and monarchs that their people did not respect and even hated.

For the purpose of the campaign, the Activist divided the state into two parts: urban and rural. While he allowed *The Patriot* to feed its urban readers with cries for change, he gave the rural people what mattered to them. His symbol was the fish. He knew that the old had voted for the fish before - that was many decades ago when Nigeria was newly independent. The people loved fish, their staple.

"All I care for is Niger Delta State. I want us to have our soil, water, and air as healthy as it used to be. We have to douse the fires that threaten our very existence," he told rural and riverine people.

"If you give me your vote, I will ask the oil companies to clean our creeks, streams, and rivers so that the fish population can return to our waters. My government will provide boats to travel about in the riverine area. We have the resources to help ourselves live better than we now live in the area," he told his listeners to loud shouts of support.

"We want him," echoed everywhere from the political foot-soldiers planted in the crowd.

The other candidates talked about bringing jobs from Abuja.

"What jobs can Abuja give us than the fishing and farming we already know how to do if the environment is right for them?" the Activist asked, to the people's applause.

"Only we can make our lives better and not Abuja that has been robbing us in the name of developing the entire country," he stated.

He talked about his plan to make the people prosper from their natural resources. He would set up industries that would make use of their water, their soil, and plants. He would establish an oil-prospecting company to compete with the foreign ones and make Niger Delta educated men and women use their education to drill oil in their land. He was aware of the economic hardship the people were going through and would award scholarships to all Niger Delta State students in any Nigerian university, he told crowds of parents and youths.

"On election day vote for me. Vote for the fish," he ended as he thrust his right fist into the air.

Ebi was always by the Activist's side and accompanied him to crisscross the state. The governorship candidate wanted his message of change to reach all corners of the state. In one of such campaign appearances, Ebi saw Udoma for the first time in more than twelve years. He had grown obese and looked dishevelled. She beckoned on him to come to her and wondered how big his son would be at the time. There was not much time to talk in a public rally but he told her that he lost his son and that he had divorced his wife, Jessica. He had been alone since the divorce. Ebi suspected he did not go back to Ezeani, as she had advised. She could not tell him that he ought to have kept to his side of the contract with the medicine man - if he did not pay for what he got, he should not blame anybody for losing the child. It was a pity that the child died, but Udoma's stubbornness caused his own loss. Ebi wondered why his pastor, a prayer warrior for that matter, did not make the child to live. The rally ended there and Ebi and the Activist continued their campaign blitz to other towns.

On Election Day the fish was not difficult to recognize. Old habits die hard and most people in the rural part of the state chose fish over abstract ideas. Other candidates had picked horse, a storey house, phone, and other icons that the people had never seen. The people of the state had not seen a horse, since tsetse flies had never allowed horses to come as far south. The rural people had not seen a phone set. One of the candidates had a knot as his symbol and it was too abstract for the electorate to decipher. In urban areas, the cry for change echoed all over and became the theme song of voters.

The Activist whose campaign had drowned the other eleven candidates' voices comfortably won the governorship race and became the first elected governor of the state in all its history. The state had been created by a military decree and its governors before then had all been middle-level military officers appointed from Lagos and later from Abuja. Such appointees were always from outside the state and they did not understand the problems of the people. Most of them saw their governorship of the rich state as an opportunity to siphon as much money as possible into their own private accounts overseas. For once, Niger Delta State had its own native son elected to rule it.

After he was sworn in, he gave up his partnership with Pere in the Delta Cartel; they arrived at an amicable settlement. Pere's chain of hotels in Warri, Port Harcourt, Lagos, and Abuja would be used for official state events until the government built its own guest houses in different parts of the country. Pere gave a discount to state guests in his hotels and did not treat them as he treated Bell Oil guests.

The Activist brought major changes to the State government. He had taken his office as a challenge. He restructured the government ministries and agencies in place before his election. He found them constrictive and introduced a system that he felt would make his rule most effective. He created a Ministry of Environmental and Mineral Matters to deal with many of the problems of the Niger Delta. This was a ministry more than any other that the state needed to harness its natural resources and also to clean the polluted soil, water, and air and put out fires from gas flares and oil blowouts.

    The newly elected governor brought back Dennis Ishaka from Amsterdam where he had remained without work in a big office after Erika took maternity leave to deliver a boy. The Governor appointed Dennis the commissioner of the new ministry. As the Commissioner for Environmental and Mineral Matters, Dennis Ishaka oversaw the creation of the Niger Delta State Oil Corporation invested with enough capital, authority, and support to prospect for oil in the state. Dennis was waiting for oil to be struck in his family's farmlands and hoped his father in the other world would now nod his head and smile because of the new turn of events that had brought him closer to achieving the deferred dream. He believed that his father would forgive him for having Erika now stuck with him. Their son, Fredrik, handsome and possessing Ishaka features, would gladden the grandfather's heart.

    Three months after Dennis assumed his new position in the state, Erika was appointed the Public Relations Officer of the Niger Delta State Oil Corporation. She was to mediate between the corporation and the other oil companies around. She also had the portfolio of managing the image of the new corporation. She enthusiastically accepted her new responsibilities and set herself ready to make the corporation succeed in all ways possible.

    A year into the Activist's governorship of the state, he was invited to speak at the annual convention of the Niger Delta People's Association in Washington, DC. He had left the United States nine years ago for good. He had never felt all the time he had been back in his home country any urge to still return to where he had studied and taught. He had missed nothing in the United States that many of his countrymen and women were still fleeing into. He had felt like one relieved of a burden. Yes, to him living in America was an emotional, if not a psychological, burden. Often those who were not smart enough to give it up as early as he did got crushed. He knew some and had heard of many other Nigerians who had been in mental asylums in America. Such people were lost in the American Dream! Some other Nigerians there suffered from depression almost every season. The Activist felt happy that he left when he did.

Now that he was fully a Niger Delta person, the state's chief executive, he could travel to the United States on his own terms and return. He took a two-week leave and planned to address the convention before travelling to where he used to live. The trip would be partly official and partly private. He wanted to see how things must have changed since he left. Of Barber College, he still did not care if it had long closed for reasons of bankruptcy or lack of accreditation. Those two problems had remained intractable all the years he taught there. He would also see his fellow Africans, especially Nigerians. As his people say, you show off ivory bangles by wearing them. His former colleagues and friends would hear him addressed as "Your Excellency" and need not ask him whether home was fine for him or not. From the Excellency prefixing his name, they would tell on their own how he had fared wonderfully well since he returned to his Niger Delta home.

He and Ebi might visit New York. Nobody could deny the city's wonderful places, especially in Manhattan, but those were countered by the ugly sides of Brooklyn, Bronx, and Harlem. He did not want to live there like all big cities but only visit as a tourist. He had more than enough personal money to spend, but he was not sure he would buy anything. After all, what he needed was always available in Nigeria.

The Activist made the flight, and, as protocol required, he and Ebi flew first class on British Airways from Lagos to London and then changed planes to Washington, DC. The governor lamented the fact that his country had no airline and the nation of so many travellers had to throw away so much money to foreigners to build up their economies. It was one of the reasons he disliked Abuja and its legislators: the inability to discuss the country's problems and solve them. A rich country of travellers without an airline! Maybe someday, he thought, after completing his term as a state governor, he might run for the presidency of the nation and make the nation a model African state. That was a tall dream, but in politics nothing in the future was ruled out, he told himself.

The Nigerian Embassy in Washington had been notified of his trip and so prepared adequately for his arrival. He was booked into Hilton Towers, where a limousine was rented for his local travel. The Activist felt embarrassed by the huge but sleek car that cost more than two thousand dollars a day and asked it to be given up. He asked for and got one of the embassy's cars. After all, he did not come with a delegation as many governors did on their overseas trips. He came only with his wife, who was now popularly called the State's First Lady.

The Activist's speech as Governor of Niger Delta State questioned assumptions in his people's culture. After noting that the wrapper, also called Dutch wax or Hollandais, the traditional dress of all groups in the state, was manufactured in England or Holland, the hat in India or Pakistan, he threw a challenge at his audience. It was not enough for men to sew their dress shirts in Victorian style and call it Izon, Itsekiri, or Urhobo. Nor was it enough for the women to wear a three-piece dress of head-tie, blouse, and wrapper, none of which was homemade, and call it theirs. They even claimed imported Schnapps and Gordon Gin as their traditional gin!

"Don't you see the anomaly?" he asked. "If you knew the origin of those drinks, you would boycott them and make something of your own," he added.

He challenged his people to come out with ways to make new climbing ropes for palm oil production, new ways to preserve their fish, write down their languages, and power their boats. He wanted them living in a technologically advanced country to apply their learning experience to the needs of their Niger Delta State people at home.

He advised the Niger Delta people abroad to see themselves as one and to mobilize all the Niger Delta State's people abroad to help the state. He asked them to invest at home by promoting industries that related to the people's lives. He also declared that any of them who wanted a job, especially the professionals, was welcome and would be given a job for which his or her skills had prepared him or her.

"Together we will always be strong and win our struggle as true Niger Delta people," he concluded.

The Activist was given a tumultuous ovation at the end of his speech. He was overwhelmed by the applause. Ebi, in the United States for the first time, walked through the crowd and showed great affability. She and the Activist mixed freely with the Niger Delta indigenes who were surprised at how both of them spoke all the languages of the State. He had over the years learnt from Ebi the other languages that he had not known how to speak.

There was a coincidence that the Activist did not want to go by and he told Ebi about it. There was one of those annual joint meetings of the World Bank and the International Monetary Fund going on in Washington. Protesters were assembling. After they went back to the hotel, the Activist could not resist his old passion. He told Ebi that he wanted to go and carry placards against the evil angels, his new name for the capitalist institutions that did so much damage to other economies in the name of assistance. One of the sustaining aspects of their relationship as companions and then spouses had always been mutual support. Ebi had seen so many women among the protesters and wanted to see for herself the nature of protest in a developed country. They put on simple dresses and walked to join the protest.

Pennsylvania Avenue was crowded. One could barely distinguish curious tourists and passersby from the protesters. The police were in full gear to prevent any disruption of the meeting. The Activist led Ebi to a section of the protesters that had the formation of ATTACK. Soon the protesters advanced with slogans against the Bank and the International Monetary Fund. Some of their placards read: "NO TO THIEVES," "STOP IMPOVERISHING THE REST OF THE WORLD," and "LET OTHERS ALSO LIVE."

The Activist felt like he used to feel in those old days. His adrenalin level rose high. He felt so exhilarated by the tense mood that he picked up a placard that had fallen down and held it high EVERY LIFE MATTERS. There were cameras clicking. Journalists from all over the world were there to capture the rowdy scene. Very soon the police felt their red line was being crossed and released water hoses on the advancing crowd. The Activist and Ebi were doused with cold water but like the other protesters were determined to go on with the protest. Fortunately, none of the protesters was arrested for disorderly conduct. The water-splashing scene was boldly captured by state-of-the-art digital cameras that had become necessities of contemporary journalists.

News often travelled faster than its makers and, in recent years, correspondents had acquired the magic ability of instant transmission of events worldwide. Before the Activist and Ebi returned home, their pictures were already splashed all over the national papers in Nigeria. Even The Patriot, courtesy of Associated Press, printed some pictures on its back page with the caption, "Niger Delta State Governor and First Lady had fun in Washington, DC." *The Activist* and Ebi would certainly concur.

Effurun, Nigeria - Charlotte, USA. July, 2004 - May, 2006